Never Nap in a Casket

J. W. Hodge

Kenmore, WA

CAMEL PRESS

A Camel Press book published by Epicenter Press

Epicenter Press
6524 NE 181st St.
Suite 2
Kenmore, WA 98028

For more information go to:
www.Camelpress.com
www.Coffeetownpress.com
www.Epicenterpress.com

Cover design by Scott Book
Design by Melissa Vail Coffman

Never Nap in a Casket
Copyright © 2025 by J. W. Hodge

Library of Congress Control Number: 2024940171

ISBN: 978-1-68492-230-7 (Trade Paper)
ISBN: 978-1-68492-231-4 (eBook)

*This book is dedicated to All of my family and friends.
I wouldn't be a writer without your
love and encouragement.*

Acknowledgments

Thanks to the very helpful and encouraging Executive Editor and Associate Publisher Jennifer McCord. Thank you to officer Gary White who answered questions about police procedure with patience and humor. As always a big thanks to my special critique sisters Barbara Larson and Georgia Wright, without their love and support my writing would not be possible. I am truly blessed by your friendship. Thank you to all the readers who have taken Sadie into their hearts and spread the word that she's worth reading about. I can't thank you enough.

ONE

MANY FAMILIES USE CERTAIN EVENTS LIKE births, graduations, and deaths as demarcation lines in their lives: Uncle Joe moved to Alaska and joined a fishing fleet in 2002 because that's when so-and-so was born. Cousin Jed married his first wife the year Aunt Amelia tried to stop the city snowplow and ... well you get the idea. I come from two generations of morticians and since death is our business, it rarely rates more than a nod let alone a demarcation mark. However, murder is a whole different ball game.

I'm Mercedes McCambridge Harrigan, named after my mother's favorite female actor, and this time the body before me was not that of an elderly tenant, but one of a vital, thirty-something woman—naked, spray-painted metallic gold, and draped over a Mercedes-Benz G-class shiny black steering wheel. Looking at the dead woman didn't freak me out; my grandmother, Cassandra Harrigan, the only female mortician in Portneuf Gap, Idaho, had already introduced me to my share of dead bodies. And, due to the gold paint, which covered any trauma or natural discoloration, she didn't look dead; she looked more like a life-size trophy. I would've found the manner of her death bizarre but also intriguing if the SUV wasn't parked at my apartment complex. Last fall, the above-mentioned elderly tenant had been murdered, and the possibility of another murder at my apartments had my anxiety meter soaring like the wicked July temperatures in Portneuf Gap. Soon only ghouls and necromancers would answer my rental ads. Sounds cold, I know, so let me start at the beginning while all the details are as clearly etched in my mind as dates on a tombstone.

I remember the D.J. on KZBQ chortling the time: Eight a.m., and the temperature: eighty-nine, climbing toward the 103 predicted by noon. People who live in Portneuf Gap come from sturdy stock. We can withstand single-digit temps in the winter and continue about our business. But let a week of triple digits invade our space and the general population switches from surly to psychotic real quick.

I'd passed the nasty-mean phase and was teetering toward settling minor disputes with a baseball bat. My arms ached from scrubbing a filthy oven, while rivulets of sweat trickled down my neck and pooled in the cleavage created by a snug sports bra. I could feel my skin and ponytail absorbing grease and Easy-Off fumes like a fast-food French fry. Melvin Schmunk, aka Pig-boy, had split in the dark of night, stiffing me for half a month's rent.

Schmunk had forfeited his cleaning deposit.

Big-freakin'-deal!

That paltry sum would barely cover the cost of paint. I didn't have a legal eagle in my corner to sue his sorry ass for damages, and no idea where to find Schmunk. A voodoo doll fashioned from fermenting grease and the hair clog from the bathroom sink seemed my last resort. I wasn't familiar with the ins and outs of black magic, but if I threw in the toenail clippings littering the kitchen floor, I bet I'd have enough to give the sucker an eternal rash in his most private areas!

The kitchen screen door screeched open and a familiar voice hollered, "Girlfriend, get your pathetic head out of that oven, suicide is _not_ painless. Besides, hello, electric!" Rebbie Russell, best friend and wannabe comedian, stepped into the room humming the theme from *Mash*.

"Ha, ha." My voice echoed as I squirmed out of the stifling box and sat on my heels.

Dressed for success in black linen pants, red silk blouse cut to display a tantalizing peek at her goodies, and knockoff Prada pumps, Reb leaned against the doorway, arms folded, nose wrinkled. "Gad, you look like something the cat wouldn't drag in."

I stood, stretched a kink from my back, and eyed her perfectly pressed ensemble. One quick swipe with my grime-encrusted rubber-glove would adjust Ms. Haute Couture's attitude. "Come closer and say that." I shucked off my crusty gloves, grabbed a water bottle from the counter, and took a lukewarm swig.

Rebbie has been my best friend since sixth grade when we cut our thumbs, mixed our blood, and recited some mumbo-jumbo Reb swore would bond our friendship for infinity and beyond. We're often mistaken for sisters due to our similar coloring. Except her sable hair bounces in perfect curls, while my locks are stick straight. I take comfort from the fact that her thirty-six D's are the best a brief stint dating a plastic surgeon can buy. Mine are the real deal.

Reb scooped two bottles of cherry Pepsi from a squat red cooler she'd carried in and tiptoed through the industrial-strength cleaning paraphernalia littering the floor. "Thought you'd enjoy a break from cleaning up this Petri-dish."

I grabbed the icy bottle and rolled it across my forehead. "Okay, you're my hero. I take back all my nasty thoughts."

Reb opened her Pepsi and took a sip. "Speaking of nasty, guess Cary and his girlfriend," she sketched quotation marks in the air with her fingers, "will be doing the mattress mambo in the apartment next door instead of in your house?"

A shudder ran up my spine. I glared at Reb. "Bite your tongue off."

My twenty-five-year-old brother, Cary Grant Harrigan, a dedicated California surf bum, was coming for a brief visit with his latest squeeze. Their ETA was sometime today.

I'm not naive, I know Cary lost his virginity to Mindy Bartholomew the summer between his sophomore and junior years of high school. That info doesn't erase the fact that he's my baby brother and the thought of him doing the horizontal tango between the sheets on my bed sort of creeps me out.

"What's his new babe like?" Reb asked, dusting off a spot on the ancient, yellow-tiled counter before leaning against it.

I shrugged. "He didn't say much about her, except she's made big bucks operating different Internet companies, and she has a plan that's going to bury them up to their eyeballs in Moolah."

Reb tilted her head. "Hmm, sounds interesting."

I pointed to her outfit. "You had a psychic moment and decided to dress-to-impress Ms. Frobi Fisher?"

"That *cannot* be her real name." Reb tucked a lock of curly, dark hair behind her ear and smoothed an imaginary wrinkle from her pants. "All of us multimillion-dollar realtors dress for success."

"What?"

"In thirty minutes I'm meeting with a couple of suits from The Phoenix Corporation. They flew in from Tucson to check out that bunch of vacant warehouses on Second Street."

"Who or what is the Phoenix Corporation?"

"Some outfit that buys old warehouses and turns them into ultra-chic mini-malls with loft apartments. They're interested in old man Bernhagen's property."

"Money-bags Bernhagen? The guy developing all the ground above Pheasant Ridge?"

Reb lifted an eyebrow and grinned. "One and the same. When Bernie sees how I handle this warehouse sale, bet he'll give me an exclusive listing on his new subdivision." Her eyes glazed over and I could almost hear the dollars ka-chinging in her head.

"Holy crap, Bernie Bernhagen." I held up my Pepsi. "Here's to my millionaire best friend who won't forget me when she's rubbing elbows with the rich and famous."

A blaring horn cut off Reb's reply. Wiping damp hands down the side of my jeans, I hurried to the picture window in the front room.

A guy dressed in a white golf shirt, light gray Dockers, and burgundy tasseled loafers climbed out of the driver's side of a gleaming black Mercedes-Benz G class SUV. His sun-bleached hair was styled to bank-president perfection and his mirrored sun glasses screamed expensive.

Reb leaned into me. "Who's the hunk? And if he needs a maid for this apartment, I'm available."

I shook my head and scissored a wider opening in the grimy mini-blinds, trying to make sense of the sight before me. My brother, the beach bum, wouldn't be caught dead in a golf shirt. And tasseled loafers? Puh-leeze!

"Holy Hawkeye," Reb gasped. "That's Harry Cary! When did the brat morph from slug to corporate hottie?"

Cary opened the passenger-side door and helped a petite, curvaceous woman out. Dressed in a low-cut, belly-skimming peach tank top and black capri pants bonded to her like she'd been shrink-wrapped, she sauntered to the sidewalk in strapless black Prada sandals with spiked four-inch heels. A long waterfall of burgundy hair tickled her waistband and matched Cary's cordovan loafers.

Reb groaned and clutched her chest. "He's dating a Kardashian wannabe with a really bad dye job."

We reached the front door and cried, "Cary?" in unison.

He threw open his arms, his trademark smile dimpling his cheeks. "In the flesh!"

I opened my arms to give him a hug, but he held up his hands. "Wearin' white, Sis! Doesn't mix well with your greasy cleaning lady."

"You're cruisin' for a bruisin'," Reb said.

Cary grabbed Reb and swung her around. "Good to see you too, half-pint." He set her down, smoothed his shirt and said, "Sadie, Rebbie, I'd like you to meet Frobi Fisher." He slid a possessive arm around his companion's shoulders. "Frobi, meet my sister, the horror writer, and her evil twin."

"The dastardly duo I've heard so much about," Frobi said and stretched her lips in a toothpaste-ad smile. "Cary, honey, did you lock the SUV?"

"Relax, this is no-worries Portneuf Gap." He tilted his head back and inhaled. "Just smell that smog-free air."

"Just the same . . ." Fisher shrugged off Cary's arm, went to the SUV, and returned with a butter-cream leather laptop case slung over one shoulder; slut meets Madison Avenue. I fought to keep my jaw shut.

Clutching the case, Frobi peered into the apartment. "Um, someone, please tell me this is *not* where we're staying."

"No, you're next door." I pointed to the right. "I'm still working on this one."

My apartments were built during WWII and comprise four single story four-plexes that form a horseshoe around the parking lot. Beautiful, vintage buildings that have classic, sturdy red-brick exteriors, arched maple doors with matching arched white wooden screen doors. I grumble about the storm windows that have to be taken down each summer and put back each fall but never fail to keep the howling winter wind at bay. Located in the middle of Old Town Portneuf Gap, I considered the complex a beautiful landmark surrounded by unique architectural homes.

Frobi stepped from the stoop, shaded her violet-blue eyes, gave the twelve-plex a once over. "Uh-huh." Obviously she didn't share my love of vintage.

"Sadie's in the process of remodeling this old place." Cary placed his hand on Fisher's tiny waist and guided her to the adjoining unit. "My sis is a whiz with a paint brush and plumber's friend. Let me show you what she's done."

The glow from Cary's praise followed me into Number Ten's tiny entryway. I'd recently ripped the nuclear-green shag carpet from the living room, two bedrooms and hallway, and replaced it with oak laminate floors. For the walls, I'd chosen a creamy Navajo white. Fisher walked down the short hallway, heels clicking smartly against the wood. She peered into both bedrooms and then the bathroom, which boasted a new toilet, sink and tile counter-top. "Interesting," she said and entered the kitchen.

I stood ready to humbly accept a compliment or two on the transformation.

"Quite the revamp. Did you do all the work yourself?"

"Everything but the floor, one of my renters helped me put it down."

"You are one industrious woman."

"Thank you."

"Are you leaving the kitchen as is? Old linoleum is a perfect breeding ground for cockroaches." She faced me, nose wrinkled, eyebrow arched. A perfect passive-aggressive stance. "You have sprayed, right?"

"The tile I want is on back order," I said. Okay, maybe not exactly back ordered, but I knew what I wanted to put down once I had the money to do it.

"Mercedes, Mercedes!" Agatha Heckathorn, my tenant in Number Seven, burst into the room, face flushed, eyes bright, waving a small notebook. "Where is she?"

"Who?" I asked.

Agatha adjusted her Dolly Parton-style wig and peered past Cary down the hall. "Sherrilyn Sanborn of course."

Of course. "Agatha, she goes by Sherri and her last name is hyphenated, Sherri Sandborn-Sweet."

Agatha let out a tortured grunt. "Not the Channel Six weather gal who lives in Number Eight. I'm talking about Sherrilyn Sanborn. Southern gal on the cooking channel, has that yummy show "Butter is Always Better." Agatha cut her eyes to the open door and lowered her voice. "Rumor has it she's rented a unit here. All very hush-hush so the paparazzi won't follow her from Sun Valley. There's a Mercedes-Benz SUV outside." Agatha cocked her thumb at the picture window and beamed. "Who else would drive such an expensive vehicle?"

I rolled my eyes. Agatha has a black belt in gossip and her neighborhood gossip squad would put any high-tech intelligence agency to shame.

"Sherrilyn Sanborn *here*?" Fisher said. She looked up at Cary with a perplexed frown and shook her head. "Interesting concept."

The look Reb leveled at Fisher would've melted hard water deposits off corroded pipes. "Sadie's apartments would make a great hideaway."

"Hold it." I brushed back a hank of sweat-soaked hair. "No one's using my complex as a hideout."

"Uh-huh. Nice try, Mercedes." Agatha puffed out her concave chest and straightened to her full five-foot height. "I met one of her biggest fans this morning. Nice young fellow, Albert something. He gave me the straight skinny. You know he once sat next to Ms. Sanborn, I'm talkin' cheek-to-cheek on a bus in L.A. when she was all incognito. Guess he knows what he's talking about." She winked at me and held up the notebook. "All I want is her autograph. Then, I promise, mum's the word." She mimed zipping her lips.

"Sorry, but the SUV belongs to me," Cary said, flashing his trademark grin. He gently clasped Agatha's hand, looking like he might bring it to his lips for a brief kiss. "I'm Cary Harrigan, Sadie's brother. My fiancé and I are here on business." He dug into the front pocket of his slacks and brought out a roll of butterscotch Lifesavers. "Care for one?"

Fiancé? Fiancé!

My heart did a jackknife dive to my knees. The air seemed to whoosh out of the room while I steadied myself against the doorjamb.

Agatha gazed up at Cary, accepted the offered candy, and gave Fisher a quick squint. "You don't say. Damn!" She tucked the little notebook in her pocket. Her eyes softened as she looked again at

Cary. "Well, Mr. Harrigan, it's a good thing I caught you before you go gallivanting around our fair city. Watch out for those itty-bitty cameras mounted on some of the stoplights. They're set to catch speeders and people running red lights."

"Agatha, those are *not* cameras," Reb said. "They monitor the traffic patterns to help the stop lights work better."

"Uh-huh. That's what the mayor *wants* everyone to think."

Fisher coughed, hiding a laugh. It took great effort not to join her.

"Yo, Sadie," a rich, male voice with an East Coast staccato accent called from the open doorway. Todd Sudi, renter in Number One opened the screen and stepped in.

"Oops, didn't know youse was busy. Just thought I'd drop off my . . ." He didn't finish the sentence but stood, money in hand, gaping at Fisher.

Fisher glanced toward the doorway and gave Todd a quick once-over before turning back to watch Agatha's antics.

He tapped the wad of bills against his palm. "I might be a little short. I'll catch up later." He mumbled, running a hand through his curly, black hair, as he backed out the door. The wad of bills disappeared into his back pocket as he took off at a trot across the parking lot.

Talk about things that make you go hmm. "Todd, wait," I called after him. He just walked faster.

Agatha nodded at Fisher and shook Cary's hand. "Mind those cameras, young man. Don't let our greedy mayor go fishin' in your wallet." She sprinted after Todd, warbling his name.

Reb touched Cary's arm. "Gotta run, too, Harry-Cary, big meeting with some suits." She wiggled her eyebrows. "Before I go, give me a hint about your new business venture."

"A hint?" A mischievous glint lit his baby blues. "Okay, Batgirl, riddle me this; the man who uses it doesn't see it. The man who made it doesn't want it. The man who buys it doesn't use it."

Reb's faced scrunched with concentration. Her lips moved as

she silently mouthed the riddle. She stopped. Her eyes widened. "A casket!"

Cary nodded and gave her a high five. "We're diving into the retail casket biz."

Two

"CASKETS? THE BOY'S SELLING CASKETS? Out of some damn warehouse?" Grandma Cass, my favorite mortician, turned from the oven with a tray of plump cinnamon rolls clutched in red oven mitts that matched her gingham apron. Her dark irises looked ready to spark lightning.

My mother, Willie, usually refers to Grandma Cass as "that big tub of lard." I think of her as opulent and lush. Cassandra Viola Harrigan carries her weight proudly and moves through life in a swoosh of silk and cloud of Poison perfume. My Grandpa Harrigan went to the great funeral parlor in the sky before I was born, but I've been told Gram didn't miss a beat. She took hold of the Harrigan Funeral Home reins, hired a couple of assistants, and never looked back.

"Your brother has the brain function of a corpse. Hell, he wouldn't know how to pour piss out of a boot if the instructions were printed on the heel!" She blew an errant strand of salt-and-pepper hair out of her eyes, then poked it back into her French twist.

I'd tuned Gram out, choosing, instead, to revel in the luscious yeasty, cinnamon smell of her kitchen while wrestling with possible titles for my latest horror story. The boot remark brought me back like a slap to the head. When it was called for, Gram could swear with the best, but she rarely used the "P" word.

"No wonder he didn't let me know he was coming." She banged the tray on a cooling rack hard enough to make the rolls bounce, grasped the last cookie sheet of unbaked heaven, and shoved it into the oven with a clatter. "Reputable casket companies will not deal with anyone who isn't associated with a mortuary." Her eyes narrowed. "Hell, I hope he hasn't involved the Harrigan Funeral Home in this cockeyed endeavor. What company is he using?"

I shrugged and reached for a roll. Gram slapped my hand with the floured spatula. "Mind your manners, Mercedes McCambridge, these are for company."

She drizzled creamy glaze over the pastries and shot me a steely glare. "Your brother and his, uh, *friend* will be here any minute."

I nodded, happy I was merely the warm-up act for Gram's wrath. Cary was smack in the middle of her bullseye.

"If he wants to work in the mortuary business, he could move here and give me a hand. I'd offer him the same deal I've offered *someone* else." She gave me a sideways glance. "Send him to the finest mortuary college, all expenses paid."

I sighed and kept my eyes on the sweet rolls. This was a sore subject between the two of us. Gram wanted me to follow in her footsteps and take over the family business when she was ready to step down. But, and we're talking a humongous *but—*, the sight of blood has always made me woozy. Using a Trocar stick to suck out various body fluids wasn't on my to-do list.

"I bet this is another one of his get-rich schemes," Gram groaned. "I know he's got a good brain in that obstinate head of his. Just wish he'd get off his lazy behind and use it."

The phone rang. Gram swiped her hands across her gingham apron, picked up the receiver, and in a polite, well-modulated voice said, "Hello." The woman could be cursing the devil, but whenever the phone trilled she'd switch into perfect Funeral Director decorum.

"Ok. Where?" Her brow wrinkled and her knuckles whitened as she clutched the receiver. "Fine. Mercedes and I will be there." She hung up and turned to me. Her face had changed from fierce to frosty beneath finely arched black brows.

"Your brother has run into a snag. He won't be coming by. We'll meet him for dinner at The Sandpiper at seven. If you've got a conflict, cancel it. He's buying."

I eyed the tray of plump cinnamon rolls. Fine, more for me.

CARY'S SLIGHT EYE-TWITCH CONTRADICTED his happy façade. He wore tan chinos and an unlined, cream linen sports coat with the sleeves pushed up. Very retro-*Miami Vice*. An open-collared, teal knit shirt and leather sandals completed his vintage Don Johnson look. He kissed Gram on the cheek, tucked her pudgy hand through his arm, and led the way to a row of tables next to a wall of windows with a panoramic view of the Portneuf valley. I tagged along, watching Cary gesture and chat as he led Gram down the narrow, carpeted aisle.

The Sandpiper is one of the better restaurants in Portneuf Gap. The exterior draws you in with its weathered wood siding and nautical bric-a-brac. Inside is a pleasant mix of cozy-but-elegant with burgundy linen tablecloths draping each table, and napkins folded origami style. Their prime rib is to die for.

Outside, the hazy inferno still held the valley in a death grip, shimmering over dusty cement, melting road tar, sucking the energy from everything it touched. In the Sandpiper's dining room the temperature was close to nirvana. I plucked at the burnt-orange silk tank top clinging to me like a leaden blanket and reveled in the cool air sweeping across my sticky body.

Cary stopped at a table for four and my heart fluttered with confusion and hope. The woman seated at the table, with shiny platinum, shoulder-skimming locks couldn't be Fisher. She turned from gazing out the window and fixed root-beer brown eyes on me and smiled. My hopes cracked, then shattered. Cary pulled out

Gram's chair, indicating she should sit next to him. That left me sharing elbow space with Fisher the Chameleon.

Cary did the introductions and both Gram and Fisher smiled politely, however, Gram's ramrod posture transmitted tension like static electricity.

"Nice to finally meet you. I hate clichés but Cary has shared so many warm memories of you, I feel I know you." Fisher said, reaching a hand across the linen tablecloth. Her French-manicured nails sported medium-length, squared-off tips.

Gram smiled and grasped Fisher's hand in a no-nonsense grip, and then visibly relaxed in her seat. "I'm guessing you had a hand in my grandson's lifestyle and appearance transformation."

"He didn't need much help," Fisher said winking at Cary. "He was ready to shuck his surfer persona and reach his full potential. Right, babe?"

Cary nodded. "Right. Frobi has opened my eyes to a world of exciting possibilities." He nudged me with his knee. "She's a wonder at transforming her looks whenever the mood strikes. Like tonight. She's got great tips for revamping your image, Sis."

"What's wrong with my image?" I asked.

"Well, it's sorta . . ."

"I was telling Cary you have exotic cheekbones and with the right hairstyle . . ." Fisher fingered a lock of my hair. "Have you ever considered what a difference a wig might make?"

Gram leapt in before I could respond. "Am I correct when I say you and my grandson have come to Portneuf Gap seeking your fortune . . . *in caskets?*"

Fisher took a sip of ice water. "We had a very productive meeting with three partners in different senior health care corporations today. They were very impressed with what we have to offer."

"Senior care facilities want to offer discount caskets?" I said.

"Why not?" Cary grinned and patted Frobi's hand. "When my little entrepreneur sets her sights on something, she's simply golden. I swear she's been blessed with the Midas Touch."

Frobi reached into the butter-cream bag leaning against her chair, pulled out a hot pink laptop and plunked it between her water glass and silverware. "Let me show you what we have to offer. Once you see the craftsmanship I think you'll agree that it's an excellent line."

Gram shook her head and unfolded her napkin. "Let's eat first. Propositions are better on a full stomach."

Fisher snapped the laptop shut and put it away. "I'm guessing all of this might sound strange to you. You've built a successful business, why change something when it's not broken, right?"

Before Gram could answer, our waiter appeared and took our drink preferences and asked if we were ready to order.

"We need just a moment," Cary said. "But please start us off with an order of hot wings and artichoke dip. I've been craving these all day."

"Like I said, why change what has worked well for years?" Fisher said after the waiter left. "However, I know that as an astute business woman you want to keep on top of changes in the industry that can bring more profit."

Gram tilted her head and seemed to consider Fisher's comments. "I'm always open to new ideas as long as they're not a passing fad."

"I assure you this is the wave of the future." Fisher said.

Gram steepled her fingers, nodded, and I wondered what had happened to my astute grandmother. At an early age she'd taught me the meaning of cynical; yet it appeared she was taking everything Fisher said at face value.

Cary raised his iced tea. "Gram you can't go wrong with whatever Frobi proposes. Midas Touch."

I choked, gulped some water, excused myself, and headed for the restrooms. Everyone seemed enthralled by Fisher, but she was too smooth, too slick, too something for me to feel comfortable. I reached the door marked Women, pushed inside, and rooted through my purse until I found the Excedrin bottle. Using my palm as a cup, I tossed a couple of pills into my mouth and chased them down with a slurp from the sink faucet.

I looked at my reflection in the mirror. My hair might be suffering from the heat, but I was *not* drab. I added some lipstick to prove my point and fluffed my hair.

Screaming sirens rent the air when I opened the restroom door. I had a pretty good view of the parking lot through the double glass entry doors and it looked like a cop convention. Strobe lights flashed from the three black and whites blocking the entrance. Slamming doors, shouting, and running feet provided background for the chaos outside.

I went out the nearest glass door and weaved my way through a crowd of looky-loos. A thin man rolled on the ground, screaming and cursing. His sunglasses hung askew from his bloody nose and his right hand was pressed against his head. Blood oozed between his fingers. A second man with a swarthy complexion and black hair hanging in his eyes had assumed "the position" against the furthest police car while an officer performed a pat-down as another uniform looked on.

I inhaled heated air and checked the rest of the parking area: No sign of Grandma Cass, Cary, or Fisher. I glanced back at the squad car and my heart skipped a couple of beats. The tousled hair and sexy stance of the second officer reading the Miranda rights belonged to my favorite officer, Jack Killian. Jack boarded his horse, Eclipse, in my barn. The man could scramble libidos with one dimpled smile or wink from his intense green eyes.

At that precise moment he raised his head, caught my attention and gave me one of those smiles. My insides quivered while a *Beware, Extreme Danger* sign flashed in neon across sensible parts of my brain. Jack is a gorgeous threshing machine of heartbreak, cutting a wide swath wherever he pleases.

I wasn't ready for his kind of games.

An ambulance eased into the lot; two paramedics jumped out and trotted over to the writhing man.

"What's going on?"

I turned and found Cary and Fisher wending their way toward me. "Not sure," I said. "I'm guessing the guy being frisked did something horrific to the guy bleeding and clutching his head."

"Thought this was a real white-bread, no worries, Norman Rockwell kind of place?" Fisher said, a touch of anxiety in her voice.

"Where's Gram?" I asked Cary.

"Back in the restaurant sipping iced tea. If needed, I'll ring her cell."

The swarthy fellow was handcuffed and tucked into the back of Killian's cruiser. Killian spoke briefly to his partner and then turned toward us, oozing confidence with each step, gun belt riding low on trim hips like an Old-West gunslinger.

"Hot time in the old town," he said, wiping his forehead with his arm. His damp hair settled above his green eyes in tantalizing disarray.

"What's the deal?" I asked.

"The guy we're hauling away had a beef with that fellow the paramedics are treating. Seems they're neighbors and share a well. Something to do with a dead cat poisoning the water. They started quarreling at the Exxon station, then one chased the other across the street. They did a face-off, and traded punches until the perp bit part of his neighbor's ear off."

I winced and shuddered.

Fisher cocked her head. "Mike Tyson have a boxing school nearby?" Her voice lowered to the perfect pitch and timbre for telling ghost stories after dark. *Interesting.* I sounded like Minnie Mouse when stressed.

Jack looked at me with one eyebrow cocked. Right. I gave proper introductions all around. Jack and Cary shook hands; Jack took Fisher's hand and held it a moment longer than necessary. Fisher took a deep breath, extending her amazing assets.

"Frobi, what an unusual name." His gaze lingered lower than her face, and if asked, he probably couldn't tell you the color of her eyes.

I cleared my throat and Jack let go of her hand. "My partner's waiting. See you later." With a little salute, he turned and left.

"Boyfriend?" Fisher asked, her gaze following Jack's remarkable assets.

"Friend. He boards his horse in my barn."

"Yeah." Cary nodded and grinned. "I knew I recognized the name. Mom told me about him."

Mom?

When had Cary started calling our female parent Mom? Since my birth, she'd made it clear her name was Willie. Not Mom or Mama. And never, ever Mother. Willie.

"Seems like a *very* capable fellow." Fisher said. A smile curved her full lips.

Cary cut his eyes in her direction. His baby-blues turned to churning-sea-gray. "Capable?"

Oh-oh. I wasn't the only one suffering from the clutches of a green-eyed monster.

Fisher turned and took his hand. "Relax, babe. Cops are supposed to be capable but no one's like you."

"I found it." One of the EMT's held something that resembled mutant Play-Dough high in the air and gave it a shake. The victim's ear. Bile rose in my throat. As far as I was concerned, dinner was over.

My cell phone growled Darth Vader's theme, signaling a renter in need. Their needs ranged far and wide, from backed up plumbing to losing their keys. I glanced at the caller I.D. and answered, "Yes, Dexter?"

Dexter and Violet Zoetwilder live in Apartment Four. Dexter's in his early seventies with a lean build, white crew-cut, and rigorous posture that makes the Semper-Fi tattoo on his bicep stand at attention. He's Neighborhood Watch Captain and runs the Watch group like a well-trained platoon.

"I caught him. Caught him red-handed. The S.O.B. was trying to pry off Sherri's screen, break into her apartment, little pervert!" Dexter hollered.

"What little pervert?" I asked, mentally crossing my fingers it wasn't Sherri Sandborn-Sweet's ex-hubby, Mark. She'd gotten a restraining order but . . .

"Some little sawed-off runt. Claims to be her biggest fan."

Huh? Our local weather gal had fans?

Oh crap!

Agatha's babbling about a rabid Sherrilyn Sanborn fan was valid?

"Where is he, Dexter?"

"Got him tied to a chair at my kitchen table."

Great. Just great. Would the guy sue me, Dexter, or both of us?

"Untie him, Dexter, but keep him there. I'm on my way."

I tucked my phone into my purse and turned to Cary. "Please take Gram home after dinner. I have a minor situation at the apartments."

"Doesn't sound minor. Want help?" Cary asked, cracking his knuckles.

"No. Enjoy your dinner, catch up on stuff with Gram. I'll see you later."

Fisher gave me a little finger wave, turned, and sashayed back inside The Sandpiper.

THREE

"**O**NE CONVERSATION WITH SHERRILYN, that's all I'm asking. Then I might forget about pressing charges. I happen to have a recipe handed down through many generations that I *guarantee* she'll want to add to the latest cookbook she's working on."

Like Sherrilyn hadn't heard that proposition before.

Albert Lechman sat on Dexter's couch rubbing his left wrist. His wavy blonde hair was expertly cut to caress his ears and accentuate his strong jaw. Some might consider him nice looking, maybe even handsome, but I found his lips a little too thin to be appealing and his blue eyes a little too cold to instill trust. Right now those eyes were small and mean as he glowered up at me and continued to abuse his wrist. There hadn't been so much as a scratch on the man when I arrived, but now a dull red line marked the spot where his thumb kneaded rhythmically.

"I'll see your charges and raise you a breaking and entering," I said, squinting back at him. Lechman reminded me more of a pissed-off lawyer than a delusional fan. White shorts, spotless tennis shoes, and yellow sport shirt, all he lacked was a tennis racket to complete his how-dare-you-interrupt-my-game ensemble.

"Want me to call the Neighborhood Watch?" Dexter asked. He stood off to the side, arms folded across his sleeveless tee-shirt, running-shoe-clad feet spread, ready to pounce should Lechman make a wrong move.

Violet, Dexter's wife, fluttered in from the kitchen. This week her Brillo-pad hair was dyed to match her hot pink muumuu and flip-flops. I caught a glimpse of dark half-moon rings staining the fabric under her fleshy arms as she held a glass of lemonade against her forehead and gave a huge sigh.

"If this heat don't get me, the thugs roaming this neighborhood will."

She collapsed into her favorite overstuffed chair. "Guess you heard about the ruckus that woke the whole neighborhood last night. Men in ski masks broke into that ramshackle house over on the next block, started beating the snot out of those fellows in that obnoxious rock band. All the noise and commotion, liked to scare the living daylights right out'ta me." She patted her pink frizz and threw a black glare at Dexter. "Some Neighborhood Watch."

"I told you, the Watch don't prevent violence. We only report it to the police!" Dexter turned to thrust a tight jaw in Lechman's direction. "But we can haul low-down *sleaze balls* to the police station."

Lechman opened his mouth and then closed it.

"Did he damage the screen?" I asked.

Dexter shook his head. "Nope. Caught him trying to jiggle it loose."

I'd cursed the heavy wooden screens on my apartment complex each time I had to put them up in the summer and take down to store for winter but I had to admit, they made a great deterrent to unwelcome visitors.

I eyed Lechman, watched a bead of sweat slide from his hairline to his eyebrow, and made a decision. "Albert, I'm going to give you a break. You haul your sorry self out of here and I won't report this."

Dexter snorted. I ignored him. "If I ever catch you even looking at my property again, I'll let Dexter give you a lump on your head so big it'll need an athletic supporter." I leaned close and poked his chest with my finger. "And I won't hesitate to call the cops. Do we have an understanding?"

Lechman eyed Dexter's tattoo, nodded, and climbed to his feet. "I have other ways of finding Sherrilyn. We share a common bond when it comes to cooking and when I tell her how you've treated . . ."

Dexter took a step forward. "I believe the lady said haul it."

Lechman cut his eyes to me, ambled across the room and let the screen door slam. I watched him get into a silver Taurus and leave.

Violet gasped, clutched her chest, and shook a finger at Dexter. "You're crazy. Since you joined that Watch Group, you've gone plumb crazy!" she said while struggling to her feet. "If I'm murdered in my bed by some lunatic, it'll be on your head!"

She marched into the kitchen and Dexter grinned as we heard the back door bang shut.

"Lump big enough to need a jock strap? Good one, Mercedes." The twinkle in his blue eyes dimmed as he shook his head. "Big mistake, letting that scumbag go. There's something about him . . . I can't put my finger on it, but if I did I'd have to sterilize my whole hand."

"How'd you subdue him?"

"It's all in the thumb." He extended his callused hands and demonstrated. "Quick grab the hand, bend ol' Thumbman back, then hoist the perp's arm between his shoulder blades. Voila! You can lead the sucker around like one of your little dogs. If the perp so much as wiggles, just give his thumb another crank."

"Good to know. So what was Violet saying about intruders in ski masks?"

"You don't know? It's been all over the news."

"I've been getting Number Ten ready for my brother, and working on the mess Schmunk left."

Dexter nodded. "Schmunk, what a loser, sneakin' out in the middle of the night. Bet he stiffed you some rent."

"That's dirty water under the bridge. Tell me about the ruckus." I said pointing toward the alley which separated my apartments from the backyards of five homes on the next street.

"You remember the teenage kid who got the snot beat out of him at that elementary school parking lot?"

I nodded.

"Well, the kid's friends found out it was some of the band members livin' in the old Atkins' place who beat-up their friend. His buds came armed with baseball bats, tire irons, what have you, and busted up the place."

"Whoa. Did anyone get hurt?"

"The usual cuts, bruises, black eyes. Cops arrived before anything serious happened."

Killian hadn't mentioned anything. Of course, the last couple of days I'd gone pedal-to-the-metal, practically living at the complex. My two Dachshunds hardly recognized me. I was disappointed Killian hadn't given me a heads-up in case I had to soothe a worried renter.

"It's this heat," Dexter said. "It's like an itch that can't be scratched, makes people do crazy things."

"Dexter, come fix this fan," Violet called from the kitchen. "I don't want it stationary, I want it moving in an arc. Can't make a decent BLT with the shredded lettuce blowing about."

Dexter rolled his eyes. "Did you hear her come in?"

I shook my head.

"I swear that woman's part cat, sneakin' around, listening in on conversations." He adjusted his belt around his trim waist and went to Violet's aid.

I walked to my car, scanning the surrounding area for any sign of Lechman. If the man was skulking, he was well hidden. The sun had dipped well below the tall oaks bordering my complex. Another fevered night would soon settle on the valley accompanied by a full moon; the perfect time for more crazies suffering from heat exhaustion to wreak havoc.

I slid into my Karmann Ghia's bucket seat, thighs protesting the hot, sticky vinyl as my cell phone trilled *March of the Marionettes*. Gram's cell.

"Yello," I said, searching through my bag for car keys.

"Come get me."

"What?"

"I'm on Fifth Avenue between Putnam and Humbolt."

"Where's Cary and Frobi?"

"I'll explain later. Just come and get me before I pass out from heatstroke."

Gram clicked off, leaving me staring at the phone in my left hand as the fingers on my right hand wrapped around the elusive keys. The sun would soon be a mere memory as twilight shadows deepened.

Cary and Frobi were MIA and my seventy-one-year-old Grandmother was all alone a couple of blocks from the warehouse district, home-sweet-home to muggers, drug dealers and possibly murderers.

Streetlights blinked to life as I revved the Ghia's engine, popped the clutch, and bumped across a series of potholes on Benton Street. I put my foot to the floor and blew through a yellow light—a tad more red than yellow—hit the next light green on Main and roared across the Benton St. overpass. Railroad tracks snaked beneath the overpass and a train huffed in the night air as it ambled out of the yard.

A hard right on Second, another right on Putnam, then left on Fifth and I spotted Gram walking in stocking feet down the cracked sidewalk. She saw me and stopped, waving her sandals in the air.

I pulled to the side, my tires kissing the curb, then leaned over and opened the door. Gram maneuvered herself into the passenger seat, yanked the door closed, and turned to face me. Several limp strands had escaped her steel-gray French twist, smudges of mascara pooled in the bags under her eyes, and her face was an unhealthy shade of red.

My brother was a dead man walking.

"What happened?"

"I told Cary I wanted to walk home, and he obliged."

"He pulled over and let you out, just like that? I waved my hand in an arc. "Inches away from Mugger Central?"

Gram lifted her chin, eyes defiant. "Mercedes, don't exaggerate. I'm nowhere near First Street, this is a perfectly normal neighborhood."

Uh-huh. Normal neighborhood back in the seventies but now . . ."What happened?"

"Frobi's endless chatter about their fabulous online enterprise was exhausting, but when the two began bickering I was done."

Bickering? Hmm. "Bickering about . . .?" I prodded, rolling my hand in a come-on movement.

Gram shrugged and fiddled with the Ghia's temperamental, non-factory-installed air conditioner, turning all the vents in her direction. "When are you trading this junk heap for a decent car?"

"Uh-uh, changing the subject, not allowed."

Gram heaved a sign. "After we finished eating, Cary wanted to show me the warehouse they've rented to store the caskets. Frobi wanted to go back to the mortuary and use her laptop to show me the different products, the estimated sales with, no doubt, charts and graphs out the ying-yang. Hence the bickering and then Cary reverted to his passive-aggressive whining."

She said. "I doubt he was cuddled enough as a child!"

I raised an eyebrow.

She heaved a sign again. "For some reason Frobi didn't want to go to the warehouse, said she wasn't sure of the exact address. She'd only viewed the property on the internet, hadn't entered the information into her new cell phone . . . something along those lines. That started the argument, Cary didn't believe her. The real kicker was when Cary accused Frobi of flirting with your cop friend, Killian."

Hmm. Double hmm.

I put the Ghia in gear, eased away from the curb and headed for Harrigan Mortuary on Twelfth Street.

"Cary let you out of the SUV just like that." I snapped my fingers. Something wasn't ringing true.

Gram shrugged. "I wanted out, he pulled over, and I got out. He did offer me a roll of butterscotch Lifesavers." Gram leaned back in the seat and closed her eyes. "You know, I'm not impressed with the way that SUV rides. I thought about getting one until tonight."

Gram and her lead foot in a Mercedes-Benz G? I shuddered and blinked the image from my mind.

"What if you hadn't been able to reach me? Did you expect to walk all the way home?"

She opened one eye and gave me the look that had squelched many a feud between "grieving" family members.

"Mercedes McCambridge, you are the most pugnacious . . . leave it be!" She closed her eye and settled deeper into the seat.

"And, for your information, I could walk this whole town if I put my mind to it."

That much was true. Changing Gram's mind was on a par with carving granite with a butter knife.

"Besides, if I hadn't reached you, Yancey would've picked me up." I smothered a sigh.

Yancey Candlemass. My grandmother's head assistant.

Yancey was oil, I was water. Mix us together and things got ugly. Gram had lured Yancey away from Wayco Funeral Home with the promise of a higher wage, a free apartment above the four-stall mortuary garage, and anything else she could entice him with. Yancey's ability to make uncle so-and-so look like he was merely napping in a casket, even if poor uncle had gone through the windshield, bordered on uncanny. I suspect Yancy had been dabbling with makeup while other little boys were playing with trucks.

We pulled under the left portico of the Harrigan Mortuary and I shut off the Ghia, hoping Gram would invite me in for tea and the rest of the sordid Cary and Frobi saga. I rolled down my window and inhaled the light fragrance. Years ago, Gram had started each Irish Gold rose from a mere twig, and now the bountiful bushes formed an aromatic hedge.

The right side of the double, leaded glass front door opened and Yancey poked his head out, expertly tousled tawny hair shining under the portico spotlights. Thanks to his English heritage, a patrician nose graced his lean, pale face.

"Thank God you're here. I just took a call from the hospital. Mr. Youngstown has passed on." He paused and looked skyward, right hand pressed to his heart, pure avarice dancing in his glacial blue eyes.

"Gimme a break," I muttered. Gram swatted my knee.

Yancey sauntered to the end of the porch, placed a hand on the white wrap-around porch railing, and vaulted to the tarmac below. He opened Gram's car door with aplomb and extended his hand to help her from the low-slung seat.

"Duty calls. Thanks for the lift," Gram said, bussing my cheek before exiting. I turned the key and watched Yancey throw his arm around Gram's ample shoulders as they sauntered toward the double front door. When they reached the steps, he turned his head, mouthed "ta-ta." and blew me a kiss.

I revved the engine, popped the clutch, and squealed out of the driveway. That would show him.

My stomach growled reminding me I'd skipped dinner. I pulled into the Maverik gas station on the corner of Fifth Avenue and Center in search of some comfort food. Ten minutes later, on the outskirts of town, I ignored the posted speed limit and let the Ghia hug the winding curves, the wind blowing through the open windows as I munched on a glazed Krispy Kreme. I hoped to catch Killian in my barn tending to his horse, Eclipse. Maybe, if I traded him a couple of cream-filled doughnuts he'd use his cop skills to run a deep background check on one Ms. Frobi Fisher.

My gut instinct screamed something was out of whack with Fisher and her whole get-rich spiel. Killian would accuse me of sticking my nose where it didn't belong. And I'd remind him that the last time my gut instinct hollered, I'd helped him take down a psychotic killer. Besides, I was worried about the welfare of my baby brother. If anyone was going to kill him, it was going to be me.

I pulled down the long driveway and parked next to my two-story 1920s farmhouse. No sign of Killian's black truck. Damn! I gathered my goodies and headed for the backyard. Bogart, my black and tan Dachshund, and Bacall, my long-haired red, greeted me, hopping on stubby hind legs, scrabbling with fat front paws in the hopes of scaling the chain-link gate.

"Move it or lose it," I said, pushing the gate open and then closing it with my hip. I petted and fed my happy duo a couple bites of doughnut. "Now, this is only to ease Mama's guilt for leaving you alone so long," I warned.

Bogart wagged his tail while Bacall rushed through the dog door only to return with her empty food dish. I heard Eclipse nicker from the corral. "Hold your water, big guy."

Inside, the light from my ancient answering machine blinked in the dimness. I hit the kitchen light switch and glanced at the digital readout: six messages. Either a couple of elderly tenants, who preferred to use my landline, had a problem, or all six messages were from telemarketers.

I pushed the play button, scooped dog food into Bogart and Bacall's dishes, and listened to my renter Agatha ask me if she could trim a bush beside her front door tomorrow. I'd deal with her floral obsession later.

I deleted the next five, which sounded vaguely like the same guy making pre-recorded sales pitches for various companies.

I checked my cell and was surprised to find I'd missed three calls. The first message, from Cary, informed me he and Frobi would look for other accommodations tomorrow.

Yes.

The last two were from Rebbie. In the first one, she sounded elated, telling me to call her ASAP. The second call was mostly static, mixed with . . . was that panic in her voice?

I dialed Reb's number and it went straight to voicemail. Hmm. I left a message.

Exchanging my black wedge sandals for pull-on mud boots, I walked up to the corral. Eclipse hung his beautiful black head over the top corral pole and nudged my hip, looking for a sugar cube.

"Sorry, buddy. I'll bring a handful in the morning." I went into the barn and checked to make sure Killian had fed him. Yup, fresh water and hay. Here and gone, I'd have to hunt the man down tomorrow. The only thing left was to finish the last glazed doughnut and plop my body in bed.

I munched the rest of my dinner over the kitchen sink, chased the last bite with Cherry Pepsi, and glanced out the window at the black clouds smothering the stars. Not high in nutrition but in some circles considered the breakfast of champions. My cell rang. Probably Reb.

A female voice said, "Mercedes, I'm so happy I caught you."

Not Rebbie, and I had no idea who was thrilled to find me.

"This is Ester Clemmens from the Humane Society. I'm in a bit of a spot. I'm fostering a mini-Schnauzer until I can find him the right home. He's exhibiting small dog syndrome, keeps nipping at my Great Dane and German Shepherd. So far both dogs are being extremely patient but, I don't want to risk a problem."

Ester lived across the river behind my apartment complex. President of the local Humane Society, she had an assortment of dogs and cats, and she'd helped me out a couple of months ago by finding a home for a cranky cat left by a deceased tenant.

"That's too bad," I said.

"Remember when you said you'd love to give us a hand? Well, now is the time to come to the Society's aid."

I didn't remember saying anything of the sort, but that didn't mean much. I tend to say things in the heat of the moment. "So, what can I do?"

"Take this little sweetheart into your home until the Society's next adoption day, which is in two weeks. I think he'll feel more at ease with dogs his own size." Ester's perfectly modulated voice floated through my receiver. I pictured her in her immaculate kitchen in a perfectly coordinated outfit with just the right accessories.

"Ester, right now isn't the best time. My brother . . ."

"Great, I'll bring him over in the morning. Thanks so much. Bye."

I stared at the phone wondering if all the sugar and caffeine had turned me mute. Hadn't I just told the woman *no*?

Upstairs in my bedroom, I angled a standing floor fan to blow a cross breeze over the bed and opened the windows. Shucking off my black capri pants and silk tank top, I pulled on an old tee shirt and lay down on top of the covers, staring at the long crack in my ceiling. The air drifting through the windows teased with the scent of impending rain. Glorious rain that would cleanse away the dust and cool the earth. If only the rain could seep through my brother's thick skull, wash away the alien businessman he'd morphed into, and turn him back to his lazy, haphazard self.

I flipped onto my stomach and thought about Cary and Frobi meeting on some surfing website. With her toned body she'd look great in a bikini but I had a hard time picturing her getting slammed by waves, spitting out saltwater, and keeping with the program until she could successfully navigate the waves upright on her board. In the morning, I planned to Google Fisher. Where did she come from? Did she really have a knack for turning internet companies into money makers? What made her pick Cary for her instructor? His bio and picture caught her attention or had she sensed an opportunity to turn my carefree sibling into her corporate minion?

I turned on my side, thrashed around, seeking comfort where none existed. To distract myself from the thin film of perspiration laying on me and my snoring dogs, I replayed Reb's last strange voicemail. Did I detect panic in her voice? Was she okay? I had to believe yes, or she would have called me back. Right?

Heat, worry, and too much sugar equaled a sleepless night.

My eyes snapped open to Darth Vader's theme. I groped past sleeping dogs for the phone and groaned when I spotted the digital readout on my bedside clock. 2:30 a.m. This could not be good!

Dexter's gruff voice jarred me. "Mercedes, there's been another 187."

"What?"

"We've got a DOA in the parking lot."

"A DOA? As in dead person?"

"—'fraid so. Agatha says it's that gal who came here with your brother."

FOUR

"**D**AMNDEST THING I'VE EVER SEEN," DEXTER said, eyes narrowed, head cocked to one side. We stood together in front of his apartment on the sidewalk that divides my apartment complex from the asphalt parking lot which, at the moment, resembled any popular police drama with multiple PGPD cruisers and emergency vehicles. Flashing red and blue lights gave a surreal cast to the crowd of gawkers gathered beneath the swollen, obsidian sky watching as police, forensic team, and investigators milled or scurried about.

"It's just plain crazy, stripping the clothes off the poor girl and then painting every inch of her gold," Dexter said. "Killer must be a die-hard James Bond fan."

I could only nod in mute agreement. With the exception of her extraordinary breasts, Frobi resembled a life-sized Oscar statue, draped artfully over the steering wheel . . . an urban legend for the internet.

It was the first time I'd seen Frobi without a wig. Her real locks were pixie-short and plastered to her head by the gold paint. She had tiny, well-shaped ears and what I guessed were diamond stud earrings. The killer had taped her eyes shut with duct tape. I found that more disturbing than the paint.

The interior of the SUV was devoid of spray paint, so Frobi had been coated elsewhere. But where? And why?

"Quite an audience," Dexter said, motioning to the curious crowd that had doubled in size since I first arrived. "Emergencies act like magnets."

In the distance, a bolt of lightning competed with the colored lights from the official vehicles. Each flash from the forensic technician's camera added to the light show. The wind had picked up, rustling the yellow crime scene tape stretched between emergency poles surrounding the SUV. Any minute the various professionals searching for evidence would be S.O.L.

"Better go check on Violet. An officer was questioning her when she nearly collapsed and two paramedics had to help her into the house with a 'sick headache.'"

Dexter walked a few steps then stopped and scratched his chin. "I told a couple of officers about Lechman the peeping Tom. Something's not right with his story. Better watch your back, you hear?"

Despite the humidity, a chill slithered down my spine. I nodded.

A news van bearing the Channel Six logo screeched to a halt in the alley which ran behind the left side of my complex, a reporter in a short dress-for-success suit jumped from the passenger side with a lone cameraman close behind her. Barbie Honeywell, the blonde piranha of Channel Six.

Crap! My nightmare had gone from bad to worse. Barbie had been a thorn in my side since we attended grade school together. I ducked in behind a fire engine and sat on the curb hoping Barbie hadn't noticed me. She either knew I owned the complex or she'd soon find out.

Reb appeared at my side. "Had to park down the block, got here soon as I could. OMG is that . . .?" She pointed to the SUV then plopped beside me on the curb.

"Yes, that's . . . um . . . Frobi Fisher." I looked closely at Reb, still dressed as she had been earlier with hair and makeup intact. No sign of bed head or smeared mascara. At three a.m. what was the deal with that?

"Where's Harry Cary?" Reb voiced the gnawing concern I'd had since I arrived. Where was my brother?

I stood, grabbed her arm and pulled her behind the bush Agatha wanted to scalp, away from prying eyes and ears. "I don't know. He isn't here, no one's seen him since he left."

"Left?"

"Yeah, seems Fisher and Cary had a very vocal fight in the middle of the parking lot sometime around midnight. Agatha heard it all, watched Cary stomp off and Fisher storm inside the apartment." I gulped in an ozone-tinged breath.

"Did Agatha witness . . . that?" Reb pointed to the SUV and shuddered.

"No. She went to bed after Cary took off. Dexter got a call from someone in his Neighborhood Watch group asking if the naked lady in the parking lot was some kind of prank. He called me before he called 911."

"And you've called Cary?"

"Multiple times, left multiple messages. Where could he be? What if he's dead too?"

"Uh-uh." Reb threw her arm around my shoulder and squeezed. "Let's not leap off that cliff just yet." she held me tighter. "Willie needs to know about this. And it should come from you, *not* the news media."

She nodded as another news van parked across the street. "Portneuf Gap rarely makes the national news unless the event is too juicy to ignore. Fisher's death, the way she was murdered, might register above the high-juice mark."

Of course Reb was right. The thought of having my vintage apartment complex splashed around national media outlets was both depressing and terrifying. But the thought of bringing Willie into this mess boded far worse. I felt all the air rush from my lungs, leaving me light-headed and wishing for a paper sack to breathe into. My fifty-something mother lived in a little bungalow in Southern California, where she studied classic movies from the 40's and 50's, occasionally appeared in commercials, and lived out her delusional femme fatale life.

"Cary could still show up. No need to bother Willie just yet." I said.

Reb rolled her eyes.

From my hiding spot, I watched Barbie Honeywell shove a microphone close to Dexter; he was puffed up like a rooster and, looking serious for the camera, answered each question as though rattling off his rank and serial number.

I pulled Reb deeper behind the bush. She pointed at the scurrying police and EMT's. "What's the consensus from our men in blue?"

"No one is saying anything but I'm betting that Cary's Numero Uno on their suspect list."

Reb pursed her mouth and nodded. "Of course, always look at the husband or boyfriend through a microscope."

"S.O.P.," a deep male voice said. Reb squealed and whirled into Jack Killian.

"Don't do that!" My voice came out sounding like Minnie Mouse. I glared at Killian. "I hate when you sneak around. And for your information, standard operating procedure doesn't apply in this case."

Killian rocked back in his worn cowboy boots. A black-tee, tucked into worn Wranglers, stretched to cover abs of steel. He hooked his thumbs in the belt loops of his jeans. "Why doesn't it apply?"

"He's my brother." I sniffed and swiped at a tear. Another one leaked out to take its place. Killian leaned forward to brush it away with a calloused finger-tip.

"Sadie, that doesn't mean . . ."

"He's my brother," I said, louder to combat the rest of the tears threatening to spill. Killian pulled me into his arms and I laid my head against his solid chest, my tears seeping onto said black tee shirt. He smelled of Ivory soap, sun-kissed laundry, and the cologne he favors, a strong, no-nonsense smell I could lose myself in. I wanted to stay in his embrace, if only for a while. That scent and his strong, capable arms could hold the monsters of this night at bay, at least for a time.

"What are you doing here?" Reb asked.

"Heard the call go out on my scanner. Thought you might need a friendly face," Killian said.

Friend. Right.

I stepped from his embrace, scrubbed my face with both hands, and tried for a smile. "Thanks."

Reb took Killian's hand between her palms. "You are just so thoughtful." Tilting her head, cute little worry lines between her eyes, she licked her lips.

Okay, Reb and Killian had been an item on and off for the past year. Lately they'd been more off than on. Looked like the tide was changing.

An anguished howl erupted from the back of the crowd standing in the parking lot entrance. A disheveled man made a dash for the SUV. A young cop stepped forward to intercept him, the man tried to sidestep and ended in a heap on the pavement. He lay on his back, hands covering his eyes, crying, "Sherri, I told you, an' told you, an' told you!"

"What the hell?" Killian started forward. I grabbed his arm.

"That's Mark Sandborn, Sherri Sandborn's ex. He's shit-faced, but harmless. Sherri lives in Number Eight, but she's out of town."

Two officers helped Mark to his feet, and guided him over to the curb, where he fell to his knees. "That's my wife," he cried, struggling to pull his stained tee shirt over his skinny white gut. "I have to cover her. For God's sake, someone cover her!"

Agatha shuffled across the parking lot to Mark. Her flowered cotton robe blew around skinny ankles while she squatted down beside him, grabbed his cheeks, and put her forehead smack against his. "Look at me, you big oaf. That's not your wife! You hear me? Not. Your. Wife. Now haul your kiester on home and sober up." She gave Mark a good shake and pointed to the street. "Go on, before the cops arrest you for drunk and disorderly."

Mark squinted at Agatha. "That's not my lil' Sherri?"

"No!" Agatha stood and crossed her arms across her concave chest.

Mark climbed to his feet, and wiped his nose on his shirt. Two officers took him by the arms and led him toward a police cruiser with Barbie Honeywell on their heels shouting questions.

"Hey, Killian, didn't know you pulled a double shift," Detective Mick Stayner said as he ambled toward us. At six-foot-three, and solidly in the three-hundred-pound range, Mick carried his weight well on his large frame. Stayner's hair, eyebrows, and mustache were bushy and peppered with gray. He reminded me of a big, friendly Saint Bernard.

"Just here as a friend," Killian said. "I board Eclipse in Mercedes' barn."

"You know the brother?" Det. Stayner asked, pulling out a worn notebook.

"He has a name, you know. Cary Grant Harrigan," Rebbie said.

"Right," Det. Stayner said.

"Cary just arrived in town. Jack doesn't know him." Rebbie said.

"Right," Det. Stayner said.

Jack patted Rebbie's shoulder. "I did meet Mr. Harrigan and the victim, Ms. Frobi Fisher, earlier this evening when I answered that 415 at The Sandpiper."

"Yeah, I heard about the rabid neighbor chewing some guy's ear off." Det. Stayner whistled and turned to me. "The deceased wasn't one of your regular tenants, right?"

"No. She and my brother are . . ." I sucked in some air and blew it out. "They were here on a working vacation for a couple of days, staying in apartment number three."

Det. Stayner jotted something in his notebook. "And you met Ms. Fisher when?"

"Yesterday morning. She and my brother arrived in that SUV," I waved my hand at the crime scene. "Sometime after ten."

"Okay." He tucked the notebook back in his jacket and held out his hand. A large raindrop bounced off his palm. "Looks like we're in for it. Hope Forensics is done gathering evidence. I'm gonna have a look around the apartment. Don't leave, I've got more questions." He ambled toward Apartment Three.

Det. Stayner wouldn't find much. As soon as I'd arrived, before the first patrol car appeared and Dexter was calming Violet, I had ducked into the apartment for a quick look-see. I know, I know, possible crime scene, but I'm the landlord and I had the right to check in case Cary was inside. Except for their luggage and the furniture that came with the apartment, I'd discovered the place empty. The only odd item was a suitcase, open on the bed, full of wigs in various colors and styles. A couple of contact lens cases lay on the bathroom counter.

Above the background noise came the unmistakable sound of the body bag zipper, followed by a clattering of the gurney headed for the hearse. On the rotation schedule the Waygo Funeral Home had been called. The body would be put in their cooler until the medical examiner could perform an autopsy. I watched a couple of Waygo assistants help the coroner load the body then slam the rear door. One assistant tipped me a two-finger salute before climbing behind the wheel. The red taillights of the hearse hit me like a kick to the stomach; Fisher was dead.

And my baby brother was MIA.

Killian followed Det. Stayner to the apartment door and pulled on the gloves Stayner slapped against his chest before they disappeared inside.

I called Cary, again. His cell went immediately to voicemail. "Frobi's dead. Where the hell are you? Call me!"

Hating the panicked squeak in my voice, I hung up, tried my

land line and left the same message on my machine, just in case Cary happened to be in my kitchen raiding my fridge.

The clouds burst open and rain poured in earnest, sending the news crew and looky-loos scurrying for cover. Reb and I ducked into the vacated apartment, where the heat and humidity enveloped us like a soggy blanket.

"Open some windows before we all die," Reb said, trying to heft the smallest living-room window.

Killian pulled her away. "Don't touch anything!"

Det. Stayner stepped in from the hallway. "Nothing here, far as I can tell. Cell phone isn't in her purse. Other than that nothing seems to be missing. Money and credit cards appear to be intact." He shrugged. "Forensics will do their thing but I don't see any signs of a struggle. No gold paint."

If he found the assortment of wigs odd, he was keeping mum.

"Look, Detective, let's talk facts. The paint proves my brother's innocent," I said.

He raised a bushy eyebrow.

"Painting a person takes creative thinking. Originality is not Cary's strong point, unless he's on a surfboard."

Det. Stayner nodded but didn't reach for his note book. I bit my lip and swallowed the rest of the argument he didn't want to hear.

Killian stood by the front door, hands in his pockets, looking at the knob. "Lock wasn't engaged, no sign of forced entry." He looked at me. "Did you unlock it?"

I shook my head. I wasn't lying, I'd found the apartment open, which struck me as strange, since I'd witnessed Fisher insisting everything needed to be locked up tight.

"First unit found the front door unlocked but the back deadbolt engaged." Det. Stayner walked into the kitchen, and tired hinges protested as he unlocked the deadbolt and pulled the door open. He consulted his notes. "Screen door's latched, too. Looks like the victim knew her assailant well enough to open the front door." He relocked the door and gave me a pointed look. "Was Ms. Fisher acquainted with anyone here besides your brother?"

"I don't know."

A young female cop stepped into the apartment, blonde hair plastered to her head. An evidence baggie dangled between her thumb and forefinger. "Found this in the victim's left hand." She handed the baggie to Det. Stayner.

Half a roll of butterscotch Lifesavers lay in the bottom of the bag—butterscotch, Cary's favorite since we were kids. My stomach lodged in my throat, while my heart slammed against my chest like a trapped animal.

"Find anything else?" he handed the evidence back.

The young cop shook her head. "Tow truck's on the way. We'll know more after we process the vehicle in impound."

"Do you have a current picture of your brother?" Det. Stayner asked.

I shook my head, not trusting my voice to answer. He nodded, took out his wallet, and handed me a card. "Call me as soon as your brother contacts you or you learn his where abouts. Come to the station in the morning I'll get your statement." He said goodnight and hurried into the rain.

"That detective has a bulls-eye painted on Cary," Reb said, pacing to the kitchen sink and back. "He'll toss Cary in jail before the boy has a chance to explain."

Killian ignored Reb's rant. "Why don't we call it a night?" he said, turning off the kitchen light. "Nothing more to do here."

Yeah. Right. His lips said *go home*, but his eyes were in cop mode, brain working the scene.

Reb looked at her watch. "Damn, almost four. I have another meeting with the big boys at nine. I need to look sharp, be sharp. Can't do that with baggage under my eyes." She yawned and sighed. "I'm out'ta here. We'll talk later. Okay?"

My B.S. radar pinged. "Wait," I said. Reb had arrived dressed for success, strange considering the early hour. Now she planned to mosey home and grab some sleep? Uh-uh. "I recall a frantic message earlier demanding I call you. What's wrong?"

Reb frowned and pursed her lips. "Nothing."

"Nothing? Really? You sounded . . ."

"Oh, wait." Reb thunked her head with her hand. "I had a curt 'call me' message from Bernhagen. Guess I sorta panicked, thought he wanted to break the deal." Reb shrugged. "Turns out he's a little antsy about the meeting today, just needed a little reassuring. Call me ASAP when you find Cary." She blew an air kiss and popped out the front door.

Killian stood, arms folded, eyes narrowed, staring at the doorway. *I wasn't the only one with suspicions.*

He looked at me and his face softened. Throwing an arm around my shoulders, he gave me a squeeze. "You okay to go home alone?"

"Yeah. I'll go see if my brother's hiding under my bed."

Killian turned me to face him. "You *will* call me with any news, right?"

"Of course," I said, taking a step backward.

Killian frowned. "Sadie, you've got to trust me. I can help Cary, but only if you keep me in the loop."

"I'll call, I promise."

After Killian left, Dexter came out of his apartment to watch the tow truck winch the SUV onto a long flatbed. The rain had eased to a light drizzle and the moon peered between tattered clouds.

"Hell of a night," he said.

"Dexter, if Cary shows up . . ."

"I'll give you a jingle."

"Don't let him leave. Sit on him if you have to."

"I'll handle him, not to worry." He patted my back. "Now you run home and get some rest, you look about done in."

I gave him a quick hug and got into my car. Questions spun in my head faster than a windmill in a storm. Rest was the last item on my agenda. Checking my cell, I saw I'd missed a call from Gram. I put the Ghia in gear and headed for the Harrigan Funeral Home.

FIVE

"IT'S ABOUT TIME," GRAM SAID WHEN I opened her kitchen door. "Take a seat and tell me what the hell happened."

I slipped into a chair at her 1946 chrome and Formica dinette set. A china cup, saucer, and small plate sat before me on a cross-stitched placemat. I inhaled the aroma of Earl Gray tea and felt my muscles relax a notch. A warm cinnamon roll with butter oozing down the sides covered the plate. Is it any wonder I love this woman?

"There was a murder at my complex," I said, snatching two sugar cubes from the footed sugar bowl and stirring them into my tea.

"Enough with the Joe Friday imitation. Yancy woke me and explained all about Golden Girl."

Of course he did.

Gram stood, reached into a white kitchen cabinet drawer and pulled out a large dishtowel. "Here, dry your hair before you catch your death. Then tell me everything."

As I toweled my hair, I let my gaze wander across the black and white tile floor, up the white cabinets to the yellow tile countertop, trying to decide how to phrase the problem. "Dexter found Frobi Fisher slumped over the steering wheel of the SUV they'd rented.

She was nude, painted gold, and D.O.A. Cary and Fisher had a fight in the parking lot sometime around midnight. Now, Cary's disappeared and he's not answering his cell."

Gram drummed her fingers on the Formica. "Your brother's really stepped in it this time. He's most likely holed up somewhere, afraid to show his face." She reached up to adjust a loose pink sponge curler on her head. "Any ideas?"

"No. Fresh out." I laid my spoon across the saucer and raised an eyebrow. "How about you? Any spare guests who're still breathing?"

"Mercedes McCambridge Harrigan, how can you even think I'd harbor a fugitive?" Gram sat up straighter, dabbed the corners of her mouth with a linen napkin, and pinned me with a no-nonsense glare. "I do not flaunt the law like some people I could name."

I did a mental eye roll. "Stop fuming. We both know Cary couldn't murder anyone . . ."

"Especially someone he's planning to wed. At least I hope not," Gram murmured, brushing an imaginary speck from her pink chenille bathrobe.

"But the cops have him in their sights. And being kin and all, you'd feel obligated to hide him, right?"

Gram laid her hand over her heart. "I wish he *had* come to me. I could help him."

"Then, either he's hiding somewhere or . . ." I did a palms-up, refusing to consider the other possibilities.

"I'm betting Frobi's death wasn't random, few murders are. She'd just arrived and was supposedly new to our town." Gram took a sip of tea and pursed her lips. "And, assuming Cary didn't commit this heinous crime, then someone's privy to their travel itinerary. Could there be another partner in this ludicrous casket venture?"

"Cary didn't mention anyone."

Gram frowned, stirred her tea. "Do you know if they met with anyone else besides the assisted living group to hawk their caskets?" She said the word casket like it tasted bad.

I shook my head.

"You need to call your mother."

Another vote for alerting Willie. I raised an eyebrow. "She'll insist on coming here. Then the drama will really hit the fan."

Gram folded her arms under her abundant breasts and chewed on her lip. When I was twelve my father took off for places unknown, never to return, and accusations as to why he left flew between Willie and Gram like migrating geese. Gram had mellowed some in the following years. Willie still blamed Gram for every ill that plagued the world. Frosty was a polite way to describe their relationship.

"Her son is not only missing," Gram paused, a pained look on her face, "but is also the lead suspect in a murder investigation. She must hear this from a loved one. Not the news media!"

Is that how Gram had found out my father was missing? From a news report? Neither she nor Willie talked much about the first couple of weeks after my dad disappeared.

Lightning lit the night and thunder boomed a couple of beats later. Appropriate. "Okay, I'll call her when I get home."

Gram narrowed her eyes.

"I will. I promise," I said, holding up my right hand.

"Time's ticking, let's move. You can check out the surfing website where Frobi and Cary hooked up. I'll have Yancy check her background in the morning, after he's finished preparing Mr. Youngstown for tonight's viewing."

I rolled my eyes so far I could see my eyebrows needed plucking.

"Oh, stop. Yancy's absolutely brilliant at digging around computer sites. If there's any dirt on the woman, he'll find it." She stood and put the remaining rolls into a plastic bag. "Now get home search the website and your property. He gets hungry he'll turn up. Not that many places he's familiar with."

I took the bag and headed for the door.

"And call your mother," Gram hollered as the screen slammed shut.

The Portneuf Gap airport accommodated only small planes. If Willie Dearest decided to catch a flight, it would be from San Diego to the Idaho Falls airport, sixty miles to the north. I had time on my side and essentially two options: either find Cary and clean up this mess before she arrived or commit hara-kiri. Option two seemed more appealing at the moment.

My asphalt driveway looked freshly paved after the rain, no dusty tire tracks or brother-on-the-run footprints. I pulled next to the backyard gate, cut the engine, and heard the familiar greeting of Bogart and Bacall as they bounced against the fence. I slipped into the backyard and sat in the wet grass, my shorts sucking up the cold water like a thirsty sponge. Both dogs leapt into my lap, licking my face with abandon. I needed this unconditional love before I made *The Call*. Unconditional love, a shower, and a couple of the rolls Gram had sent.

Inside, my answering machine blinked madly in the pre-dawn light filtering through the kitchen blinds. The first message was my own panicked voice beseeching Cary to call. The second was strange: "Hi. Name's Martin Mangum. I heard about the murder at your complex and since I'm doing research on paranormal psychology, I'd like to meet with you to discuss . . ." I hit the delete button.

"Time to get a life, Martin."

The wall clock read five forty-five; four forty-five in California. Dealing with Willie when she's fully awake is hard enough, best to wait for a decent time to ring her bell. Cary could show up on my doorstep with an explanation that would solve everything. Or I might win the next Powerball lottery. The odds were about the same.

I checked every corner of my house and barn for signs of my fugitive brother, then hurried upstairs to the bathroom, stripped, and let the power-head shower beat on me until my skin turned a nice rosy hue and some of the cobwebs were cleared from my brain. After toweling off, I shrugged into Levi shorts and a red tank top, and padded down the stairs to feed the hounds, fix coffee, and watch Linda Hamilton in *Terminator Two*. Watching her decked out in full commando gear, biceps bulging, I always feel stronger, more in control, ready to kick some ass.

As the movie began, I grabbed an envelope from the pile of papers on my kitchen table to jot down places Cary might be holed up. I settled on the couch, bookended by Bogart and Bacall. When the credits rolled, I shut off the TV and looked at the blank paper. Damn. Hamilton had once again saved her son and the whole world. I, on the other hand, couldn't figure out where my own brother might hide out. The only ass kicked so far was my own.

The clock on the mantle read eight-forty-five. It was time. I clutched my phone, mentally girded my loins, and dialed Willie. She answered on the third ring, and her sleepy voice had me praying she was alone in bed.

"Hey, Willie."

"Mercedes? What time is it?" I waited as she fumbled for the clock on her nightstand. "Why the hell are you calling so early? Is something wrong?"

"Have you heard from Cary?" I crossed my fingers and silently chanted *please, please, pretty please with sugar,* while steeling myself for hysterics.

"Heavens, no. Why would he call when he and his new paramour are busy making tons of moollah?"

"Uh . . . there's been a slight change in the moollah-making plans." I took a deep breath. Best to rip the Band-aid off quick. "His paramour is dead, he's missing, and the police think he may have killed her." I squeezed my eyes shut and gritted my teeth.

Silence.

I peeked one eye open.

Eerie silence. No eardrum-shattering, end-of-life-as-we-know-it scream.

"Willie?" I relaxed my jaw and opened the other eye.

"When did this happen?" Her voice was calm, controlled.

I told her what I knew.

"I'll check airline schedules and get back to you." Click, the line went dead.

Okay, who was this rational woman and what had she done with my drama-queen mother?

I went into the kitchen, poured another cup of coffee, nibbled on a roll and tried Cary's cell again. Voicemail. I walked out onto the back porch and stared at the distant hills, watching a hawk soar above a group of juniper trees. Who would Cary turn to besides me or Gram? Had he kept in touch with friends from middle school? Not likely. My phone rang and I nearly dropped it in my haste to answer.

"Turn on channel six," Reb said. "Cary's the top story on the early news."

I ran into the living room and clicked on the TV. Sure enough, there was Cary's high-school graduation picture enlarged for the viewing audience. Next to it was a picture of Frobi, wearing a long platinum wig and dressed casually in jeans and a pink tank top shrink-wrapped to her body. She was with a group of people standing outside some bar. Someone at the station had been busy digging up photos.

"He should've left his hair long. The corporate look just isn't him. His face is perfect for longer locks, sort-a like Liam Neeson," Reb said.

I half-listened as Barbie Honeywell, looking perky as ever, explained all the bizarre details of the murder and how Cary Grant Harrigan was a "person of interest."

Speaking of hairstyles, why had Fisher owned so many wigs? Did she have a bizarre hair fetish, or a frequent need to change her appearance?"

"It's a good thing the news used his high-school picture. Doesn't look a thing like him now." Reb said.

"Might buy us some time," I murmured.

"Gotta run. If he gets in touch let me know. I'll call when I'm done meeting with the Suits from Phoenix. Wish me luck."

"Luck," I said to the dial tone.

I clicked off and the phone jingled before I could put it in my pocket.

"It took some doing, I had to wheedle a *bunch* of favors, but a friend of a friend will let me hitch a ride in his private plane." Willie said. "I should get into Portneuf Gap around two."

"Right. I'll pick you up."

"No, you stay put in case your brother contacts you. I'll rent a car, one with a civilized transmission. I refuse to wrestle with that ancient jalopy you insist on driving."

"Willie, the Karmann Ghia is a classic. I've seen Ghia's in dozens of movies," I lied.

"Well, you'd never catch Elizabeth Taylor driving one."

I couldn't argue with that logic. We said our goodbyes and I trudged upstairs to my office to let my fingers do some snooping. I logged onto the surfing website. The homepage was impressive, so I clicked on the questionnaire. It looked fairly basic, and the price was reasonable. Hmm. With a couple more clicks I could sign up for a fun-filled week of lessons choosing from four different beach locations along the California coast. Meals and snacks were included and, at the end, a cookout dinner on the beach would cap off the perfect surfing experience. The website had three pages of male and female instructors to choose from, depending on which beach one chose.

Cary's bio paragraph was impressive, his picture displaying his sexy dimples and long, sun-kissed hair. Even if Channel Six had used this recent shot it would be hard to match this carefree beach bum with the ultra-conservative executive he'd become.

As if on cue, my cell rang and I wasn't surprised to see a call was from Channel Six. *Uh-uh, Ms. Honeywell. No time to say, "No comment." I had to figure out where Cary was, try to save him from a prison sentence, then deal with my mother. Talking to Barbie fell somewhere below arranging my sock drawer on my to-do list.*

Frobi had signed up for surf lessons, talked my brother into leaving his passion and going into business with her; now she was dead. Dead in a very bizarre fashion. Had she picked Cary as her instructor at random? If only I had enough info to run a credit check on her, so much information available if one knows the tricks.

I crossed my fingers and tried my luck with Google. Lots of info on people with the last name of Fisher but no matter how I spelled Frobi, Google couldn't find a match. I sorely lacked the computer gene most of my generation were born with. Sad to admit, Gram had a better grasp on navigating her way around Google and Facebook than I, and she could Tweet with the best of them. This part of the search could use a computer-whiz. Like Yancy. He'd probably hunt up all sorts of good stuff, including the type of toothpaste Fisher preferred.

I Goggled Albert Lechman, Sherrilyn Sanborn's biggest fan. Maybe I'd find him in a police log for stalking charges. He was creepy enough. I didn't find Albert Lechman but I did find an Al Lechner, business development consultant in Mississippi who was accused of murdering his father, Mathers Lechner, and possibly starting a fire to disguise the murder. The case never reached the courtroom. Not enough evidence. Lechner could become Lechman if the circumstances were right but judging by Mathers age, his son Al had to be much older than Albert Lechman, Sherrilyn Sanborn's biggest fan.

I logged out and looked down at the letter next to my keyboard from the editor of *Thriller Night*. The man had rejected my latest fiction story, but stated he'd like to see anything else I had that would fit their future themes. Trouble was, real murder and mayhem had my muse in a headlock leaving me with nothing but a few rough ideas. I caressed the letter, sighed, and stood up. Maybe I should switch to writing true crime. Ugh.

Both dogs bounded up the stairs barking, turned in circles at my feet, then raced back down. I jogged downstairs and looked out the dining room window as Ester Clemmens' white Cadillac pulled into the driveway. Damn. I'd forgotten about fostering the Schnauzer. Ester angled out of the car and gave me a wave. Dressed in black shorts, white golf shirt with matching tennis shoes, and socks with those annoying little balls at the heels, she clapped her hands and a gray fur-ball with an extreme punk hair-cut bounded out.

I turned to Bogart and Bacall. "We're having company. I want good behavior." With cocked heads, they furiously wagged their tails. I opened the front door as Ester stepped onto my porch.

"Good morning, Mercedes. Lots of excitement at your complex last night. All of the flashing emergency lights both intrigued and terrified my pack. Too bad about the murder. Very bizarre." I steeled myself for a barrage of questions. She surprised me by pointing to the little guy sniffing my porch. "This is Mr. Wiggins."

My shoulders relaxed. Thank goodness murder took a backseat with Ester whenever she was on a mission to help an animal.

"Was his owner English?" I asked, watching Bogart, Bacall and Wiggins say hello with a three-way doggie butt-sniff.

"No, his owner was an asshole. Wanted this adorable little guy put to sleep ASAP. Poor darling is so on edge he's been pulling out patches of hair."

That explained his weird trim. Ester walked into my kitchen and dumped a bag of dog food, two plastic dishes, a bed pillow, and red plaid blanket onto my table. I didn't see a single animal hair on her outfit. Amazing. No one would ever guess she's the current Humane Society president and that she houses at least six dogs and cats at any given time. She's also gifted with great genes, making it hard to judge her age. Fifty-something was my guess.

"Now don't worry about a thing. Mr. Wiggins will be my responsibility to adopt out. Just think of yourself as his temporary mama for now."

The three dogs raced into the kitchen and out the doggie door.

"See, he's much happier here, already becoming one of the pack. Call if you have any problems." With that Ester said goodbye and let herself out the front door.

I stepped into the back yard to make sure things in doggy-land were okay and watched Ester's Caddy pass a shiny, black truck heading up the road. Killian. He parked behind my car and stepped out. He wore the same clothes from last night, which meant he wasn't on duty, a definite plus. He opened the gate into my backyard. I gulped and frowned. Not heading for the barn meant this must be an official visit.

"Hey," I said.

"Hey, yourself. What's with the new mutt?" he asked, nodding at the trio racing around the back yard.

"I'm helping the Humane Society." I held the back door open, an invitation to join me inside.

He raised an eyebrow and sauntered past me, opened the fridge, and grabbed a Pepsi. "Heard from your brother?"

Was that a loaded question? Was Cary in a jail cell dodging advances from some brute named Bubba? "No."

"And you don't have any recent pictures of him?" He stood in the doorway that separated the kitchen and living room, his eyes taking in every surface.

"No. But he's on a surfing website. I can send you the link."

Killian shook his head. "Tech guys are on it. How long has your brother been mixed up with Frobi Fisher?"

I shrugged. "Maybe six weeks."

"Uh-huh." Killian took a long pull from the Pepsi and burped. "Has he ever mentioned Gretchen Grimes?"

I shook my head.

"How about Dana Davis? Millicent Moore?"

I crossed my arms and leaned against the counter. "Killian, stop with the name game and tell me what you want."

"Those are different names for the same person, Ms. Frobi Fisher or rather Kate Fitzsimmons, if that's her real name. The woman had a real gift as a con artist. Started scamming people when she was fourteen."

"What?"

"Yeah, she made a very good living duping people. Old, young, even corporations. No one was safe."

Gram's original suspicions were right. The casket thing was a fraud. Did Cary know?

As if reading my thoughts Killian continued. "Losing money is one thing, losing money while losing face in front of loved ones makes people angry. Crazy. Sometimes crazy enough to kill."

My legs went rubbery, my palms damp. "Reb was right," I said, sinking to the floor and wrapping my arms around my knees to stop the quivering.

"Rebbie knew Cary was mixed up in a con game?"

I shook my head. "She never believed Frobi was her real name.

SIX

"**M**ERCEDES MCCAMBRIDGE HARRIGAN, HOW COULD YOU?" I stared at my petite mother standing in my entryway. She'd chosen a red fitted suit with a plunging neckline and a skirt slit up the side to show off her gym-rat, tanning-bed legs; perfect ensemble for rushing to the rescue. If I was betting, I'd plunk down serious money that the pilot friend of a friend was male and Hollywood handsome.

Long blonde hair, no doubt extensions, newly inflated lips (perfectly contoured and colored Risqué Red), and angry blue eyes with enough mascara to lengthen the lashes of a small village completed the image. Surrounded by three large suitcases and a carryon, Willie looked ready to hunker in for the duration.

"What?" I asked. "No smoochy air-kiss?"

"How could you put Cary and poor, poor Frobi in that death trap?" Willie folded her arms, aiding her over-taxed push-up bra.

"My apartments are not death traps." I said, mimicking her stance.

"Oh, really?" She fisted her hands on her hips and tapped a Prada-clad foot. "What about the old broad who got snuffed in her apartment by that disgruntled employee?"

"A freak incident. Thanks to Reb and me a dangerous psycho now sits behind bars."

"You listen to me, little girl. I've rented from plenty of landlords, in L.A. mind you, and nothing like this has ever happened. Ever!" Willie waltzed past me wafting a trail of Crystal Noir perfume. She positioned herself in a languid pose on my sofa and heaved a dramatic sigh. "What have you got to drink? My nerves are just shot."

My shoulders relaxed and I breathed a sigh. Exit Rational Willie, the one who'd made it a priority to get here ASAP. Enter Drama Queen Willie, the familiar one I knew and loved. I rummaged through the fridge. "What's your preference? Cherry Pepsi, iced tea, or milk?" I eyed the expiration date on the milk, took off the lid and sniffed. "Nix the milk."

"Don't you have any Scotch or Bourbon? Something a grown-up would imbibe?" She absently stroked Bogart's long ears as he sat beside her and fawned for attention. Mr. Wiggins lay on his back near her feet, pawing the air and grinning. Typical male response. Bacall sat next to the fireplace, ears and eyes alert, ready to pounce should this she-devil try anything strange.

I fixed two iced teas and placed them on a tray along with a bowl of lemon wedges, long spoons, napkins, and a plate of sugar cubes. Gram would've been proud. I set the tray on the coffee table and took a seat in my favorite overstuffed chair across from Willie.

Willie squeezed a lemon wedge into her tea, stirred, and took a sip. "At least it's cold." She dabbed her lips with a napkin, pushed both dogs away, and leveled an icy blue stare at me. "What have you done to locate your brother?"

"I've enlisted the help of a special tactical National Guard team to comb Scout Mountain," I said.

"Mercedes McCambridge Harrigan, I will not stand for any impertinence." She banged her glass down on the coffee table and tried to look stern; a recent Botox treatment ruined the effect.

"Well, hell, Willie! What do you want me to say? I'm tired of being my brother's keeper. He's a big boy, time to deal with his own mistakes."

Willie shook her head. "Maybe . . ."

"Maybe, nothing." I placed my glass on the floor, leaned forward, resting my elbows on my knees, and began ticking off points on my fingers. "First, if Cary's *not* guilty, the coward could turn himself in and *help* the police locate his fiancé's killer. Second, looks like he's up to his baby blues in a huge scam to swindle money from unsuspecting elderly people. And three . . ."

"Mercedes." Willie picked at some lint on her skirt. "We both know your brother's a knucklehead. You've always been the practical, pedantic one. The one I could count on to . . ."

"Be boring as hell?" I cocked an eyebrow, happy my face was totally mobile.

Willie sniffed. "If you're going to treat your brother's disappearance as a joke . . .," she took her glass and rolled it across her forehead, her heavily made-up eye-lids closing to half-mast.

I swallowed a frustrated sigh. "Willie, I *have* searched for Cary." I spread my arms in an encompassing gesture. "The house, barn, and surrounding land. He's not here, and he's not at Gram's."

Willie opened an eye. "How is the old battle-axe?"

"Hold it!" I stood. "Calling Gram names not allowed . . . even under your breath."

"Is she willing to abide by the same rules?"

I folded my arms and stared at Willie Dearest.

"Whatever." She huffed a sigh and pursed her perfect lips. "Come help me unpack and then we can go into town for supplies. Later, I want to go to the crime scene. My last psychic reader said I have the gift."

Willie psychic? Psychotic maybe.

Willie rose, picked up her overnight bag and started for the stairs, Bogart and Wiggins following. She stopped at the bottom, looked at me, then at the rest of her luggage. "Be a dear and bring those to the spare bedroom."

I grabbed her medium bag, rolled it next to her toes and dropped it. "Everyone pulls their own weight around here," I said, retrieving the remaining two bags and lugging them up to the second floor.

"You can be such a brat." Willie said, huffing and banging along behind me. "I should have asked Fred to take my bags upstairs."

No surprise, Willie was on a first-name basis with the Uber driver who'd delivered her to my doorstep; men tended to buzz around her like drunken flies. That being said, I doubted the fellow would've hauled her paraphernalia anywhere for a simple kiss on the cheek. I stopped in the hallway between the spare room and bathroom. Uber driver? Would Willie pay for an Uber?

"Willie, did you use Uber to get here?"

"Of course not!"

"Then . . .?"

Willie rolled her eyes and thumped the suitcase up the final stair. "Frederick Ames, a totally charming man, approached me while I scanned the different car rental signs. He said I looked lost and offered his assistance."

"After all the stranger/danger lectures you gave me, you jump into a car with the first man you meet?"

Willie shrugged. "I can read men, darling. Fred's as harmless as an old Basset Hound." She homed in on the bathroom to lay siege. "He happened to be coming this way and offered me a lift. Too bad his final destination is Vegas," she said, opening the bulging carry-on. Soon bottles, brushes, and doo-dads jostled for space on the bathroom vanity and shelf above.

I took a deep breath. "So, you want to drive the Ghia," I said, pulling the last behemoth suitcase into the spare bedroom. "Or the truck?" Along with the house and apartments, Aunt Vie had left me a nineteen-seventy GMC pickup. The thing drove like a tank and had a cantankerous starter, but breezed through snowstorms.

"I can't maneuver either one. I'll find my own ride."

Great! Soon a parade of men, eager to play chauffeur, would be knocking down my door.

"And please do something with these two," she said, pointing to Bogart and Wiggins happily exploring the trappings left in her bag.

Relieved to have an excuse to escape downstairs and avoid an ever-popular lecture on proper skin care, I scooped the two up and headed for the kitchen. I threw a handful of liver dog treats into the back yard and locked the doggie door after the trio raced out.

While Willie finished commandeering my bathroom, I decided it was time to call my last resource, Floydean Mollicker, head dispatcher at the Portneuf Gap police station. Pumping Killian for news on Cary had been a waste, he'd gone straight to cop mode—no passing *Go*, no collecting anything. Floydean would share info. The woman was gossip central.

Hoping to catch her off-duty, I punched Floydean's home number. One of her three children answered in a nasal twang, "Mollicker residence, how may I help you?" The kids were hellions, but Floydean made sure they had telephone skills to rival the best secretary.

"Is your mother available?" I asked, throwing in my own etiquette.

"M-o-m-m-m. Phone."

"Yes?"

"Talk to me, Floydean. Tell me something, girlfriend," I said.

"Your brother's causing a real stir. No one's ever seen a corpse covered in gold paint. What is it with you two and your bent views of death?"

"We can discuss my interesting childhood later. Just give me some dirt, okay. Is Det. Stayner heading the case? What do they have so far?"

"I can only tell you what the average Joe Schmoe learns from the news. Nothing confidential, my lips are sealed."

"Floydean, I don't have time to jump through all your stupid hoops. Willie has landed and commandeered the top half of my house!" I resisted the urge to bang my head against the wall.

"Your mama is here?" Floydean sounded delighted. "Well, of course she's here, her baby's in trouble. When can I meet the Queen?"

"After you tell me what's happening," I said through gritted teeth.

"That ancient picture someone resurrected of Cary is no help. 'Cute buns' Killian says you've turned hostile, won't share any recent ones. I told him he should've tried a full-body search."

"I don't have any pictures!" I barked, trying to ignore the rush of heat in the pit of my stomach when I heard the words Killian and full body search.

"Don't cop an attitude with me, Missy." Floydean cleared her throat and lowered her voice. "Okay, the coroner hasn't released his verdict, but the real money is on death by asphyxiation. Lungs, nasal passages, throat, you name it, all coated with gold paint. No unusual purchase of gold spray paint in the area reported so far. None of the body shops missing paint or equipment. Det. Stayner is heading the case, checking with anyone who knew Cary. So far, nada." She was silent for a moment. "Would your brother take to the hills, hide out somewhere you played as kids?"

"No. He hates snakes and assumes one is coiled behind every rock."

"O . . . kay," she said. "Forget that theory. Wait, just before my shift ended last night, we got a report of a naked guy crawling out from a manhole on the corner of Eleventh and Benton. He disappeared before the squad car arrived."

"What did he look like?" I asked, my chest tight, stomach clenching. *Had Cary managed to escape from the paint-happy maniac and make his way through the sewer?*

"About six foot, matted blonde hair, scraggly beard."

I let out the breath I'd been holding. "Nope, my brother's as clean shaven as a baby's bottom."

"Knowing your family, wouldn't surprise me to learn he's part werewolf."

"Who're you talking to, dear?"

Startled, I whirled and found Willie in the kitchen doorway. She'd changed into black mid-calf leggings and a white cap-sleeve tee shirt. Both items molded to her curves like a second skin.

"A friend. Are those Manolo Blahniks?" I asked, pointing to the Zebra-print sling-backs with black leather trim and three-inch heels.

"You like?" She lifted her foot and pointed her toe.

I nodded and groaned inwardly. Willie had fantastic taste in shoes and a collection to die for. Too bad her tootsies were a half size smaller than mine.

"Manolo?" Floydean shouted in my ear. "Girlfriend, I could really bond with your mama."

"Fine. You can play chauffeur, haul her ass around, and bond away," I whispered, as Willie sashayed her way across the kitchen, heels tapping staccato against the worn linoleum.

She grabbed my keys from the hook by the door, and dangled them in the air. "Let's go to the apartment complex first. My intuition is simply churning. Who knows what vibes I'll pick up? We can stop by Budget and rent me some decent transportation later."

"Intuition? Vibes? I'll meet you at the complex," Floydean laughed and clicked off.

I snatched the keys from Willie and unlocked the doggie door. The trio burst through. I tossed a Milk bone to each one with instructions to watch for Cary and followed Willie out the back door.

When we pulled into the entrance of the apartment parking lot I had to slam on the brakes, stalling the Ghia. "What the . . .?"

Agatha, astride a mountain bike, wobbled in a crazy circle around the middle of the parking lot in the shimmering heat.

"Hand brakes. Hand brakes!" Dexter shouted from the sidewalk.

"Who is that unfortunate creature?" Willie asked, raising her rhinestone-studded, cat-eye sunglasses.

"Agatha Heckathorn. She lives in Number Seven." Decked out in a wide-brim straw hat, white gloves, long-sleeve shirt and pants tucked into knee-high boots, the woman had to be sweating buckets.

"Does she always dress like that?" Willie asked, trying to furrow her brow.

"She's sort of eccentric. Thinks she's allergic to the sun." I started the car and coasted over to Dexter. "What gives?" I asked, opening my door.

Dexter opened his mouth, caught sight of Willie angling out of the car, and froze, struck dumb on the spot. He straightened and the Semper-Fi tattoo on his bicep snapped to attention. "Agatha has signed up for that la-de-da bicycle ride, wine-tasting tour hosted by the Chamber of Commerce. I'm loaning her my bike, *if* she can learn how to stop the dang thing."

Willie sauntered over to Dexter and removed her sunglasses. She tilted her head and gave him a well-practiced, coy smile. "Well, aren't you sweet."

"Just being neighborly, ma'am," he said. "Name's Dexter Zoetwilder, retired gunny sergeant, USMC, at your service."

I sighed with exasperation. If he'd been wearing a hat, he'd have tipped it.

"Dexter, this is my mother, Willie." She shot me a sideways glare. "Willie, Dexter and his *wife*, Violet, live in Number Four."

As if on cue, Violet appeared at the screen door. Her bright purple caftan and pink flip-flops clashed with her peach lipstick. Eyes blazing, she pushed the screen open and marched over to stand beside her man. "So this is your mama. Come to help find your no-good brother?"

Willie's eyes narrowed, but she managed a sad smile as she addressed Dexter. "This whole situation is terrible. To think my sweet baby has been implicated in such a ghastly mess." She closed her eyes. When she opened them, a lone-tear slid from the corner of one eye.

I smothered a groan, but truth be known, I'd have paid good money to learn the lone tear trick.

Dexter took a white handkerchief from the front pocket of his khaki shorts and handed it to Willie. Violet's face turned an alarming shade of purple.

"Don't you fret now, ma'am. I have my entire unit on the lookout for your son. We'll have this murder cleared up before long," Dexter said.

Willie dabbed at her eyes and returned the hanky. "Are you in law enforcement?"

"Ha," Violet said. "Dang fool is captain of the Neighborhood Watch. Most of the old coots can't find matching socks, let alone some criminal."

"Watch your tongue, woman!" Dexter growled. "We've helped with plenty of . . ." A screech of tires cut Dexter off. Reb pulled next to us, and jumped from her car, eyes wild, hair disheveled, sea-blue sheath dress wrinkled and wilted.

"The whole warehouse district's ablaze!" She grabbed my hand. "Come on, my commission's going up in smoke."

"Whoa, Reb," I said, digging my heels in before she jerked me off the curb. "How are we supposed to help?"

"I don't know," she waved her hands in circles, "I must be there to comfort Bernhagen, show him I'm an agent who'll stick through thick or—oh, hell, just move your ass," she cried, heading for her car.

"Hold on." Dexter grabbed Reb's arm. "Nothing you can do but get in the way."

Reb wrenched her arm from his grasp, eyes narrowed to slits. "I'm not going to . . ." Her eyes flew open and her voice became a soft purr. "Oh, my gosh! Mrs. Harrigan, when did you get here?"

While Rebbie and Willie exchanged how's-everything-with-you, I noticed Floydean coming down the sidewalk. Dressed for work in navy slacks, white blouse, and black loafers, she stood by me and whispered, "Guess you know about the fire in the warehouse district?"

I nodded. By now, thick, acrid smoke smudged the sky to the East, turning the sun into a blazing orange ball while making our eyes water.

"Thank heavens," Reb said, grasping Floydean's hand. "Tell

me about the fire. How many warehouses are gone? Is the whole district burning?"

"I could see some flames as I drove over Benton Street-overpass. Looks like a couple of warehouses are involved, hard to tell for sure, lots of smoke and confusion," Floydean said.

Agatha stopped the bike in front of Reb's car and pulled her wide-brimmed hat off. With gray hair plastered to her head and rivulets of sweat running down her neck, she looked at the smoke-filled heavens. "Well, this sucks! I'm finally getting the hang of riding this contraption and that damn firebug is gonna spoil the Chamber's event."

"What are you blathering about?" Violet asked.

Agatha pursed her thin lips. "Don't you listen to the news? Some pyromaniac's been getting his jollies torching stuff for the past week."

Violet huffed and folded her arms. "I knew that."

A pyromaniac? Here in Portneuf Gap? Dexter was right, I'd been so caught up in cleaning apartments it was like I'd just emerged from a cave.

Agatha handed the bike to Dexter, turned to Willie and stuck out her hand. "You must be Sadie's mother. I'm Agatha Heckathorn. I've lived in this complex forever. You want to know anything, ask me."

Reb and Floydean were behind me but I could feel their eyes rolling.

"That reminds me, Sadie," Agatha said. "I taped that early news bit about your brother. Wanna come see it?"

"You have my poor baby on tape?" Willie said. She shaded her eyes and scanned the complex, a look of pain stretched across her face. For a brief moment, I wanted to put my arms around her, hold her tight, find solace together. Willie licked her lips and the pained expression disappeared behind phony pleasantry.

Reality check, Harrigan. Willie was not the hugging type but she was always on . . . always aware of her audience. She agreed with William Shakespeare, 'All the world's a stage.'

"Come on over to my place, take a load off, get out of this heat. I've got some organic lemonade with a pinch of ginger, good for the whole system," Agatha said, wrapping an arm around Willie. Willie threw a panicked look over her shoulder as Agatha led the way.

Reb sat on the curb and put her head in her hands. "I had the warehouse sale nailed. I could feel it. That commission would've made my life sweet."

"How do you know if Bernhagen's property is actually on fire?" I asked, sitting down beside her.

"Figures, way my luck's been running," Reb said.

"Oh, hell." Floydean threw her arms in the air. "I've got some time before my shift. Let's run over and check it out." She pivoted on the sidewalk and headed for her rust-eaten, four-wheel-drive truck. "Guess I'll have to meet Willie later," she called over her shoulder.

Reb jumped up, heading for her car. "Let's move, Harrigan."

I shook my head and remained seated. "Can't, I need to haul Willie around to rent a car. Call me with details."

"Right," Reb caught up with Floydean, they climbed into Floydean's truck and roared off in a cloud of exhaust fumes.

Movement in my peripheral vision made me turn my head. A young fellow emerged from behind a tree and trotted over. Looming above me, he extended his hand and said, "Name's Martin Mangum. What a pleasure to finally meet you." He shook my hand vigorously and then sank down onto the curb next to me.

I stared at him. The name Martin Mangum didn't jog any brain cells. Who the hell was this guy?

"You look confused. Perfectly understandable considering the murder." He grinned and continued. "I left a message on your machine. I'm studying parapsychology. I intend to make it my life's work. Most people cringe at my vocational choice, but you and I, uh, we're like kindred spirits."

Great. Freakin' great! Add fending off a juvenile ghost-buster to my worry list. I took a closer look at Martin and guessed him to be either a junior or senior in high school. He had a round, pleasant face, a pug nose sprinkled with freckles and black-rimmed glasses. His white, short-sleeve shirt clung to the extra pounds of baby-fat still riding his five-ten frame. He was the perfect walking wedgies target for all the school rowdies.

"Aren't you a little young to be a ghostbuster?"

His excited expression was replaced by a surly pout. "I thought you'd understand, being a horror writer and practically growing up in a mortuary."

My chest squeezed like I'd taken milk from a starving kitten. "I'm just surprised by your level of maturity with such a sticky subject."

"You do get it." Martin beamed. "Brand new spectrometer came FedEx today; I've been dying to try it out." He pulled the backpack off his back and unzipped the main compartment. "My mentor, Axel, sent this last week. Axel's extremely intuitive, and somehow, he knew I'd need this right away. He's joining me later."

I laid a hand on his arm before he could pull out the whatever meter. "Martin, right now is a very bad time. Most of the tenants are rattled by the murder. Could you hold off investigating?"

"But the vibes are strongest right after . . ."

I squeezed his arm. "Sorry but it's simply too soon. I'm talking tenant overwhelm. We will give them a little time to process everything. Some of the elderly tenants are pretty spooked." *This wasn't completely true but the only excuse I could come up with at the moment.*

Martin zipped the backpack. He stood. "I guess I see your point. When can I start my investigation?"

I shrugged. "Hard to say."

He reached into his pocket, pulled out a business card and handed it to me. His name and number were stamped in black against the gray outline of a ghost.

"Either call or text me. Otherwise, I'll be in touch." He scooped up his backpack and left.

My body felt baked raw by the heat. Agatha's swamp cooler hummed away, enticing me to seek refuge inside with Willie. Instead, I blew a strand of hair from my face and sought shelter in a patch of shade at the base of an elm tree. Braving the heat was better than listening to Willie's theatrics or Agatha's ailments. Besides, a few quiet moment would help me gather my thoughts.

Cary's only mode of transportation had been impounded by the police. He hadn't come to Gram or me for help. I couldn't see him taking to the hills, or skulking around alleys. So, where was he? Okay, time to stop speculating and look at the facts. Fact: he and Fisher had come here to peddle their caskets. They'd met with assisted living people, visited a couple of retirement homes, and they'd rented a . . . oh crap they'd rented a warehouse!

I jumped up, ran to Agatha's front door and banged on it. Agatha opened the door, in her sweat-soaked clothes. Willie peered from behind her. I grabbed Willie's arm and yanked her outside. "Sorry, Agatha, gotta run," I yelled, pulling my reluctant mother with me.

"Mercedes!" Willie snatched her hand from mine. "What is with you? These shoes are new, I don't want to break a heel."

"Cary might be at the warehouse fire!" My heart was beating so hard I could barely get the words out. Willie stared at me like I'd grown a second head. I took a breath, blew it out, and tried to explain. "Frobi rented a warehouse on First Street to store the caskets."

"So?"

"Warehouses make great hiding spots." I turned and ran for my car.

Willie beat me to the Ghia and slid into the passenger seat. Manolo heels must be made of strong stuff. Good to know.

SEVEN

"**W**ATER, SMOKE, AND SOOT-COVERED HUNKS hauling hoses, this reminds me of the "Flames of Glory" set," Willie said, sticking her head out of the passenger window, as I maneuvered the Ghia past the milling crowd held at bay by yellow wooden barriers.

"You were in the crowd scene, right?" Playing an extra in a couple of B movies basically described Willie's film career. The clock on my dashboard read four p.m., hours before the sun called it quits yet the hazy sky resembled twilight. I parked the Ghia two blocks over on Whitman Street, climbed out, and waited on the cracked sidewalk for Willie to join me.

"I had a full ten-second close-up, on the front row. Right behind the police barricade," Willie said. "They served the best buffet on that set, and I sat right across from the leading man, Dean Ford. Too bad he was married at the time."

I'd never been on a Hollywood set or in a war, but, to me, First Street looked like a battle zone. A large blaze effects people in a peculiar way . . . horrifying yet mesmerizing and beguiling. The crowd watched as torrents of sparks cascaded to the ground. Heaps of shattered glass littered the street and reflected the blood-red sun hanging above the blazing three-story building.

Debris floated in black puddles. Firemen in full gear manned hoses, scurried up ladders, and rushed to extinguish the devouring flames or sprayed the surrounding buildings in hopes of containing the monster. The indescribable acrid smell of burnt objects assaulted my nostrils.

As we neared the crowd of looky-loos, the excitement charged air and male bodies changed Willie's slow stride to a strut-her-stuff sashay. No matter what the situation, she automatically plays to her audience.

The fire had reduced a one-story office building to a mountain of rubble and moved onto the adjoining Dickson Moving and Storage warehouse. I scanned the area for Reb, halfway expecting to find her turning cartwheels. Berghagen's warehouses, located two blocks south of the fire, were safe-for the moment.

No Reb or Floydean, but across the street, I spotted Albert Lechman leaning against the rusted chain-link fence encircling the abandoned Challenge Creamery warehouse. The sight of Sherrilyn Sanborn's number one fan gave me goose bumps, while my gut instinct beeped like the blaring car alarm everyone ignores. Dexter had nailed it, there was something eerie about the man. I had no idea what his game was, but "cooking-celebrity stalker" just didn't fit. No reason for him to be here unless he had a recipe for roast something over the coals of a disaster, however . . .

Could he be the arsonist terrorizing the warehouse district? I'd read pyromaniacs had an uncontrollable fascination to be near the blaze they'd started, an almost insatiable desire to watch the flames eat and destroy.

Hmmm.

Dressed in a navy golf shirt and tan Dockers that looked pressed within an inch of their life, Lechman appeared to be just another casual observer, watching the firemen battle the blaze. Was he simply observing or was he mesmerized?

"Mercedes, don't squint like that. It's unattractive and enhances your crow's feet," Willie said.

Reality check, Harrigan. Just because Lechman irritated me didn't make him an evil firebug any more than the substitute mail carrier, who continually mixed up the tenants mail, would turn out to be a serial killer.

I widened my eyes in a deer-in-the-headlights stare. "Is this better?"

"No need to be snide. I'm only trying to help," Willie said. "My friend, Miriam, has discovered a moisturizing cream made from crushed pearls . . ."

I tuned her out and punched Gram's number on my cell. She picked up on the first ring. "There's a fire on First Street. Which block is Cary's rented warehouse on?" I asked.

"We never made it to the warehouse," Gram said. "Frobi couldn't remember the exact address, and that started the fight."

I gave myself a mental head whack. I'd forgotten the reason Cary left Gram stranded on this very block. My brother and Frobi had done nothing but fight on the night she died. Stack another brick on the motive pile.

"Who're you talking to?" Willie asked.

"Gram."

Willie wrinkled her nose. "Oh."

"Sounds like Willie made it," Gram said, her words tightly modulated. "Good."

The crowd gasped as flames shot skyward and cinders sprinkled the ground. "It's getting scary. I'll call you later," I told Gram and clicked off to dial Reb's cell. I got her voice-mail, again. "Tell me you're *not* roasting marshmallows in this firestorm. Call me!"

I grabbed Willie's arm. "Let's get out of here."

Willie nodded. "Obviously, we won't find Cary within a mile of this mess. Too much law enforcement." She pointed to four policemen wandering the perimeter, doing crowd control. "I'm starving. Let's grab a bite to eat, somewhere that is air-conditioned and serves fun drinks."

We hurried to my car, slipped inside, and my cell phone rang. "Hello."

"Mercedes, get back here pronto," Dexter said, his voice gruff with impatience.

"What's going on?" I asked.

"No time to explain. Just get back here."

I started the Ghia and looked at Willie. "I'm needed back at the apartments. Dinner and drinks will have to wait."

A semi-trailer idled in the apartment's parking lot, the trailer angled in a way that blocked the entrance. I parked across the street and jumped out. A man stood beside the rumbling truck, dressed in worn jeans and a wrinkled tee with a company logo printed across the left pocket. A fedora, circa nineteen-thirty, was perched at a rakish angle on his head. Give him a whip and he could pass for a poor man's Indiana Jones.

Dexter stood beside the driver, shaking his head. "Hey, Mercedes," he cried, pointing at a clipboard in the man's ham-sized fists. "Come take a gander at this."

"Why is this truck in my parking lot?" I asked the man.

He held out a work-worn hand. "Name's Jim. I have a shipment I need to unload. The whole warehouse district is closed off, what with the fire and all. Your complex is listed as the alternate address."

"I didn't order anything. What's the shipment?" I asked.

"Caskets," Jim said.

"Don't that beat all?" Dexter slapped me on the back and grinned.

Caskets? Cary's caskets? I took a deep breath, counted to ten, and looked at the truck spewing exhaust fumes into the hot, smoke-filled air while Jim and Dexter faked a cool demeanor as they eyed Willie crossing the road. I walked a couple of feet away and called Gram.

Yancy answered in his fake British accent, "Harrigan Funeral Home."

"Yancy, please get my grandmother."

"Whom shall I say is calling?"

"Not funny. Just get her."

"No can do. She's meeting with a couple who are finalizing the plans for their uncle's funeral. May I give her a message?" His voice dripped with enough icky sweetness to give half the city diabetes. I clicked my cell off and tapped it against my palm. Gram loved me but she probably wouldn't agree to store a shipment of questionable caskets. And there was no flippin' way I was going to have them at the apartment complex.

I turned to Jim. "Doesn't someone have to sign for this shipment?"

He held up the clipboard. "I have a signature to deliver, and the shipment's been paid for, but I need another signature before I can unload the cargo."

"Let me see the invoice." I held out my hand. Sure enough Frobi Fisher had crossed all her I's and dotted her T's. The deal was signed, sealed, and all but delivered to a warehouse that might be in flames.

"Mercedes, you can't let this charming man unload the caskets here. What will your neighbors think?" Willie said in a stage whisper.

Neighbors indeed! A casket-clogged parking lot wasn't the way to advertise two vacant apartments.

"Look, I have to pick up another load and haul it to Fresno. I'm losing money the longer we stand around jawin' about this," Jim said. He snatched the clipboard back. "My instructions are to deliver this shipment. Period."

Jim started to unlatch the tailgate, as a white Cadillac tried to pull into the parking lot. Great! The Kandels, tenants in Nine, had chosen this moment to return to the complex. Retired from some university in Upstate New York, they'd rented my apartment as a place to lay their weary heads while remodeling a two-story log house in Sagewood Hills.

I grabbed Jim's arm. "How many caskets are we talking?"

"Five."

I put on a no-nonsense scowl and folded my arms. "You cannot unload here." He opened his mouth, and I held up a finger. "You *can* dump the damn things at my house."

He cocked his head, a squint wrinkling the corners of his face. "You own this setup and don't live here?"

I nodded. "My house is ten minutes from here. Can you maneuver a winding road?"

"Does a bear . . . ?"

"Spare me. Just get your rig out of the way so my tenants can park." I grabbed Willie's hand and pulled her along while I did a little damage control with the Kandels. With a whoosh of airbrakes and a puff of diesel smoke, Jim backed the truck onto the street.

Later, as Willie and I watched from my front porch, Jim hoisted the last casket onto the prongs of a forklift and drove down the loading ramp to deposit it on my driveway. The five caskets, bronze tops gleaming through their plastic covering, lined side-by-side on the asphalt reminded me of oblong Lego's. Damn, now what? Gram hadn't returned my call and I wasn't about to go through Yancy again.

Jim slammed and locked the tailgate, then walked over and handed me a yellow copy of the invoice. "Five on the dot. I can just make the next pickup. Have a good evening." He tipped his hat and gave me a wink.

I slumped onto my front step and stared at the retreating semi. All this grief because I'd offered my brother a place to stay.

Willie nudged me with her toe. "Now, can we get something to eat and rent a car? One with air conditioning that could freeze a polar bear?" She wiped a drop of sweat from her hairline.

A car? I had five caskets in my driveway, no idea how to get rid of them, and Willie's only thought was filling her stomach and renting a car with air! Before the urge to throttle the woman took hold, I climbed to my feet, turned, and retreated into my house.

"Mercedes? Didn't you hear me?" Willie's whine grated down my backbone as she followed me into the foyer, where I stood gaping at the carnage.

Couch cushions lay strewn about the wood floor like gutted fish. Wads of stuffing were heaped in piles like dirty snow.

Willie clutched my arm. "Your place has been ransacked!" She grabbed my other arm and stared at me. "Are you dealing drugs?"

"No, but I'm considering it."

I pulled free and noticed two faces peeking out from the kitchen doorway. Bogart had classic Dachshund wrinkles scrunching his forehead. Mr. Wiggins had a piece of foam stuck to his whiskers. No wonder Ester wanted the little bugger gone. I was boarding the Tasmanian Devil disguised as a mini-Schnauzer.

For a moment I swear I saw red flowing like lava over everything in my field of vision. I grabbed one of the cushions and threw it against the wall, sending both Bogart and Mr. Wiggins scurrying for cover. The sound of scrambling claws above told me Bacall had retreated into my bedroom closet.

"Mercedes, for heaven sakes, get hold of yourself," Willie gasped. "This isn't like you!" Mascara-caked lashes open wide, she backed up a few steps. "But this is straight out of central casting: crazed addict tears house apart searching for drugs!"

I glared at her. "This mess has nothing to do with drugs. This is central casting for a story about a total patsy who people use as a doormat. I agree to foster a poor pooch, or offer my brother and his conniving girlfriend a place to stay and *my life, My Life*, takes a nose dive into the toilet. Genghis Khan never had this problem!" I stomped outside, tore the plastic covering off one of the caskets and opened the lid. The white satin lining looked sub-standard and the poor excuse for a pillow resembled a fluffed pancake.

"Cary," I screamed. "You are beyond dead." I kicked the side of the offensive box and the entire side panel fell to the ground.

What the hell?

I dropped to my knees and looked inside. Two long cardboard tubes were taped to the bottom of the casket.

"Mercedes McCambrige Harrigan. Get off the ground this instant. Throwing a hissy fit is *not* going to help." Willie stood over me, shaking a chewed-up sandal in the air. "You have got to get rid of that furry menace, he ruined my best . . ." Her voice died in mid-rant. She sank slowly to her knees beside me. "That's strange. Cardboard tubes inside a casket? Is that normal?"

I pulled the closest tube out from the casket interior. Probably forty inches long and twenty inches circumference. I picked it up, not heavy but not empty either. "We need to open this." I carried the tube into my house, Willie followed rattling off questions I couldn't answer.

A box cutter made swift work of the tape and plastic stopper on the top of the tube. I pulled a translucent, glossy roll of paper out and laid it on my kitchen table. Undoing the taped ends, I gently unrolled the paper from some type of canvas which was rolled around more glossy paper and another smaller canvas.

"What is it?" Willie asked, voice hushed.

I carefully unrolled paper and canvas revealing two paintings of beautiful women in skimpy outfits sporting forties era hairstyles and saucy expressions as they performed mundane chores.

"Paintings of pin-up girls?" I held one up to admire the sweeping brush strokes.

Willie held the other one up. "Mercedes . . . if these are originals you've got artwork worth at least a million."

"Million?"

"See that signature in the right-hand corner? If this is an original Elvgren it's worth money. Lots of money!" Willie reverently laid her painting back on the table. I followed her example.

"Why would someone stuff artwork in the bottom of a casket?"

"Maybe your grandmother would know."

I shook my head. "Doubtful. It's probably illegal." I punched a number into my cell phone and the screen went black. Dead battery.

I held out my hand. "Give me your cell."

She pulled it out of the side pocket of her leggings and handed it to me. "Who are you calling?"

"Reb."

"Why? Can she help?"

I shrugged and dialed Rebbie's cell. "I will keep her up to speed and she has access to people who specialize in many different areas. We're going to need someone to authenticate this art." Reb's voice mail clicked on. I hung up and punched in her home phone. The voice that answered was so familiar, I forgot what I wanted to tell Reb. I deepened my voice, mumbled wrong number, disconnected, and turned to Willie.

"What's wrong?" she asked.

"Cary's at Reb's. He's alive! I'm gonna kill him!

EIGHT

I SILENTLY INSERTED MY KEY INTO REB'S front door and rammed it open, it ricocheted off the wall and I caught it on the rebound. Cary, shirtless and wearing wrinkled khaki shorts, screamed like a girl, dropped the remote, and leapt off the couch. He scrambled into the kitchen and ran smack into Willie's open arms. *Big rule in police dramas: always park out of sight and cover all exits.*

"Oh my poor, poor baby. Forced into hiding like a common criminal." Willie pulled Cary's head to her chest, no small feat considering my five-foot mother and six-foot brother.

"Good to see you too," Cary said, wiggling away from the awkward embrace. He looked at me then Willie and grinned his disarming, double-dimple grin. "Talk about surprise. I better call Rebbie and tell her to buy more take-out."

He pulled his phone from his pocket but I grabbed it and popped it into my purse. "Uh-uh. No warning my *former* best friend."

Cary shrugged and allowed Willie to lead him back to the couch. His long body molded against the dark-blue cushions as he slumped and sighed. "Don't get pissed at Rebbie. She was just doing an old friend a favor."

I tucked my anger away and took a seat in the lipstick-red chair across from the couch. Folding my arms, I gave Cary my big-sister glare. "Favor? Your hide-and-seek gag has wasted precious time in a criminal investigation."

"There's a big reward for your capture," Willie said.

Cary looked at Willie then me. "Really?"

"Willie, enough drama. Cary, your fiancé is in the morgue! You're hiding! What the hell happened?" I said.

"Not much to tell. We had a fight. I took a walk to cool down." Voice matter of fact, Cary was the epitome of unflappable except for nervous fingers rat-a-tatting against his knee. "When I got back to the complex she was naked. Painted." He closed his eyes and ran a hand through his sun-kissed hair. "Beyond help."

"How long were you gone?" I asked.

Another shrug. "A while."

"Where'd you go?"

"Here and there."

"What'd you fight about?"

"This and that."

I stood, grabbed my purse, and hooked it over my shoulder. "Fine."

I walked to the door, grabbed the knob and stopped. Leaving wasn't the answer. Slapping Cary silly might be, but leaving wasn't. "This isn't twenty questions, Bro," I said, returning to stand in front of him. "I want answers, not bullshit."

"Un-bunch those panties, Sis. The vein at your temple is pulsing like a metronome."

I opened my mouth, closed it against the gush of hateful words, took a deep breath and plunked down on the coffee table. "Pay attention, I'm trying to help." I spoke slowly, taking his hands in mine. "You're the number one suspect in Frobi's murder. The longer you play hide-and-seek with the cops, the guiltier you look."

I stopped as a horrible thought squeezed my heart. "You're not guilty, are you?"

Cary squeezed my hands. "I. Did. Not. Kill. Her." His words whispered out between clenched teeth.

"Darling, you have to tell the police," Willie said, stroking his hair. "I couldn't bear to have you gunned down in a back alley like George Raft in *Dirty G Man*." She clasped her fist to her heart, leaned back against the plush sofa, and closed her eyes.

Cary shook his head. "No can do."

"Why?" I asked.

He looked at the floor. "It's complicated."

I stood and headed for the door.

"Sis, wait. Let me explain."

I held my hand up, fingers splayed. "Five minutes. Then I dial 911."

He pursed his lips and leaned forward, shoulders hunched tight. He studied his worn tennis shoes for what seemed an eternity then raised his head and began rocking slightly in an agitated rhythm. "Last Friday night we couldn't find the right warehouse. I knew she was lying but she blamed being forgetful on bad karma. Most of the day, she'd been antsy, nervous. Back at the apartment we got into it, right there in the parking lot. Woke up the old hypochondriac broad. She and Frobi traded insults and I left."

"Why was she antsy?" I asked.

Cary sucked in his top lip while rubbing his thighs. "You're not gonna like . . ."

The front door swung inward and Reb swished into the living room wearing peach linen pants, a silk shell, and a relaxed smile. Her eyes widened for a moment and I thought she might drop the large Wendy's bag she had clutched to her chest like a shield. An interesting shade of red colored her face while her eyes flicked from Cary, then back to the front door trying to decide between fight or flight.

I stood, balancing on the balls of my feet, ready for her to bolt. She licked her lips, shot a quick glance at the floor, straightened her shoulders and forced a smile.

"Oops. Didn't get enough for company."

Cary let out a pent-up sigh, no doubt pleased with the distraction, then stood and reached for the bag. "Just what we need, greasy comfort food." He placed the bag on the coffee table and hauled out the burgers and fries. He unwrapped a burger, removed the top bun, tore open a little catsup packet and drizzled catsup over the meat.

Willie and Rebbie each snatched a couple of French-fries and dipped them in a miniscule container of fry-sauce. I watched amazed, as fast food trumped my quest for the truth.

I leaned down and with one swipe of my arm, I sent the food, drinks, and fry sauce flying.

"Mercedes!" Rebbie's eyes bulged as she looked at the liquid drenching her pants. "These pants cost a fortune!" She grabbed a handful of napkins and swiped at the mess staining her outfit. "Son-of-a-bitch, Harrigan, what is your problem?"

I shot her a look. She shot one back through slitted eyes but clamped her mouth shut.

"No need to go postal, Sis. I was willing to share," Cary said, eyeing me as he sidled behind the couch.

"I'll show you postal if everyone doesn't stop avoiding truth or consequences here." I pointed at Reb. "Your damn pants will be the least of your worries when you're behind bars, jiving to Jailhouse Rock. Aiding and abetting! Where's your head, girlfriend?"

I turned to Cary. "And you deserve to be kicked by a jackass and I'm just the one to do it."

Cary smirked "You're saying . . ."

"That's right. I feel like a total jackass the way you two have jerked me around!"

Both tried for a contrite look. Reb succeeded. Cary didn't.

"What was I supposed to do?" he asked, molding his lean body to the sofa. Shirtless, wearing khaki shorts and sporting a five-o-clock shadow, the old Cary was back, ready to dodge responsibility.

"I called the one person who would listen, really listen, to my problem without jumping on the Cary-is-so-stupid-bandwagon. If I'd called you, or Gram, my ass would've been chewed on for hours."

"He has a point," Willie said, a sly knowing grin quirked her painted lips. She moved to the window and angled the blinds half-closed to block the dwindling sun.

I looked at the mess on the carpet and my stomach churned. I'd just pitched a classic Willie fit. *Mirror, mirror on the wall. I am my mother after all.* My knees gave way and I sat down, hard.

"Sis, you okay?" Cary asked, kneeling beside me on the floor.

"No, Bro, I'm not. Five inferior caskets are plugging my driveway. One has a false compartment and look what I found inside." I took my phone out of my purse and showed him the pictures I'd taken of the paintings. "Do these look familiar? It's pin-up art that could be worth money. Lots of money! I'm guessing the rest of the caskets also have surprises tucked inside."

His brows inched together and he sat back on his heels. "Stay out of this."

"Out of what?"

I studied his clenched jaw, the way his eyes changed from sky-blue to stormy, and the epiphany hit me like a fist to the gut. "Those paintings are stolen!"

The color leached from Cary's face. "You don't want to go there."

"Oh, no," Willie cried. "There's a police car pulling up outside."

Cary stood and dashed for the kitchen. Gathering my feet under me, I dove across the room and snagged his ankle with one hand. He slammed his sneaker-clad heel into my chin. I closed my eyes against a wave of dizziness and lost my grip.

"Sorry, Sis." His words echoed around the kitchen as the back door banged shut.

I dragged myself off the floor and gingerly touched my chin. My fingers came away red.

A swift triple knock and Killian opened the front door.

Terrific. I backed up out of sight, ripped a paper towel off the roll by the sink, and held it to my bloody chin.

Killian stood hands on hips watching Reb blotting the carpet with a towel. "Someone upset with the dinner choice?"

Willie smoothed her tank top and minced closer to Killian. She laid a hand on his arm and cocked her head. "Just a little accident, Officer."

I took a shaky breath and walked into the living room. "Officer Jack Killian meet my mother, Willie Harrigan." What is Jack's title...and use it here.

Killian nodded his head. "Ma'am."

Willie patted his arm. "Let me guess, you must be the poster model for 'bad boys in uniform,' right?"

One corner of Killian's mouth quirked, indenting a single dimple. "Whatever you say, ma'am." He removed his arm from Willie's clasp and turned to me. "What's with the paper towel? You trip and cause this mess?"

"Heavens, no. Mercedes isn't quite that clumsy." Willie said. "She and Cary had a little skirmish."

Killian's green eyes turned rusted-can sharp. "You found Cary?"

I nodded, resisting the urge to glance out the nearest window.

Killian peered down the hallway. "Where is he?"

"I hid him again so *you* could find him."

Killian reached me in two strides. Vise-like fingers squeezed my arms as he backed me against the fridge. "You don't want to piss me off, Mercedes." His voice came out low, edged with contained anger. I could feel every definition in his upper body, the roughness of his chin as his breath tickled my cheek. His eyes shimmered anger, along with . . . lust? A shiver tickled my spine.

"Sorry," I managed. He didn't move. Or blink. "I tried to stop him."

Killian sucked in some air, relaxed his grip, and took a step back.

He lifted the paper towel. "Not too bad. Butterfly ought to hold it. Your brother in the habit of knocking women around?"

"I raised my son to respect women!" Willie's exasperated statement puffed out her bangs. "This was a sibling thing."

Killian looked from Willie, to me, to Reb was scrubbing away at the stains on her carpet. "Good thing the three of you are *not* harboring Cary, or I'd have to haul the lot of you in for questioning."

Reb and Willie batted their eyes in coquettish unison and looked chastened.

I nodded. "Good thing. How come you decided to drop by?"

Killian folded his arms, making all the cop tools on his belt jingle. "I'm kind of curious about the five caskets in your driveway."

"My driveway?" *Taking the time to line the caskets up so the broken one was hidden: good. Hiding the paintings behind the furnace in the basement: priceless.*

"Yeah. We got a call from one of your neighbors. Seems she was riding her horse and they both spooked when they passed your house."

"There's a simple explanation," I said.

"There usually is," Killian said.

"That shipment was supposed to be delivered to a warehouse Cary rented. But with the fire blocking the whole warehouse district . . ." I shrugged.

He cocked an eyebrow and fingered his handcuffs. "You decided your driveway would suffice?"

"Better than my apartment parking lot." I stuck out my chin and the paper towel dropped onto the floor.

"Come with me." Killian hauled me into Reb's bathroom, opened her medicine cabinet above the sink and grabbed a bottle of Peroxide. Snatching a white wash cloth from the towel bar, he splashed the foamy liquid on it and placed it against my chin. "Hold this." He rummaged in the cabinet and emerged with a roll of gauze and a roll of white tape. He stepped closer to make the butterfly thingy, brushing my cheek with his knuckles as he tucked stray hair behind my ear. The smell of leather and cologne mixed nicely in the overheated room.

He finished and rubbed his thumb along my jaw line. "Little smear of blood here," he said, bending closer.

I held my breath and licked my lips, pulse pounding, oblivious to anything but the thought of his full mouth pressed against mine. To hell with his relationship with Reb.

"First you ruin my carpet, now my towels!"

We jumped apart and turned in unison to find Reb in the doorway, pointing at the bloodied washcloth on the floor.

"Cold water and hydrogen peroxide will take the blood out," Willie said, peering over Reb's shoulder. She inserted herself into the tiny bathroom and latched onto Killian's elbow. "Shouldn't you put out an APB or BOLO on Cary? We've got to get him off the streets before some gun-happy rookie pops a cap in him."

Pops a cap in him?

"BOLO's are only issued if someone is running from the law," Killian said. "Does he fit that description?"

"No." Reb shook her head.

Willie put her hands on her hips. "Certainly not."

Killian looked at me. I studied the tile floor at my feet. Cary was involved in something illegal and on the run. I'd say that qualified him as one supremely stupid-ass fugitive.

"Unless he's hot footing it to the station to turn himself in, then I'd say he fits . . .," Killian began. The lapel mike on his shoulder squawked and he slipped into the hall to respond.

I grabbed Reb by her shirt and hauled her close enough to whisper, "If Cary contacts you, you'd better tell me!"

She pushed me away, rolled her eyes and mouthed, "Okay, okay."

Killian appeared in the doorway. "Duty calls. Any of you hear even a rumor about Cary, call me ASAP." He leveled a steady gaze at me. "We're not done."

Oh, boy! The front door slammed shut and I let out the breath I'd been holding.

"Why's Darth Vader's theme playing in the kitchen?" Willie asked.

"That's Dexter's ringtone," I said, breaking from the group and hurrying to answer my cell phone. "Hi, Dex."

"Another mishap, Sadie, better haul on over here."

"What now, death, destruction, or bloodied limbs?"

"Todd Sudi just rammed his truck through his apartment."

NINE

"DEVIOUS. COUPLE OF HOLES IN THE brake line. Probably used an ice pick," Dexter said, as he angled the mechanic's dolly out from under Sudi's truck. That made it unanimous, every male within a twenty-mile radius who'd crawled under the smashed vehicle came up with the same conclusion.

The last vestige of the sun's scarlet rays along with the work light hooked to the undercarriage of the truck created alien shadows around the apartment parking lot. With the brake failure solved, the group of men turned their attention to the best way to plug the gaping hole in Todd's apartment. Ideas and testosterone flowed like cheap wine at a party. It was my apartment complex and I already knew what to do but listening to the different solutions was entertaining and kept my mind from exploring the insurance nightmare that was about to land in my lap.

At the other end of the parking lot, Agatha, Violet, and a couple of neighbors huddled together, tongues wagging, eyes darting between the shadows; aging vigilantes trying to decide who needed a good hanging. So far, the suspect list included the hoodlum rock group who lived through the alley; Mark Sweet, wacko ex-husband of Sherri Sandborn-Sweet; or some guy at Todd's work place who'd been giving him grief.

Todd sat on the curb, holding an ice pack to his forehead. The gash near his hairline had dribbled blood down his cheek, making his injury look worse than it was. Or so I hoped. I walked over and stood beside him. "You need a doctor. Let me take you to the emergency room."

He waved the suggestion away with his hand. "S'nuthin. I've had worse."

"At least come into Agatha's and clean up so we can see how bad it is," I said.

He shook his head and winced. "Nah, I'll use my bathroom. All her herbal mumbo-jumbo gives me da willies."

He had a point. I sat beside him and laid my hand on his arm. His rapid-fire, Jersey accent seemed more pronounced tonight. "Then let me call 911, get some paramedics to look at you. I have insurance for emergencies like this."

"No!" His large hand clamped mine, squeezing until I thought my knuckles would pop. I yanked my hand back and glared at him. He glared back. "Fugedaboudit. My truck, my problem. Whatever da cost, I'm good for it."

"Todd, come on. I'll wait in the E.R. with you, bring you straight back, scout's honor."

He held up his hand. "You call anyone, cops, paramedics, whatever, an' your premium'll climb to da stars. Do it my way, you'll maintain da same status quo, an' everyone comes out smellin' like the pervoibial rose."

I looked at him as he leaned back, his face hidden by shadows. Why so adamant about keeping the accident hush-hush? His Jersey upbringing? Or fear that whoever messed with his brake-line would retaliate?

The man had muscles on his muscles and worked in a body shop. He didn't seem the type to spook easily.

Sudi cleared his throat. "I mean, why bring in a bunch of namby-pamby adjusters to fu...uh...screw things up? These old places are solid. All it'll take is a new window, couple of boards, place'll be good as new. I know people."

I could imagine the type of people he knew: guys with even thicker "Joisy" accents who favored black suits and had the unique skill of crafting cement booties.

I did a mental head shake. Time to rein in all stereotypical thoughts.

Sudi stood and patted my shoulder. "Stop worrying your li'l head. Just leave everything ta me. I'll treat ya right." With that, he walked toward his tilted front door.

In my peripheral vision, I spotted Martin Magnum holding a black box, walking back and forth on the sidewalk in front of Apartment Two. I blew out a sigh and walked over.

"Martin what are you doing here? And what's that thing?" I pointed to the plastic rectangle in his hand.

He looked at me from beneath his bangs and grinned. "It's an I.R. thermometer. UPS delivered it today. I'm checking for cold spots. See, ghosts often use energy in the air . . ."

I waved away his explanation. "Martin, I know what cold spots are." And right now if he found one I was all for putting Willie in it so she'd stop bitching about getting a decent car with air. "But I've explained how you can't be here bothering my tenants with your thingamajigs."

He frowned. "I'm not bothering anyone. No one's paying attention to my research." He nodded toward the crowd in front of Sudi's apartment.

That was true enough. With all the excitement from the wreck, Martin could've dressed like Bill Murray from *Ghostbusters*, complete with an unlicensed nuclear accelerator on his back, and no one would've given him a second glance. I looked into Martin's puppy-dog eyes and something went all gooey inside me. Poor kid just wanted to get some experience with the supernatural. I seriously doubted he'd find anything around the complex, but who was I to say? I patted his shoulder. "Okay, Martin. Research away. Just keep it low-key."

Behind me a deep, luscious Australian accent answered, "No worries, luv."

I whirled and looked into a pair of brown eyes framed by long black lashes, the kind of eyes that could melt hearts without blinking. "You must be Mercedes. I'm Axel Danforth." He shook my hand, his warm, calloused palm sending tingles up my spine. "Martin's talked so highly of you, it's a pleasure to finally meet face to face."

I tried to come up with a witty response. "Hi," was all I could manage as I continued to hold his hand and gaze at rock-like pecks and abs of steel all wrapped up in a snug white T-shirt.

"Martin's pretty excited with the new thermometer, but we'll keep our activities on the Q.T."

I nodded, mesmerized by the accent and the lips that spoke each word. *Thank God for paranormal activity*, I thought, as they turned in unison and faded into the shadows.

"S.O.B. is back," Dexter said from behind me. I turned to see him pointing at the street.

The golden circle of light from the nearest streetlamp offered little help as I squinted to see an unfamiliar silver Taurus parked across the street. In the deepening twilight I couldn't make out the driver. "What S.O.B.?"

In one quick motion, Dexter grabbed my arm and shoved me behind him.

"Dexter!"

"Don't go climbin' on your high horse, that's Lechman's car." He turned to face me, arms folded, biceps bunched. "I think I've figured out what that no-good creep is up to."

I huffed a sigh and waited.

"I just finished reading an article about this shady landlord in Chicago who hired a hit man to rub out another landlord, just so he could have first chance on his complex."

It took me a minute to sort out the pronouns and make sense of his statement. "You think Lechman's a hit man?"

"He for damn sure is not the type to fantasize meeting some cooking-show gal."

I didn't completely buy it, but a hit man? After me? "Dexter, this old place isn't worth that kind of nefarious deal. If someone wanted the complex, all they'd have to do is offer me . . ." A look of hurt passed over his weathered face and stopped me cold.

"It would have to be an outrageous price," I said, wishing I could reverse *that* foot-in-mouth moment. This was his home, his castle so to speak, not some property to sell for a tidy profit. "Insanely outrageous."

"Sure. Right. Of course," he said, nodding his head like a bobble-head doll. "Better go check on Violet. She's probably worked herself into the "vapors." He turned and shuffled away, hands in pockets, shoulders slumped.

And for my next trick I'll take candy from toddlers and kick puppies. I thunked my forehead with my hand. Dexter was more than a renter; he was a friend.

Okay, time to take the stalker by the horns, or whatever ana-tomical part was most accessible. I stomped across the street, slammed my hands on the driver's door and stuck my face through the open window inches from Lechman's.

"What the hell are you doing?" I said through gritted teeth.

He put a finger between the pages of the paperback he'd been reading. A benevolent smile curved his thin lips. "Enjoying this fine evening. Doing some reading. Watching the ruckus in your parking lot while I wait for Sherrilyn Sandborn."

Some fine evening. Smoke from the warehouse fire lent an acrid scent to the sweltering heat that held Portneuf Gap in a chokehold.

"Cut the bull, Lechman." I peered into the backseat, looking for anything suspicious. A couple of pillows, neatly folded blanket, flashlight, and a cooler filled the backseat. Perfect gear for a stake-out. "Taking up residency?"

He shrugged.

"You can't camp here on the street!"

"No law says I can't." He turned the key in the ignition, twisted the knob on the air conditioner to artic, and rolled up the window. "Bye, bye," he gave me a finger-wave then leaned his back against the locked door.

I yanked my cell phone from my pocket and hit speed dial for Floydean Mollecker's cell. Crossing my fingers, I hoped she wasn't swamped at dispatch and could help me out.

"What now?" her voice was tense.

"Can someone camp-out in their car on the street?" I asked, staring at the back of Lechman's head.

"If the car is in running condition, yes. Bye."

"Wait, one more question."

"Make it quick, girlfriend. This heat's got people acting crazy, the emergency lines are jumpin."

"What problem did Killian get called out on about half-hour ago?"

"Why?" She drew the word out and I could imagine the big smile on her face. "You and Cute-buns got something goin' later?"

"No. I need to clear something up before he's free to hunt me down, chew me up, and spit me out."

"I expect *all* the details when I get off." She chortled through the receiver. "Let's see, he responded to the silent alarm going off at Bi-Lo's grocery. Nothing serious, some indigent looking for a cool place to spend the night. Emergency line's screeching. Gotta go. Remember, de-tails."

I shoved my phone into my front pocket and it chimed "*Funeral March for a Marionette*" as I hurried across the street. "Hey, Gram. I found Cary."

"Smart girl!"

"Yup. Then lost him again," I said.

"When?"

"This afternoon."

"And you wait until now to tell me?" Her tone was cool.

Damn, Yancy hadn't relayed my message. Figured. I sucked my

top lip between my teeth. Now was *not* the time to argue he said/ she said with Gram. "I need to run a couple of things past you. Are you home?"

"Just pulling into the garage," she said. "Had to go to the hospital and sign a death certificate. Where did you find Cary? Why did he take off?"

"I'll come over and explain everything."

That pacified her. "I'll fix some sandwiches. See you soon."

At the mention of food, my stomach rumbled. In all the excitement, I hadn't even scored any French fries like Reb and Willie. I found the duo lounging against Reb's Subaru, watching Sudi, Dexter, and various other renters nail a couple of sheets of plywood, which had appeared as if by magic, to the ruined apartment.

"Holy Hell, Mercedes!" Willie shot me a look and blew out a breath that fluffed her bangs. "Am I to die a slow death by heat exhaustion or starvation?" She dotted her pinkie finger at the melting mascara under her eyes. "We are supposed to be having a nice dinner and making plans to help Cary."

"I have to stick around to make sure Sudi's place is secure," I said, holding up a hand to stop Willie's next whine. "You and Reb can head back to my house. I've got the fixings for nachos and Reb can whip up some of her famous Margaritas."

Willie's eyes glazed over. "I'd kill for a Margarita."

Reb's eyes narrowed. "No can do. You never have any Jose-Cuervo."

I raised my eyebrows, mouthed *pay back's a bitch* to Reb, and pasted on a smile. "Swing past your house and pick up whatever ingredients I don't have. I'll meet you when I'm done. Oh, and feed the mutts when you get there."

I yanked open Reb's car door and Willie slid into the passenger seat. "At last, a car with decent air. Crank this baby up and burn rubber. An icy Margarita is calling my name."

Reb revved the engine and threw me a one-finger salute as she left in a cloud of dust.

"YOU'RE AS SOFT IN THE HEAD AS YOUR BROTHER!" Gram slammed a plate of BLT sandwiches down on the kitchen table and handed me the phone. "Call and report the accident to your insurance right now."

I gulped some iced tea and shook my head. "My insurance premium won't go up if Todd Sudi handles everything."

"Amazing. All that fine Harrigan blood in your veins, yet you remain as gullible as a three-year-old!" Gram shook her head, eyes raised to the ceiling. "Just like your mother."

"Taboo subject," I said, shaking my finger at her. "I'm here to solve problems, not start more."

"Funny you should mention that." Gram sat down across from me. "Ms. Fisher's sordid past is full of scams she either initiated or took part in. Such a shame, using her creative talents that way, and starting at such a young age." Gram tsk- tsked. "Yancy hasn't discovered anything the police don't have, but . . .," she drew the word out for affect. "Yesterday, a nasty text popped up in his email warning him to stop snooping. Yancy shrugged it off. The second one was posted early this morning."

"Two email warnings?" I laid down my sandwich.

"Both were dire and worded in a style mimicking a Dashiell Hammett mystery." She picked up a sandwich and took a dainty bite.

"Let me guess, *The Thin Man* threatened to beat Yancy to death with *The Maltese Falcon*?"

Gram scowled. "Mercedes! Murder is serious."

"Especially when it involves removing my gorgeous head from this glorious body," Yancy answered as he came through the back door. He snatched a handful of chips from a yellow earthenware bowl on the table and popped one in his mouth.

"You received emails involving decapitation?"

Yancy took a tall glass from the cupboard and poured himself some iced tea. "Yes, in graphic detail. The emails are signed, 'Torture Junkie.' Mr. Junkie thinks I have access to Frobi's laptop

. . . which he claims is his. I'm supposed to return the pink laptop to *him*." Yancy sighed and took a long drink.

"Why does this guy think you have her laptop?"

"Maybe because I've been in multiple sites searching for info on Ms. Frobi."

"If Torture Junkie is demanding her laptop he's probably involved in Frobi's murder. This is perfect. We'll get Killian to help you drop-off the laptop, catch ol' Junkie, and prove Cary had nothing to do with Frobi's death." I said smiling.

"Whoa, Holmes. This misanthrope hasn't set any ground rules yet, except, I'm not to involve the police in any shape or form. Speaking of which, did one of our men in blue happen to take a laptop from the crime scene?"

I took a couple of chips, chewed, and thought. "Can't say for sure, but I didn't see a computer when I went through the apartment," I said.

Yancy rolled his eyes to the ceiling. "You rummaged through the apartment *before* the police arrived at the murder scene?"

I shrugged. "My apartments, my brother, my responsibility. Back to the emails. In your not-so-humble opinion, is the threat of decapitation real or a prank?"

"Mercedes, to the untrained eye, I may appear completely sangfroid, but I consider this situation dire until I can prove otherwise." Yancy picked up my unfinished sandwich and took a bite. Okay by me, my appetite had disappeared. Thoughts of decapitation, even Yancy's, did that. I shoved my plate toward him.

"Any idea who might be sending the love notes?" I said.

Yancy shook his head. "Not yet. Junkie is computer-savvy. I'm having trouble tracking the origination point."

"That's terrific!" I said. Yancy and Gram both narrowed their eyes and I hurried to explain. "The police can't lay this on Cary. His computer skills are more abysmal than mine."

"Let me play Devil's Advocate for a moment," Yancy said around a mouthful of chips. "The cops might consider, I know I would, the fact that Cary's working with an abettor."

Yancy and his la-de-dah words. Why couldn't he just say assistant? "Thanks, Candlemass, I was feeling way too hopeful," I grumbled, snatching a couple of chips and popping them in my mouth. My appetite was still missing, but salt and grease helped me think.

"You said you wanted to run some things by me?" Gram said.

I cast a glance at Yancy. Oh, what the hell. Gram would tell him anyway. "A semi with five caskets arrived at my complex today." Gram raised an eyebrow, and I held up a hand. "Let me finish. One: I don't expect you to store the damn things, even though they're clogging my driveway. And B: I kicked a hole in one and found what might be a couple of stolen paintings."

"Paintings?" Gram and Yancy spoke together.

I nodded. "Pin-up artwork. Think of calendars circa 1940." I showed them the pictures on my phone.

"I knew something was wrong with this whole business," Gram said.

"The caskets are mere chicanery," Yancy said.

Gram took my phone. "Those look similar to the famous painter who started out doing calendars." She enlarged the second photo. "Yes, Elvgren. Originals are worth money. Where are the paintings now?" Gram asked.

"Behind my furnace."

Gram's brows lowered. "You hid expensive artwork in your dirty basement?"

"I wrapped both in the protective plastic covering they were transported in, all nice and neat and sanitary."

Have you contacted the police about this?"

"Not yet, I wanted your thoughts first," I said.

"I'll take *Accomplice* for one hundred, Alex," Yancy chortled.

Gram stared down at her hands clutched on the table and shook her head. "What is your brother mixed up in?"

My thoughts, exactly.

"Before we do anything, I'd like my friend, Raymond Quinton, to take a look at the paintings. Raymond works at a bank but he dabbles in fine art. Hopefully he'll be able to determine if they're true Elvgens. After that we *will* call the authorities," Gram said.

The grandfather clock in the hallway chimed 11:00 p.m. Time to rescue Reb from Willie's ramblings. I pushed to my feet. "Got'ta run. I'll bring the paintings tomorrow morning."

"If you find your brother again, hog-tie him and call me ASAP. Otherwise, be here in the morning by 7:00," Gram said, standing and taking her plate to the sink. "On the dot." She tapped a fork in her palm for emphasis.

Thoughts of Cary, a casket hiding artwork, and dire threats over a missing laptop, occupied my mind as I wove in and out of the traffic cruising Yellowstone Avenue.

The only reason someone would hide paintings inside a casket would be to keep the artwork secret. I hadn't checked the other five caskets but if they all contained paintings this couldn't end well. Were the paintings originals? Or was Cary involved in some grand forgery scheme? And where was Frobi's laptop? What information was stored on it that was worth killing for? My mind felt battered and bruised by the time I turned toward home.

I parked at the end of my driveway, close to the obscene caskets, and caught Willie's laughter pealing from the open living room side window. I wasn't ready to party, but I pasted on a smile, opened the back door, and stepped into the brightly lit kitchen. Seated at the kitchen table, a dead pitcher of Margaritas between them, Reb and Willie beamed up at me.

"It's about time, girlfriend," Reb said, holding her goblet aloft. "Grab a glass and join us. We've come up with quite a list of suspects." She fanned herself with a notebook, a dab of melted cheese smudged in the center.

"We've no doubt also solved the crime." Willie looked at the half-inch of green liquid in the pitcher and the one lonely nacho left on the platter beside her. "Oops, time for another batch, Girlfriend," she said to Reb.

I gently pushed Reb back into her seat. "Let's put that pitcher of Margaritas on hold for a minute." I held out my hand. "Give me the list of suspects."

Willie grabbed the book from Reb and clutched it to her chest. "We've worked very hard on this. You think you can waltz in here and take all the credit? No way, sister! We're a duo, not a trio. We're Rizzoli and Isles, Sam and Dean, those luscious hunks from *Supernatural*, Batman and Robin."

Abbot and Costello. I stifled a sigh and sat on the nearest chair. "Okay, Willie, the floor is all yours."

She opened the notebook and, with slightly slurred enunciation, began. "One: Mark Sandborn. Very jealous of his ex-wife and not *the* brightest crayon. Add the couple of unfastened screws rattling around in his noggin and he becomes a real loose cannon. Two: The unknown person who's involved in the casket scam. I . . ."

Reb cleared her throat.

"Sorry, *we*. We are fairly sure there's a third party because Cary is just too damn gullible, he's the perfect patsy. This third party set Cary up to take the fall for Frobi's murder."

Strange, Willie and Reb had also thought of a third party. I tuned Willie out and murmured to Reb, "Where are the dogs?" It was odd they hadn't greeted me like whirling dervishes.

"Snoring on the couch." Reb whispered.

"Tell me you didn't party with them."

"Just a little bit."

"Fine. You're on clean-up duty when the puking starts."

"Todd Sudi." Willie finished and laid down the notebook. "Oh, almost forgot. Todd wants you to call him. Tonight."

"Sudi made your list?"

Willie giggled. "Along with the rest of your renters. Do you check their backgrounds before they sign the lease?"

My tenants? I suppose including them on the list made sense

after a pitcher or two of Margaritas.

"What did Sudi want? Tell me there's not another problem like his smashed truck?"

"No. He has a couple of questions about fixing his front door. You know, while talking to the dear man, I had the most marvelous idea." Willie licked some salt from the rim of her glass. "Why not put him in your spare room while his apartment's being fixed?"

"No!" Sudi's questions would wait until morning when Willie wasn't hovering in the background. I turned to Reb. "Did Cary leave a pink laptop at your house?"

"No, why?"

"Why, exactly?" Willie raised her chin, bloodshot eyes zeroing in on mine. "Why can't Toddy stay here?"

"First, it's not wise to get that friendly with a tenant. Second, you're staying in my spare room. And he made your list of suspects."

"Come on, my girl. Live a little. Let loose. He might be on the list, but he's a total babe. I wouldn't mind sharing the guest room." Willie winked and turned to Reb. "To think I gave birth to this stick in the mud." She closed her eyes, opened them and slapped the table. "You know, Cary was conceived right here on this very table, in record time, mind you, while Aunt Vie was upstairs bathing Mercedes."

I stopped and stared at Willie. An image of her and my father writhing on *my* table made me shudder. Yuck! Suppose she decided to reenact the bread scene from *The Postman Always Rings Twice* with Sudi. My stomach quivered. Double Yuck! I jerked my hands off said table-top and wiped them against my pants.

Damn.

I loved this old table.

Now I'd have to sell or burn it.

TEN

I AWOKE TO DOGS BARKING AND SOMEONE pounding on my front door. My bedside clock read 1:30. I grabbed the .38 I keep in my underwear drawer, hurried downstairs, and looked through the peephole. A disgruntled face with angry green eyes glared back at me: Killian. I took a breath, scooted the gun under the hallway table and opened the door. "Do you know what time it is?"

Killian pushed past me and the barking trio, headed for the kitchen. He opened the fridge, grabbed a can of Pepsi and gulped a swig. He was still in uniform and the paraphernalia on his belt jingled as he crooked his finger in a "come hither" motion.

Glad I'd opted to sleep in a long tee-shirt instead of bra and panties, I stormed into the kitchen. "What the hell's wrong with you, pounding on my door at this time of night?" Okay, the bravado was fake, but I hoped a good offense would disarm some of his wrath.

"Don't give me attitude, not now." Killian drank the rest of the Pepsi and flattened the can with his fingers. Hands on hips, seething exasperation, he growled, "Dispatch has gotten calls about people seeing your brother. Most weren't worth following up. But starting around ten-thirty, dispatch logged eight calls reporting sightings of your brother that were followed up on.

Two of the calls were from this end of town. Where's Cary, and don't tell me you don't know."

"I don't."

"Mercedes, this isn't a game." He turned back to the fridge and grabbed another Pepsi. A line of sweat trailed down the back of his shirt. "Is this all you have?"

I nodded while my breath hitched in my throat. He couldn't have gotten a search warrant, not at this time of night. Right? What if he insisted on searching my house top to bottom anyway? Did he somehow know about the paintings? I felt like I was living a modern version of Edgar Allen Poe's *Tell-Tale Heart*. Distraction time, I snatched the can from his hands. "Take a break." I pointed to the tainted table and suppressed a shudder. "Let me get a glass, some ice. We'll talk."

Killian stood his ground for a heart-slamming moment, relented, sat and rocked back on the chair, placing his feet on the edge of the table. "Okay, talk."

I opened the freezer, grabbed a handful of ice, closed the door, handed the can and glass to Killian. "Do you think I'd still have five caskets clogging my driveway if I knew where my brother was?"

Killian poured the soda but remained mute.

"I do have some information if you want to hear it."

He shrugged. "Depends. Does it have any bearing?"

"You tell me." I pulled out a chair and sat down. "Yancy Candlemass researched Fisher online, discovered her shady past, and got two email threats for his trouble."

Killian dropped his feet and let the chair thud to the floor. "What type of threats?"

"Severe bodily harm, decapitation, stuff like that."

His eyebrows rose. "Just for Googling Fisher?"

"He probably did more than a Google search. Someone wants her hot-pink laptop. Was it recovered in the SUV and tagged as evidence?"

Killian shook his head. "No laptop, I'd remember a pink one

if it was recovered from the apartment or vehicle." He took a long drink. "Maybe your brother's trying to spook Yancy off the trail."

"Nope. Cary's computer skills suck worse than mine."

"So you say."

"So I know."

Killian leaned forward and tucked a stray lock of hair behind my ear. His hand cupped my neck as he pulled me forward until our foreheads nearly touched. His eyes held a wealth of emotion, and two worry lines appeared above his nose. "Sadie, you and your brother could be in real danger. I don't want to find you laid out on a slab in the morgue."

His concern sent tingles where tingles shouldn't go. If he kissed me, right here, right now, I'd spill all: the phony caskets, the artwork, my undying lust for him.

I pulled back a safe distance and folded my arms. "I'm not going to investigate the internet stalker. Yancy's the one in danger."

"Speaking of danger, I drove past your apartments earlier tonight and met your weird ghost-busting duo. Why does a man fly all the way from Australia to investigate your apartment complex for ghosts?" Killian raised an eyebrow and I read volumes in his look: irritation, fatigue, and maybe a tiny jab from the green-eyed monster after meeting Axel the Australian hunk.

"They're *not my* duo."

"Really? That's the impression I got from Crocodile Dundee." Killian smiled, but his eyes remained hard.

He was jealous! I swallowed a smile and gave him a palms-up shrug. "I just met the man."

Killian's eyes narrowed and he pushed to his feet. "Keep me updated on anymore internet threats. And I want your word you'll call me when Cary contacts you."

I crossed my heart. "Okay."

"And I'll talk to Yancy tomorrow about the internet threats he's gotten."

"Can I join this little party?" Rebbie lounged in the doorway, covering a yawn. Despite bed-head and smudged mascara, she managed to make the tee shirt I'd loaned her look sexy as hell.

Killian gave her a long, slow once-over, and smiled. "Did I interrupt a girls' night?"

"No, Willie and I were creating a list of suspects for Frobi's murder and I guess we drank a couple Margaritas too many. Sadie insisted I shouldn't drive." She took a deep breath and her nipples fairly saluted through the white fabric.

Killian grabbed her hand. "Walk me to my car and tell me about this list."

The front door shut, and I walked toward the picture window, reconsidered, and turned back to the kitchen. No way was I going to watch those two do the tongue tango. He was trying to play his own jealousy card and it *was not* working. Instead, I hurried downstairs to check on the paintings. The lone bulb at the bottom of the staircase cast a weak circle of light on the cracked cement floor. I reached behind the furnace, touched the plastic-wrapped art, and wondered if I should hide the paintings in a different, more secure place. But where? Then it hit me, the place Cary and I used to hide things as kids. I raced upstairs, grabbed a tape measure from the kitchen junk drawer, hoping the space was large enough.

In the upstairs bathroom, I opened the linen closet, knelt on the floor, pulled the towels from the bottom shelf, and lifted up said shelf. There was a twelve-inch gap between the shelf and floor. The space looked tight but it might work. I looked inside, something was on the dusty floor. I tugged the shelf out and found a fuchsia cell phone laying on top of a metallic pink laptop.

Son-of-a-bitch!

Cary *had* been here. I pulled the items out and sat on the floor. I knew I should go get Killian. Or call Floydean. Or take it to Detective Stayner. That would be the sensible thing to do. But nothing about this mess had made sense from the get-go. I went into my bedroom and shoved the laptop and phone under the bed, and called a familiar number.

"Harrigan Funeral Home," Yancy answered on a yawn.

"I found Frobi's laptop," I said.

There was a long silence followed by a snort. "Mercedes McCambridge, it's 2:30! This news couldn't wait for a civilized hour?"

I coated my voice with sappy sweetness and answered, "I thought you'd want to check out the hard drive while your precious head is still attached to your neck. Plus, added bonus, there's a cell phone with the laptop. Think of the info you can find using your wizardly skills with both."

"Are you positive both belonged to Frobi?"

"Yes."

"You'd better not be japing."

"What?"

"Look it up. Bring it when you bring the art."

With any luck, Yancy would discover what was so important about the laptop before I gave it to the authorities. I'd ruined the remainder of Yancy's night—mission accomplished.

An earlier comment from Willie had been nudging my brain. I went into my office and pulled open the top drawer of my filing cabinet. I didn't have the right program to run criminal background checks on prospective renters, but the credit checks I did run held a wealth of information. I pulled the last three renters and looked at their credit sheets. The only one that seemed a little unusual was Todd Sudi's. Starting in New York, he'd lived in six different states, never staying longer than six months to a year. Was the man a born gypsy or did this have some significance?

I decided to take the file to Gram's along with the artwork. I lifted the bedspread and peered at the laptop. Guarded by multiple dust bunnies, it seemed safe enough. Looking under the bed made me think of Cary still in hiding. He'd been here long enough to stash the laptop. He might still be holed up either in the barn or . . .? I checked on Willie and found her curled up and snoring softly. Hurrying down the stairs, I grabbed a flashlight from the junk drawer, checked to make sure it worked, then looked out the front window. Killian, Reb, and the police cruiser were gone. Figured.

I opened the back door, crossed to the back gate and let Bogart and Bacall out, leaving the infamous Mr. Wiggins whining behind the fence. My sleuthing duo made a beeline for the barn. Hmm. I caught up with them and turned on the light to look around. Eclipse hung his head over the stall door and nickered softly.

"Sorry to wake you, Buddy. Have you seen a worthless-looking excuse for a human?" He nudged my hand and I soothed his sleek, black neck as I scanned the place. Bales of hay piled to the ceiling lined the back area. No real place to hide there. The loft ladder was not hooked to the loft's iron rail but was still hooked to the far wall. I bent down to examine the old wood floor. A myriad of different prints in a kaleidoscope of dust made it impossible to tell anything. I stood, sneezed, and decided if Cary had hidden here earlier, I'd missed him. So much for sisterly intuition.

The dogs were sitting up, front paws quivering as they looked wistfully at the shelf where I keep a box of sugar cubes. I shooed them out, kissed Eclipse on the nose, told him to go back to dreamland, and turned out the light. At the back fence, all three dogs were busy sniffing along the gate. Probably on the trail of a squirrel. "Why can't you act like Bloodhounds and find Cary?"

Bogart lifted his head, let out a woof, and pawed at the gate. "It's way too early for breakfast so cool your jets."

I opened the gate, Bogart beat Bacall and Wiggins through the dog door. Okay, it wasn't their fault they hadn't unearthed my brother. Maybe a treat was in order. I opened the backdoor and stopped. Bogart and Bacall were doing their dance of joy around the sneaker-clad feet of some guy rummaging through my fridge.

"Hungry?" I asked, leaning against the screen door.

"I'm turning myself in. Being on the run is too hard." Cary stood with a carton of yogurt in his hand and tapped the lid. "Is this the best you have to offer? Pitiful."

I handed him a spoon. "Been too busy looking for your sorry ass to go to the store. Where the hell have you been?"

"Here and there." He plunked down at the table and finished the yogurt in a few bites.

"Hiding where?" I picked a banana from the fruit holder on the counter. "Want a PBJ?"

"Sure."

I spread the peanut butter thick, topped it with grape jelly and sliced banana, cut the sandwich and placed it on a paper towel in front of Cary.

"Hiding where?" I repeated.

Cary held up a finger as he dug into the sandwich. He swallowed and gave a contented sigh. "First I hid at the mortuary, but napping in a casket is the pits. So I came here and tried camping out in the barn until that huge black beast started throwing a hissy fit in his stall. Made enough racket to wake the dead. I let myself in through a basement window and I've been waiting for daylight to turn myself in. What have you got to drink?"

"Two choices, milk or water," I said, opening the cupboard and handing Cary a glass. "Killian drank my last Pepsi."

"I know. I'm talkin' intense heart failure when that dude came busting in. Then you come tromping downstairs. Doesn't anyone sleep around this place?" He stood, grabbed the carton of milk from the fridge, sniffed, shrugged, and emptied it into the glass. "You found her laptop and phone, right?"

I nodded. "Truth or consequence time, brother. You tell me the truth and I won't have to beat you 'til you can't grow anymore." The old bluff I'd used when we were younger brought a smile to his weary face. "The caskets are a total scam, right?"

He nodded; mouth too full to talk.

I narrowed my eyes. "What about the artwork hidden inside?"

He gulped some milk and stared at the glass.

I folded my arms and waited. He took another bite, chewed, and drank more milk, the whole time refusing to look up. He finished the sandwich and cleared his throat. "I did *not* know about the paintings until the night Frobi died."

I snorted. "Right."

"I told you earlier, she'd been antsy all day. When she finally let me in on the deal, well, that's why we were fighting in the parking lot."

"You really did not know until that night?"

He shook his head and raised one hand. "I swear."

"Okay, you didn't kill her. So, why run and hide like you're guilty?"

"It's complicated." He stood, rinsed his glass and filled it with water.

"Complicated? A maniac turned your fiancé into a metallic corpse! How much more complicated can you get?"

He huffed a sigh and plopped onto the chair he'd vacated. "You want it, you got it. The old broad comes out and tells us to take the fight inside. We're disturbing her sleep. She and Frobi get into it and I leave to cool down. I need some space before I can wrap my head around the artwork part." He paused, took a deep breath and let it out. "The real kicker . . . I don't know if the paintings are originals and stolen or excellent fakes. Frobi always claimed to have the Midas-touch, so either scenario would work. I was okay with hawking inferior caskets, but dealing in stolen or phony art, even I know that comes with serious prison time." He took a long drink.

"I walked for a long time thinking, trying to decide if I should stay or split. When I came back I found her dead." He winced.

"Painted head to toe. That freaked me out. I found a note under the windshield wiper. I'm shaking so bad I can barely read it." He ran his fingers through his hair, stood, then sat back down.

I reached across the table and grasped his hand. "What did the note say?"

He squeezed my hand. "It was printed in some fancy script. Short and simple. Said I needed to hand over the laptop or I'd end up like Frobi. I panicked and ran."

"Where's the note now?"

"I stuck it in my pocket but it must've fallen out or something. It's gone."

"Let me get this straight. In your panicked state you still collected the laptop and her cell phone?"

"I happen to have a high sense of self-preservation. Killer wants the laptop, right? Whoever has it has the power to negotiate."

"You don't negotiate with a murderer!"

"I'll use it as bait."

"Why didn't the killer grab the laptop when he murdered Frobi? She must've had it in the apartment, right?"

"When we got back from dinner, Frobi hid it in that deep kitchen cabinet by the stove. She even went into the apartment next door, took some of your cleaning stuff and stacked it in the cabinet as camouflage, said it was the perfect subterfuge, sort of a 'hide in plain sight' plan."

I thought two days ago my biggest worry was cleaning a filthy apartment. "I can understand the lure of going for the fast buck, but scamming people? Come on, Cary!"

"Giving people something that looks as nice as one of Gram's caskets for a cheaper price isn't really scamming. The lining's substandard? And the walls sort'a fall apart underground: Unless the family is into grave robbing, who's to know? Or care?"

There was so much wrong with his way of thinking I didn't know where to start. "But why give up surfing and join Frobi in the first place?"

"I know you think it was all about her fantastic bazoombas and world-class ass, and sure, the sex was unbelievable." He stared at the ceiling for a moment, then leveled his eyes at me. "But the biggest hook . . . she made me feel smart. Intelligent. She claimed I had more untapped potential than anyone she'd ever met. After a while, I believed her."

I patted his hand and opened my mouth to tell him he was smart.

"Don't!" He snorted and snatched his hand away before I got the first word out. "Don't start with the 'Cary, honey, you are smart' bit. I didn't come here for a pity party. I know everyone thinks I'm a lazy surf bum. That's okay."

It wasn't okay, but Cary didn't want to hear my sisterly thoughts on the subject.

"What do we do now?" He asked.

"Figure out what secrets her cell and that ridiculous pink laptop are hiding."

ELEVEN

"**FINE ART APPRAISAL IS AN ART UNTO ITSELF.**" Raymond Quinton, retired loan officer from Keybank, slowly circled Gram's kitchen table looking at the painting on display. His thin shoulders hunched and a lock of white hair fell across his high forehead as he learned in for a closer look at the cursive signature with a magnifying glass. Either passion for the subject or Gram's breakfast casserole had his baby blues dancing behind round-rimmed glasses.

"If this signature is Gil Elvgrans, this painting was produced during the years he worked for Bigelow. If it's an authentic Elvgren it could be worth close to half a million."

Cary let out a low whistle. "Half a million? Who'd pay that much for an old-fashioned girl blowing soap bubbles?"

"You'd be surprised," Mr. Quinton said. "There are several art collectors in Portneuf Gap who would consider it a privilege to have this painting grace their walls."

For my taste, the true selling point was an adorable black Dachshund snapping at the bubbles blown by the shapely lass. I'd even entertained the idea of buying it but with that hefty price tag this 30 X 24 painting would not be gracing my walls anytime soon.

"Oh yes, Elvgren is very popular in both pop culture and Americana." Quinton handed the magnifying glass back to Gram. "I wish I could help, Cassandra, but I'm not equipped to access whether this painting is authentic or an excellent forgery."

"How might we find out?" Gram asked.

"The nuclear bomb tests were actually good for something; radiocarbon dating or C14 is a fool-proof way to date almost anything." He beamed as though he'd given Gram the secret formula for the fountain of youth. "However, there's only a few places that have the capacity to run C14 tests on art, and the last time I checked there was a substantial waiting list. I doubt you'd want to shoulder the cost of such an experiment. If there are more paintings, I'd love to see them."

"They're in the dining room," Gram said leading the way.

I'd known Mr. Quinton for many years, his house is behind the mortuary through the alley, yet I'd never seen him this animated.

After examining each painting, he took his glasses off and nodded. "This Elvgren right here might be worth more than the one in the kitchen. Notice, it lacks a signature which means it likely dates from his years with Louis F. Dow." He pointed to the two western paintings. "Walter Ufer is another wonderful artist, his paintings are also sought after. One of his paintings recently sold for $175,000.00." He slipped his glasses in his vest pocket. "You found all four hidden inside a shipment of caskets?"

"Yes." Gram flushed and drew in a deep breath "I can assure you Carrigan Funeral Home had nothing to do with any of this. My grandson and his fiancé were . . . uh . . ."

Cary put his arm around Gram. "Mr. Quinton, my grandmother had no idea the caskets held expensive paintings. I had no idea until Frobi broke the news to me. I thought we were starting an internet mail order casket business to help cut costs on, well, you know." His last words came out in a mumbled rush. He dropped his arm from Gram's shoulder, shoved his hands in his pockets and studied his sandal-clad feet.

Quinton looked from Gram to Cary. "You have no idea where this artwork was going or where it came from?"

Cary shook his head.

"And you didn't find any paperwork, perhaps letters or photographs, with the paintings?"

Cary shrugged. "Not so far. Sadie and I searched each casket, but we didn't examine the lining. Maybe . . ."

Quinton held up his hand. "I'm not saying paperwork would help, I remember a case of a fake Jackson Pollock which had both letters and photographs guaranteeing the painting had lain hidden in Castro's estate for over fifty years. Turned out to be a brilliant scam that rocked the art world. This could be an another absolutely devious scheme to bilk the unwary." He paused and looked at Gram. "My dear neighbor, please be careful. If these paintings prove to be authentic or not, reputable people do not ship anything in the bottom of caskets. You are planning on reporting this to the authorities, right?"

"Absolutely." Gram and I said in unison.

"Let the FBI use their considerable resources to authenticate this artwork." With one last fond look at all of the paintings, he went out the back door.

At eight-thirty in the morning, this info was all fine and good if I was studying for an art exam, but it wouldn't solve our dilemma.

Soon we'd turn the whole mess over to the police, who would then bring in the Feds. Now, the only thing standing between Cary and prison time was his word. After three days on the run, would anyone believe he didn't know about the hidden paintings until the night Frobi died? Hell, I was still having trouble with that myself.

My phone rang and I looked at the caller I.D. Oh-oh.

"Hey, Willie," I said.

"Don't you 'Hey Willie' me, little girl. What's with the secret meeting at the fat lady's house?"

"Excuse me?"

"You heard me!"

"And you know the rules." I hung up and started counting. I'd reached twenty when the phone rang in my hand.

"Sorry. Oh-kay? I just hate being left out." A tortured sigh resounded in my ear. "Why did you and Rebbie sneak away this morning? You know I can't drive that old, beater truck behind your garage."

Reb's car was gone. Damn. A bored Willie, left to her own devices spelled trouble. I walked into the living room away from Gram and Cary, looked at my watch and made a hasty decision. "Cary and I will come and get you." I intended to become Cary's conjoined twin until we cleared everything up at the police station.

"You found Cary? Praise the Lord!"

Before she could launch into some sort of gospel song, I filled her in on the latest developments.

She gasped and I pictured her standing with one hand clutched to her breast. "I need to be with my baby when he turns himself in. Give me thirty, no make that forty-five minutes, then pick me up."

I hung up and went back to the kitchen. Gram was clearing the breakfast dishes while Cary slouched at the counter, eating the remaining casserole straight from the pan.

I watched him shovel in the last bite. "How can you still be hungry?"

"I don't know what they serve in jail. I am stocking up."

"No one's going to jail." Gram put the last plate in the dishwasher, dried her hands on a towel, and patted her hair. "As a personal favor, my lawyer, Mr. Worthington, has agreed to meet us this morning in the lobby of the police station." The faintest blush colored her cheeks as she spoke Barkley Worthington's name. If pressed, Gram would describe him as her dearest old friend. Most people who knew them let the description go with a wink and a nod.

"When you and Frobi met with different businesses to discuss mail-order caskets, was there anything she said that could've also applied to selling artwork?" I asked.

Cary swallowed the last bite and gave Gram the casserole dish. "I only went with her to a couple of assisted living places. She gave her spiel and I handed out the brochures. I didn't go and meet with the CEO of Hooks Specialists and Surgery Center."

"Why not?" Gram asked. "I thought you were a team."

"Frobi said it would be better for her to finesse the CEO in a one-on-one atmosphere. She could get a better feel for what the Center wanted."

"You didn't think it was odd for a surgery center to be interested in caskets?" I clasped my hands in front of my waist and adopted a posh accent. "I'm terribly sorry, Ms. Smith, that your husband did not survive the procedure. However, here's a lovely brochure featuring caskets in case you're interested."

"Hey, I wasn't thinking about the details. Frobi said it was a golden opportunity. I trusted her." Cary said.

Yancy came into the kitchen with deep smudges under his eyes and clumps of hair sticking out like a jumbled haystack. He laid the pink laptop on the table and rubbed his eyes. "I've found a couple of passwords but there's more. The woman had a password for her passwords. I have half a mind to comminute it and be done!"

Cary scowled. "You want to what?"

"Pulverize," I said, wishing Gram hadn't given him the Word-Of-The-Day desk calendar last Christmas.

"Plus, I found this little present attached to the garage door with duct tape."

Yancy held up a headless Ken doll. Red globs oozed from where the head had been and trickled down the neck, staining the doll's sweater.

Cary touched a blob with his finger and stuck it in his mouth. "Hunts—no—Heinz," he said. "What neighborhood punk have you pissed off, Candlemass?"

"It's a warning," I said, the breakfast casserole riding uneasy in my stomach. "We think the same sicko who threatened you with a total body paint job wants to behead Yancy."

"Why?" Cary asked.

"He wants Frobi's laptop," Yancy said. "We cannot, under any circumstances, let anyone know we have either her laptop or cell phone."

My phone shrilled startling all of us. I didn't need to look at caller ID, the urge to groan told me it was Willie.

"I don't need a ride. Rebbie's here and she's simply a mess, poor baby. Once I get her calmed down, she can give me a ride."

"What's the problem?" I asked.

"Something to do with a big deal falling through," Willie said. "Oh, there's the kettle singing away. I'm making her tea."

Willie making tea? I could have a complete nuclear mental meltdown and not get any tea, let alone a "poor baby."

I turned my pent-up rage on Cary. "I'm done. You help Yancy with that stupid pink laptop right now before I wring your neck!"

He ran a hand through his hair. "Two-seconds on the phone and you morph into Super Bitch. What did Willie want?"

"She doesn't want a ride, Reb will bring her to the station." I took a breath and blew it out, closed my eyes and rubbed my temples. "I no longer live with her! Why's she still pushing my buttons?"

I felt Cary's strong hands on my shoulders. "Cause she installed 'em," he whispered, slowly kneading tense muscles with his fingers.

I opened my eyes, turned and wrapped my arms around his waist, squeezing hard, feeling comforting warmth. "Sorry, Bro . . ."

He grinned. "'S okay. But, I swear, I'm totally in the dark about that f . . ." he glanced at Gram. ". . . uh, stupid laptop."

"That horrible doll has all of us on edge. Put it in here." Gram handed Yancy a plastic bag. "We'll take this atrocity to the police along with the paintings and that garish pink computer. You have one hour before we meet Barkley Worthington at Police Headquarters. If you're intent on digging deeper, you'd better get busy."

"Cassandra!" Yancy's eyes sunk deeper into their sockets as his face turned a sickly shade of pale. "Don't be obtuse. You cannot turn the laptop over to the gendarmes. If word leaks out, who knows what this cyber stalker will do? Besides, once the authorities take possession, we'll never know why someone is threatening me. Or Cary." He held his arms out in an imploring gesture. "I can access the info. A day. Two at most, please."

Gram's spine stiffened and she turned slitted eyes on Yancy. "I've told Barkley we'd bring the laptop. I intend to keep my word."

"Yancy's right." Gram turned her high-watt glare on me. I knowing I'd hate myself for agreeing with the man. "Just let him fiddle a little longer. We can always turn it in later."

AN HOUR LATER WE WENT TO THE Portneuf Gap Police Headquarters. It shares a cinderblock building with the City Offices. The tan building spans about a city block. On the public side, trees and flowers bloom under the watchful care of some green-thumbed employee. The double-entry doors open to a lobby decorated in a pastel color scheme with couches and decorative end tables littered with various magazines. I suppose the mellow colors are meant to relax Joe Public who comes to bitch about water bills or meet with the mayor.

The police entrance is another story. The sidewalk is littered with discarded cigarette butts that spill over into flower beds and the sparse mulch surrounding tree trunks. Inside, the floor is institutional gray linoleum, and the walls are white, adorned by two display cases on opposing walls. The cases hold memorabilia and pictures honoring various officers for their achievements. A single door located on the rear wall accesses the inner workings of the station. A black intercom next to the door lets John Q. state his business and gain access if need be. The lobby is empty of furniture except for an information desk opposite the entrance. The desk is manned by volunteers from different citizen watch groups.

I opened the outside door for Gram and Cary, spotted Barkley Worthington talking to the volunteer behind the desk, and sucked in a breath. Dexter. He caught my eye and gave a nod. I felt my face redden. Unlike his wife, Violet, Dexter didn't go in for gossip. But to have him privy to our family's sordid laundry made me feel itchy inside.

Barkley strode to our little group and grasped Gram's hand. "Cassandra." His voice was soothing and tinged with compassion. Today, his trademark three-piece suit was light gray with a narrow white pinstripe. It draped his wide shoulders and rangy body with elegant precision. "And Cary, my boy. How are you holding up?"

Cary shrugged, feigning nonchalance, but his jaw twitched, and his smile came out bleak and tight-lipped.

Barkley clapped him on the shoulder with a big, square hand. His periwinkle eyes, which peered from beneath heavy salt- and-pepper brows, sparkled with confidence. "Please step over here and you can fill me in. Just set the paintings next to this wall. Not to worry, this will soon be over."

My cell phone rang from the depths of my bag. I fumbled around until my hand snagged it and I prepared for another Willie tirade. "What now?"

"Mercedes, this is Martin. Axel and I found a cold spot, definite energy manifestation. An entity is here!" Martin's voice cracked with excitement.

Axel Danforth. An image of the sexy ghost buster flashed through my mind, making me wish I was there hunting cold spots and entities instead of waiting for Cary to face his fate.

"The cold is stationary, surrounding a car that's parked on the street. Axel's asking around, he's talking to your renters to determine who owns the car."

Martin's nasal voice jogged my tired brain. "Car? What kind of car?"

"Um, a silver Taurus. See, we decided to try out my I.R. thermometer around the . . ."

"Is anyone in the car?"

"No. Unless you count the entity."

Lechman's car? Had to be. I suppose cold-blooded "biggest fans" might register on I.R. thermometers. Lechman's vacant vehicle made me antsy. Dexter sat not ten feet from me so I couldn't ask him to check around the apartments.

"Martin, do me a favor. You and Axel walk around the complex and let me know if you see a blonde, preppy-looking guy on the property."

"Want me to let you know about any other cold spots?"

"Sure." I clicked off and walked over to Dexter. "Did you notice Lechman's car on the street this morning when you left?"

"No. He disappeared last night after we got Sudi's apartment squared away. Is that asshole back?"

"His car is."

"I'm manning my post for another couple of hours. If you need me to search the complex, I can bring in a replacement. Pronto." His blue eyes sparked with excitement.

I told him to hold his post for now and turned toward the sound of the door opening beside the intercom. Killian, followed by Det. Stayner and a fellow I didn't recognize came into the lobby. The other guy wore a suit almost identical to Stayner's, standard detective uniform right down to his black wingtips. They'd come for Cary.

I inhaled sharply and Dexter patted my arm. Barkley was a good attorney, a great attorney. Could he convince the authorities that Cary was an innocent pawn in an unknown game? A cold dread seeped into my body.

Killian walked over and put his arm around my shoulders. His solid comfort made me want to lean against him. Except, he had on his cop face. Was he now the enemy? I wasn't sure.

"Don't worry, Sadie. If he's innocent, this won't take long."

If. There it was. One little word that could ruin our friendship and my brother's life.

I nodded, not trusting my ability to speak. Every head turned toward the outside door as a whirlwind of commotion burst into the lobby. Willie, dressed as conservatively as Willie can, in a white, curve-hugging dress that stopped just shy of her kneecaps, rushed over and threw her arms around Cary. Rebbie followed, eyelids puffed from crying, face solemn.

"My baby! Did they hurt you?" Willie gave all the males in the room a withering glare. "Did they use rubber hoses?" She spit the words in Det. Stayner's direction.

Det. Stayner struggled to hide a smile. "He hasn't given us his statement yet."

"We did away with the hoses . . . too many visible marks," the fellow next to Det. Stayner said. When no one laughed, he cleared his throat and Barkley Worthington stepped forward to perform the introductions all around.

Detective Norton, the wannabe comedian, opened the door and motioned for Barkley and Cary to enter. Willie linked her arm through Cary's and started forward.

"Sorry, ma'am." Det. Stayner held up his hand and stopped her progress. "Only your son and his attorney are allowed right now."

Willie took a deep, unsteady breath and released her hold. "We'll be right here, baby." She turned to Det. Stayner, opened her mouth then clamped it shut. Barkley and Killian divided the wrapped paintings between them, nodded at Cary, and together they walked to the door that led to the inner sanctum.

"I'll keep you posted." Killian said trailing Stayner over the threshold. The door whooshed shut and the lobby settled into an eerie silence. Dexter busied himself shuffling papers. Willie and Gram studied the different display cases while studiously ignoring each other.

I walked over to Reb. "What's going on?"

"The deal fell through."

"Remind me . . .?" I began.

"Bernhagen's multimillion-dollar warehouse deal!"

"Oh, that deal."

"My biggest sale ever! Flushed right down the crapper. All the opportunities with Bernhagen gone! Crumbled, like a giant cookie, and not a damn thing I could do to fix it." A tear leaked from her left eye. She swiped at it and took a deep breath.

I put my arm around her. "Bernhagen backed out?"

"No. Bernie said the Phoenix Corporation did some sort of financial analysis and decided the market wouldn't support such a lofty project." She huffed a sigh. "Stupid bean counters. Stupid arsonist." She cut her eyes to where Willie stood studying the nearest display case. "Willie has helped me finally see the light. It's time to switch professions."

"What?"

"Yes, she helped me pinpoint my basic problem. You know how lately my sales have been down?"

I nodded. "Economy's a little flat right now."

Reb shook her head. "That's not the problem. See, I have an artistic nature that needs to flow with the cosmic shifts. I need to allow my inner self to expand and grow." She stretched her arms out. "Selling real estate is too stifling. My chi energy is in danger of shriveling." Her arms collapsed to her side.

"Nothing worse than a shriveled chi," I said, hoping for a smile. Reb remained mute.

"You're serious?"

"Absolutely."

I wasn't up to talking Rebbie out of a Willie-induced-life-altering funk. I looked outside at heated air shimmering off parked cars and softened road tar. My once normal little reality seemed to be melting along with the asphalt.

Forty-five minutes dragged by before Barkley strode into the lobby and the whole room gasped a sigh of relief. He walked straight to Gram and took her hand. Killian was right, the process hadn't taken long. Reb, Willie, and I looked at the door waiting for Cary to emerge.

In my peripheral vision, I watched Barkley lower his head and murmur in a voice too low for anyone besides Gram to hear. She stiffened and went pale. My heart started hammering double-time.

"What's wrong?" I asked. "Where's Cary?"

Barkley cleared his throat. "The police have reasonable suspicion to detain Cary while they conduct their investigation into the murder of Frobi Fisher."

TWELVE

For the umpteenth (if there is such a word) time, I looked at my bedside clock. 2:30 a.m. The real hour of darkness. The hour of the wolf—according to some big-time film director from the thirties. It was also the hour when irrelevant trivia sneaks from the dusty hidey holes of one's mind. Cary had been in jail for fourteen hours. Fourteen hours! Cooped up with the likes of Bubba and the boys, dressed in a horrid orange day-glow jumpsuit.

The chaos in the police station lobby had been, well, chaotic. Despite all the wailing and gnashing of teeth, calm voices competing with hysterical ones, Barkley Worthington had eventually explained that detainment is simply a process that Cary brought on himself by not coming forward when he first discovered his fiancé.

"I'm confident that once the police examine the evidence, they will find Cary guilty of fraud and we will address that accordingly." Barkley's reassuring voice dropped like a stone in my stomach.

"My son is innocent. He's incapable of committing murder!" Willie cried. "Can't you get him out on bail?"

Dexter came out from behind the desk. "Ms. Harrigan, Cary hasn't been charged with anything yet, hasn't even been read his rights. Consider this a precaution taken to make sure he doesn't disappear again while the detectives complete their investigation."

Willie grabbed Dexter's hand, tears flowing down her cheeks. "But isn't detainment the first step in the arrest process? I mean, why look any further now that my baby's behind bars?"

Dexter shook his head. "You need to have a little faith in our detectives. I do. I've worked with some of them for quite a while and they're not going to stop sifting and gathering evidence until they're satisfied they've covered everything."

Willie sighed and Dexter patted her shoulder. "You go home with Mercedes, take a couple of aspirin and put your feet up. That always helps Violet."

With those words of wisdom our sad group had left the police station. Later, two F.B.I. agents, straight out of central casting for a walk-on roll for any of the *Men in Black* movies, had come to my house to question both me and Willie about the caskets. Since we knew nothing of importance, the caskets were loaded into a couple of big black vans and taken wherever questionable paintings and shoddy caskets are taken. It would've been an amusing scene in a movie . . . in real life not so much. Cary was not only a suspect in Frobi's murder but he now had to explain the paintings to the Feds' satisfaction. My poor clueless brother was in for more grief and grilling.

I slipped away from my sleeping Dachshunds, tiptoed to the guest room and peeked in. A sliver of moonlight illuminated Willie's pink silk P.J. top. She lay on her back, snoring softly, the sheet tangled around her legs. Looked like the sleeping pill had worked. Good thing. Come morning, she'd be rested for round two of pacing, crying, accusing everyone connected with the law, and general handwringing. If this sounds cynical on my part it's because I'd witnessed the same histrionic performance when my dad disappeared sixteen years before, and enough mini versions since then that *Cynical* had become my middle name.

I eased the door closed and crept downstairs. In the living room, wispy shadows skittered across a patch of moonlight on the rug. I plunked onto the ruined cushions of my couch and watched through the window as raven clouds smothered the moon. Mr. Wiggins whined from the dog carrier in the kitchen to which he'd been exiled after his chewing rampage. I felt a pang of sorrow for both him and Cary, locked away for acting on some misguided snap decision. Who knew what urge had driven Mr. Wiggins to chew up my furniture but I was fairly sure Cary was regretting meeting Frobi Fisher and joining in her get-rich-quick scheme.

In the distance, lightning flashed, and I began the grade school count, one-one thousand, two-one thousand, waiting for the answering boom of thunder. Attempting to snuggle deeper into the couch, I let my mind drift as the storm crept closer, shut my eyes, listened as the thunder slowly advanced, tried to regulate my breathing. My eyes popped open. Sleep wasn't happening.

I stood, padded into the kitchen and turned on the light above the sink. Grabbing a pad and pencil, I sat at the table and began listing events, people, anything connected to Cary and Frobi. I hoped something might jog my mind. Something out of the ordinary that I hadn't noticed at the time. Something that would help me prove Cary's innocence. I had several pieces; they just didn't make a picture . . . unless you like Jackson Pollock paintings, in which case I had the makings of a masterpiece.

Mr. Wiggins whined again. Poor little misguided dog. I freed him from the carrier, went to the pantry, opened a new package of chew bones, and handed him one. "Chew on this, buddy." The stump of his tail waggled his little behind as he grabbed the bone, turned around three times on the rug in front of the sink and settled down with his prize.

Nails scrabbling down the stairs alerted me that my daring duo had heard the bag rustle. They stopped in the kitchen doorway, heads cocked opposite directions, looking like a pair of Dachshund bookends. I tossed each a bone with instructions to not bother anyone until daybreak then I returned to the table to jot down events, impressions, smiley faces, anything that came to mind. The wind

howled like a banshee and my mind whirled along with it. I studied
the name on my list that didn't make sense. Hooks Specialist and
Surgery Center. I needed to find out why Frobi was interested in
that particular medical facility and a Google search wouldn't cut it.
However, I couldn't waltz in and start asking questions. I required a
plausible cover. Maybe I could make an appointment for Yancy, have
him complain about symptoms of some exotic disease. Or better yet,
Rebbie could pose as an insurance adjuster and check the place out. I
sighed. *Come on, Harrigan, no time for the whimsical. Think!*

"Mercedes McCambridge Harrigan, are you trying to give me
a heart attack?"

I jerked awake and stared, bleary-eyed at Willie. She stood in the
doorway, hands on hips, looking refreshed and ready to do battle. I
peeled a notebook page from my cheek, yawned, and unfolded my
stiff body from the chair. "How am I causing your heart problems?"
I asked, squinting at the sun shining through the window. The clock
over the stove read 8:00 A.M.. I opened the back door, stepped outside with the dogs, and inhaled the morning air, pulling the invigo-
rating, earthy smell of rain-dampened sagebrush into my tired body.

"I found your bedroom empty. Not even a furry mutt in sight.
What was I to think?" Willie called to me.

That we might be downstairs? I shook my head, hoping to stim-
ulate a little brain function, and went back inside. "Want coffee?"

"Are you still buying that inferior grocery store brand?"

I took the Dunkin' Donuts ground coffee from the fridge and
held the bright orange bag aloft.

"I suppose it will have to do."

So that was to be the tone for the day: Bitch, bitch, bitch.

She settled into the chair I'd vacated and picked up the notepad.
"What's this?"

"A list of suspects, people to interview, things to double check."

"Pathetic. My list of suspects is more detailed and complete."

I refrained from doing an eye roll or barking a snide comeback,
started coffee brewing, and went upstairs to take a shower. Willie

could stay here and stew in her misery. I had things to do, places to go, people to annoy. The police couldn't hold Cary indefinitely as a person of interest. The next step . . . I didn't want to think about the next step. I had to find something that would prove Cary not guilty of murder. Stupidity, yes. Murder, no.

Despite the heat radiating through the top floor, I took a long, hot shower. The steam knocked a few cobwebs from my brain, and I felt better prepared to tackle the job of proving Cary's innocence. I toweled off, added gel to my hair before blowing it dry and even pulled out my electric curlers. While they heated, I carefully applied the correct makeup for a kick-butt landlord/sleuth, including lip liner and a new power-red lipstick.

My cell phone jangled Gram's ringtone. "Yancey's worked all night and he's finally cracked a couple of passwords on that stupid laptop," she blurted as I brought the phone to my ear.

"Great. Any info that could free Cary?"

"Not yet. He said there's some type of hidden something that he suspects could harm something or other."

A crystal-clear explanation like that would clear Cary in no time.

"He's mulling over the problem while he prepares Mr. Kent for the viewing tonight. A raging alcoholic, the man is completely jaundiced from cirrhosis. And you know what a perfectionist Yancey is. Kent will look normal and serene by the time he's finished or Yancey won't allow an open casket."

I shuddered, trying to dispel the image of Yancy jamming a Trocar stick into a jaundiced liver. "Anymore threats or presents from the cyber-stalker?"

"No," Gram said with a yawn. "Excuse me. Guess I'm a little pooped from all that's been going on."

"Did you get any sleep last night?"

"A couple of winks. Barkley talked with Cary this morning, reminded him that all conversations had to be with his council present. I hope your brother listens to Barkley."

We talked about maybe meeting somewhere for a quick bite to

compare notes and about how Willie was holding up, before Gram clicked off.

I took the curlers out, bent from the waist, and gave my hair a couple of shots of mega-hold hairspray, today was not a day for any faint-hearted curls, then stood and did a quick finger-comb. I slid into a short white skirt and red tank top, then added four-inch spike-heeled sandals that could aerate a small lawn in no time. The phone rang and the caller I.D. announced that Reb was at least stirring.

"Yello," I answered.

"Damn, Skippy, but you sound way too happy. What are you on and where can I get some?"

"Good morning to you, too."

"So what's on the agenda for today?" she asked.

"I have to place an apartment ad on a couple of sites, make sure last night's storm didn't knock any shingles loose at the complex, grocery shop . . ." and *snoop out Frobi's killer.*

"Is Willie tagging along?"

"No. She'll probably stay here and do the usual: pace, wring her hands, grieve. What're you up to?"

"Doing some soul-searching about my new career."

"You're still on that kick?"

"Yes. Maybe. That's where the soul-searching comes in. Hey, you haven't finished cleaning Pig-boy's apartment, right? You could hire me. I'll work cheap."

Talk about desperation.

"Reb, your perfect nails would be history in five minutes. Plus, you haven't seen the bathroom yet. His toilet alone is worth a month of nightmares. You could come baby-sit Willie and soul-search at the same time."

"No thanks. And don't try the 'you owe me' routine. The Margarita and nacho fest stamped my debt paid in full. Has Killian been by to feed Eclipse yet?"

"I haven't seen him," I said.

"When you do, tell him I'm sorry for going ballistic last night." Reb sighed into the phone.

"Total ballistic?"

"Sort of half-ballistic. I lumped him into the "all men are jerks" category."

"An apology from you would hold more weight," I said.

"I know that! He's not answering my calls." This was said with faint sniffling.

Too bad Reb didn't want to be with Willie. They could wring hands and commiserate together.

"I'll tell him if I see him."

We clicked off and I click-clacked my way downstairs.

Willie stared at me over the rim of her coffee cup. "Finally, my daughter decides to dress for success." She sat the cup on the counter, walked over and poked a mutinous bra strap back under my tank top. "You could use a red bra with this."

"I don't have one."

"No problem. We can stop by the mall on our way to rent me a car." She freshened her coffee, then padded toward the stairs. "I'll be ready by the time the stores open. We both have to look good when we go see your brother."

I sucked in a sigh and poured coffee into a travel mug. I didn't know if Cary was allowed visitors but getting Willie a car was not on my to-do list today. Before her top priority became mine, I snatched my keys, scribbled a quick note explaining my hasty departure, and hurried out the door. Mr. Wiggins made a dash for freedom, little legs pumping hard. I shut the back yard gate behind me and quashed his escape.

Bending down, I finger scratched him through the chain link. "Take a chill pill, Mister. No chewing while I'm gone or Willie will have you stuffed and mounted!"

"Sounds familiar. You part of the H.A.M club too?" Killian asked.

I whirled and watched him walk around his truck, a shiny,

black saddle draped over his left arm. Terrific. If I was oblivious to the roar of Killian's truck, how did I imagine I could catch Frobi's killer?

"What ham club?" I asked, smoothing a wrinkle from my skirt.

"Stands for Hate Anything Male." He looked down at Mr. Wiggins while tossing the saddle on top of the fence. "Better watch it, buddy. Women around here are out for blood."

He stood before me in black jeans, black muscle shirt, black cowboy boots and a sexy five-o-clock shadow, despite the nine-fifteen showing on my digital watch. The smudges under his lower lashes suggested either a double-shift or trouble closing those gorgeous green eyes.

"Reb says she's sorry," I said, tracing my finger along the saddle's tooled skirt, wondering if I should mention Yancy's headless doll.

"She does? What about you?"

"Me?"

"Yes, you." He quirked an eyebrow and hefted the saddle from the fence. "You're outfit says "Hello boys" but there's distinct smell of annoyance in the air. Has every authority figure become a scapegoat or just me?"

"Oh, puh-leese! I'm not mad at you. I don't live in Pettyville like some people." I walked to my car, slid behind the wheel, and missed jamming the key into the ignition on the first try.

Killian sauntered over and stuck his head in the passenger window. "Sorry. I know this is a hard time. One word of advice: don't drive angry." He leaned in and gave me a quick chuck under the chin.

I gunned the engine and backed down the driveway, wishing for gravel instead of smooth blacktop so I could spray the smug grin off his face. I'd sooner tell a neophyte meter-maid about Yancy's headless doll than confide in Officer Killian. Halfway down the mountain road, realization smacked me between the eyes; the man had purposely picked a fight.

Why?

I mulled this over as the Ghia hugged the curves, turned onto Bannock Highway, and shot toward town. We always chatted when he came to ride Eclipse, but today he'd goaded me to leave because . . .? He wanted alone time with Willie? Ugh! I scrubbed that thought. Killian loved women, but even he had standards.

I pulled into the semi-crowded Winco parking lot, wondering if I could find a couple of food items to make Willie's exotic taste buds happy. By now the paintings had been turned over to the Feds. Did Killian know something important? Maybe. Something he didn't want to share? Oh, yeah.

If he thought juvenile tactics could throw me off the trail, he had another think coming.

I swung through the double doors and stood in the lobby absorbing the cool air. To the left was a row of active checkout stands manned by five checkers deftly taking various items from conveyor belts, scanning them, and placing them back on the counter to be bagged. A well-oiled operation that would increase as the day wore on.

One of my favorite checkers, Mary Lou Hutchings, finished ringing up her last customer and motioned me over.

"Hey, you. How're you holding up?"

Not sure how to answer, I did a palms-up.

Mary Lou nodded, her auburn-corkscrew curls bobbing with the effort. She pursed burgundy-lined lips. "Understandable. Have you heard from your brother?"

I shook my head. At least the gossip grapevine didn't know that Cary was being held for questioning.

She touched my arm and lowered her voice. "I don't believe Cary turned that girl into a vintage "Goldfinger" victim. If you need help with anything . . . I mean anything," she squeezed my arm, then turned to ring up the next customer with a large vegetable tray sliding on the conveyer belt.

Wait.

Perfect solution for Willie, a veggie tray. She could nibble away while she paced. I grabbed a cart and forty-five minutes later I'd added a selection of fruit and what I hoped would pass for exotic cheeses and crackers to go with the veggies. Two large jars of peanut butter rode proudly among Willie's stuff. Desperate times, desperate measures. I had to have my peanut butter comfort food or my brain wouldn't function under the stress that weighed on me like a wet, wool blanket.

Mary Lou waved me to her lane. "Shame about Bernhagen's deal falling to pieces. Lots of people were hoping he'd score big and create jobs. What did he expect? Build a house of cards and sooner or later they tumble."

"The warehouse deal wasn't legit?" I was all ears. Mary Lou had her finger on the pulse of Portneuf Gap and wasn't prone to wild embellishments like Agatha.

"No, the warehouse deal went south when the investors learned about his development above Pheasant Ridge. Bernie hired some cut-rate sewer company and major bathroom problems are springing up like May flowers. The current homeowners are suing for damages and the remaining lots aren't selling."

No wonder Reb was in a deep funk. "Is Winco hiring?"

"Only baggers. You need a job?"

I shook my head. "Inquiring for a friend."

She frowned as she totaled my purchase, then smiled. "Good for you, Sadie, make jokes, keep things light. Best way to handle life when you get buried under a pile of lemons."

If she only knew the whole story.

I told Mary Lou goodbye and left with Willie's expensive food, which I hoped would survive the heat while I made a quick stop to inspect the apartments for storm damage.

Dexter popped out of his front door as I pulled into a vacant space.

He held up a couple of shingles. "That was some windstorm last night. Found these next to the fence in the backyard."

"Terrific." Dexter handed me the shingles and I noted two were pretty ragged. A new roof for the apartment complex was something I'd been hoping to avoid for another year. One look at the shingles and I knew waiting was no longer an option. I'd have to call a couple of guys, have the roof examined, get bids, etc. I shoved that thought away and turned to Dexter. "The night of the murder, did you or Violet hear anything unusual?"

Dexter scratched his head. "Not that I recall. Violet claimed she heard Cary and Frobi fighting. She thought of going outside to check until she heard Agatha's voice and decided to stay in bed." He leaned close and whispered, "But we both know, if she heard anything juicy, she'd have been out snooping."

"I could use your help, Dexter." I walked to the back of the complex looking for any further storm damage needing attention. Dexter followed. "Think back to that night. There's an argument, Agatha gets involved and Cary leaves. He comes back several hours later and finds Frobi dead. I'm trying to figure out what happened within that time period. The police think Frobi knew the murderer but there's no gold paint anywhere near the complex so she must've either gone willingly with that person. Or maybe she was drugged? You're sure you don't remember anything?"

"Let me think on it. Something might come to me." Dex stopped and looked out across the river. "Very dangerous waters you're diving into, Mercedes. It would be best to let that lawyer, Barkley, and the police handle the investigation."

"I'm only collecting facts to prove there's someone other than Cary to investigate. Think of me as an older version of Nancy Drew. I'm looking where the police don't have the time or manpower to cover."

Dexter quirked an eyebrow. "As I recall, Miss Drew always ended up in hot water when she did her snooping."

My cell played Gram's tune. "What's up?"

"Oh, Mercedes, I don't know. . . .I've always purchased from the same company, and nothing like this has ever happened." Gram's voice trembled and her words ran together in a rush. "What if Mr.

Brestlin had been in the hearse? No. I can't think about that. Now the attendant won't allow me to ride in the ambulance."

Ambulance! "Gram, are you hurt? What happened? Where's Yancy?" I took off for my car, Dexter at my side.

"He's in the ambulance, headed for the hospital. Luckily, he wasn't sitting behind the wheel."

"What wheel? Where are you?"

"Two blocks from the mortuary. That's where the hearse blew up."

THIRTEEN

I RACED AROUND THE CORNER AHEAD of Dexter and smacked into a firm chest and six-pack of utter maleness. Strong hands grabbed my forearms, saving me from ricocheting onto my butt, but not from dropping my cell phone. I looked up into the stunning brown eyes and sexy grin of Axel Danforth. Martin Mangum peered myopically over his shoulder.

"Mercedes, you've got to see this reading," Martin said, shoving some type of ghost-hunting EMF gadget at me.

I batted the thing away and bent to retrieve my cell phone. Axel had the same idea. We smacked heads and I sat down hard on the grass. Rubbing my smarting scalp, I squinted at Axel through tearing eyes. "Wow you've got a hard head!"

He chuckled and held out his hand. "That's what me mum always says."

His mellow voice with its seductive accent washed over me, making me tingle in places that shouldn't tingle, considering recent events. I let him help me up, and then redialed Gram.

"I'm coming to get you. I'll take you to the hospital, just sit tight," I said, hurrying to my car. As I hung up a wave of dizziness hit me. Reaching for the Ghia to steady myself, I missed and landed on my butt. Again. Firm hands stopped me from climbing to my feet.

"Just sit still, luv." Axel knelt beside me, tipped my chin up, and peered intently at my face. Humiliation heated my cheeks as I returned his gaze. And what a gaze! His brown eyes held concern, as well as a promise of something I didn't have time to explore right now.

"Pupils look okay, but your color's a bit off. I don't think you should drive right now," Axel said.

"Phone call has her in a state," Dexter said, kneeling down opposite Axel. "Who you haulin' to the hospital?"

"Gram. One of the hearses blew up. She's not allowed to ride in the ambulance with Yancy. I have to go get her." I stopped and swallowed the lump clogging my throat. A traitorous tear slipped down my cheek. "What if she'd been behind the wheel when. . . ?"

"Look, Sadie." Dexter took my hand and gave it a gentle squeeze. "Concentrate on the facts, not the *what-ifs*. Let's get you inside, out of this heat."

Regretting my short skirt, I let Dexter and Axel help me to my feet to save my dignity and gently pushed Dexter's hand away as he tried to guide me toward his apartment. "Gram's waiting for me. I have to go." I retrieved my keys from my shoulder bag.

Dexter stood immobile in front of me. "Let me give Violet a heads-up and I'll drive you."

Peripheral movement caught my eye. Across the street, Lechman leaned against an oak tree, arms folded, watching with the stillness of an experienced predator. Why? Why now?

I touched Dexter's arm and nodded toward Lechman. "I'd rather you stick around here. Keep an eye on things."

Dexter looked at Lechman then back at me. "You okay to drive?"

"No worries, I'll take the Sheila." Axel dug keys from his cargo shorts.

"No need," I said, opening my car door and sliding behind the wheel.

Axel leaned in and placed his palm against my forehead. "Clammy and pale, not a good combo."

"You really don't look so good," Martin said, hovering behind Axel.

"It's the heat." I turned the engine over and shifted into reverse.

With a shrug of his broad shoulders, Axel shut my door.

I studiously ignored Lechman as I pulled onto the street and sped through the yellow stoplight on the corner. Two lights later, I noticed a dirty green jeep a couple of cars behind me. Axel and Martin. One block later they were riding my tail. Terrific. Add Bill Murray and Dan Akroyd, we'd have a ghost-buster mini-parade.

The wet street surrounding the scorched hearse shimmered like a mirage. An officer directed traffic around two fire trucks and the smoldering hulk. I spotted Gram talking to a fireman under the shade of a cottonwood tree. I pulled to the curb, cut the engine, and scrambled from behind the wheel. We embraced on the sidewalk, holding tight, our eyes shut with relief as we breathed in the acrid scent of a near tragedy.

After a moment, Gram said. "I've learned all I can from the officials for now. We'd better go see about poor Yancy."

"How bad is he?" I asked, looking at the hearse and fearing the worst.

She dabbed her eyes with a lace hanky. "Singed some, but alive. He was on his way to get the tires rotated at Big O's. Luckily he stopped and got out to check out a strange noise in the rear," Gram said, easing into the Ghia's passenger seat.

I took a last look at the smoking wreck. Lucky was an understatement.

I PULLED INTO A PARKING SPACE a couple of rows back from the emergency room entrance, and Axel's green jeep slipped neatly into the empty right-hand slot. He slid from behind the wheel, opened Gram's door, and offered his hand.

"Mind the gap, mum," he said as he helped Gram out of the low-slung passenger seat.

"Thank you, young man," Gram said, holding Axel's hand a tad longer than normal while studying his rugged face. Affinity for an Aussie accent seemed to run in the family.

"I bet I can pick up all sorts of spectral readings here," Martin said. He stood at the rear of the jeep, shading his eyes with his hand while gaping at the eight stories of red brick like he'd discovered Mecca. "Especially in the hallways by the morgue."

"Hold off, mate," Axel said, snatching the EMF gadget from Martin's hand. "We're here to make sure Sadie and her grandmum reach their destination."

"Excuse me," Gram said, a puzzled frown puckering her brow as she looked from me to Martin and then Axel.

I made introductions and gave her the Reader's Digest Condensed version of Martin's quest at the apartment complex.

Gram nodded. "If you want to study paranormal activity, you should visit my embalming room sometime."

Martin's eyes glazed and his mouth tipped in an awe-inspired grin. Axel offered Gram his arm, she took it and we hurried toward the emergency entrance.

Inside, lingering antiseptic odors mingled with the smell of illness and fear under unforgiving florescent lights. Gram's shoes squeaked across the shiny linoleum as she headed for the information desk. I stood back trying not to look at the fellow sitting in the lobby, head down, staring at his dusty work boots with a bloody towel wrapped around his hand. A baby cried in outrage somewhere behind the double doors that led to the examining areas. My stomach rolled. I took a deep breath and studied the beige-on-beige floor pattern in an attempt to ignore the nausea that threatened.

Gram turned from the desk. "Yancy's been admitted. He's in room 506." She headed down the hall at a brisk walk.

I turned to follow and Axel grabbed my hand. "Two shades whiter, luv. What say we step outside for some air?"

I pulled my hand from his and pinched the bridge of my nose. "I'm fine. Thanks."

I caught up with Gram, who stood waiting in front of the double elevators. The doors on the right opened and a nurse got off pushing a wobbly-wheeled gurney. A man helped a very pregnant woman shuffle off, Gram and I entered the empty box. Axel and Martin followed.

Looking politely, but pointedly at Axel, Gram hit the *open door* button preventing the elevator doors from closing. "I'm sorry, young man. I appreciate your help and concern, but I know Yancy and he will not welcome strangers right now," she said.

Axel lifted an eyebrow. "Right. Time to go, Martin." He gave me a wink and salute as the doors slid shut. The elevator rumbled upward.

I was relieved to find Yancy propped up in bed, glaring from beneath singed eyebrows. He made quite the patriotic and pathetic statement lying against a white pillow with his red face and angry blue eyes. My heart lurched just looking at him.

"Just in time, Cassandra. I knew you'd spring me from this horrid place."

Gram shook her head and patted his shoulder. "One night for observation and you'll be good to go."

"Then at least take pity and bring me my burgundy lounge set," he said, plucking at the one-size-fits-no-one hospital gown. "And something edible for dinner. Your famous fried chicken ought to suffice."

"You look better than I expected, Yancy." I said, trying for perky. Yancy shot me a look that would melt the Polar Ice Cap.

"But, considering what you've been through, I imagine something fried would be off your list," I said, wandering over to check out the air conditioning unit under the window. The room was warm and would only get warmer with a west-facing window.

"Why is she here?" Yancy asked Gram. He looked at me with as much disdain as his red face would allow. "Dressed all hot to trot like her cougar mother?"

I clamped my lips shut and took pleasure in noting that the air-conditioning knob was cranked to maximum cool. The nursing staff was in for a long night; Yancy would soon be sending Morse code with his call button.

"We're here to help so quit being a baby. You're alive, be grateful," I said, sitting in the requisite uncomfortable corner chair.

"Grateful for a concussion? Grateful for broken ribs? Grateful for this?" He pointed to his face, which had turned a darker shade of fuchsia with his outburst. "Tell me how I'm supposed to work with cremated appendages?" He lifted his bandaged hands.

"I am truly sorry, Yancy." He was a pitiful sight and probably in discomfort despite whatever drug he was being given to help suppress pain.

"Mercedes is right," Gram said. She folded her arms and narrowed her eyes at Yancy. "None of your injuries are permanent. You're young, you'll heal."

Yancy closed his eyes and eased back against the pillow. He took a shuddering breath, winced, and exhaled. A lone tear slipped down his salve-smeared cheek.

Gram held his right hand gently. "Just rest for a bit. You've been through quite the ordeal."

"Speaking of which," I pushed myself up from the lumpy Naugahyde chair and stood at the end of the bed, "What happened with the hearse?"

Yancy opened one eye, then shut it. "Started the engine and it purred like always. After I turned left out of the driveway I noticed a funny rubbing sound. I pulled over, got out, and checked the left rear tire. Nothing. I was walking around to check the right rear tire . . . next thing I know, I'm on my face in the street, ears ringing." He opened his eyes. "The freakin' hearse was blazing like Hell's Kitchen."

"Could the gas tank have gone bad?" Gram said, staring at the I.V. bottle as though the answer was slowly dripping into Yancy. "You are using premium gas, right?"

Yancy's face remained neutral, but I could hear the implied eye roll in his, "Yes, Cassandra."

"Any theories from the fire department?" I asked.

Yancy shook his head. "If they have any info, they're playing it close to their soot-smeared vests. I gave a brief statement to some cop before I was loaded into the ambulance. Too bad it wasn't your friend." He sketched quotations marks in the air and smirked.

As if waiting for his cue, the door opened and Killian burst into the room. Dressed in the same clothes he'd worn this morning; he gathered me into an embrace that would've melted my resistance under different circumstances.

"Mercedes!" he said, his breath warm against my cheek. He held me at arm's length, giving me a quick once-over, before crushing me to him in an even tighter embrace. The sweet scent of horse and leather teased my senses as his heart pounded against mine like he'd run to the hospital straight from my barn.

"Hey, Constable-on-Patrol. I'm the injured party here," Yancy groused.

"Right," Killian murmured against my hairline as his breathing slowed. "Thank God for wrong info. I was told you were . . . never mind. Doesn't matter."

Despite our earlier confrontation, I would've gladly stayed wrapped in his arms, but Gram cleared her throat and Killian released his hold.

Killian turned to Gram and took her hand. "Cassandra, good thing your vehicle was the only loss."

"I just don't understand how this could've happened," Gram said. "That coach is a Cadillac. Top of the line."

"Could've been a lemon with faulty wiring or maybe the battery shorted out," Killian offered.

"Here's an idea, Jack. Why don't you play detective, find out what the official verdict is, and get back to us." The pain meds were finally kicking in, giving Yancy a dose of false bravado. He waved Killian away with a dismissive gesture.

Killian's jaw tightened.

"I think its best we all leave Yancy alone to rest." Gram placed her hand on Killian's elbow and steered him toward the door. "I need to go home, regroup, and get things ready for Mr. Brestlin's viewing tonight."

"Oh no!" Yancy moaned. "Mr. Kent is el perfecto, but I'm only half-way done with Brestlin. Mr. B's makeup isn't finished. Cassandra, the viewing must be postponed!"

"No need to panic. I'll prepare Mr. Brestlin," Gram said over her shoulder.

"But you have so much to do," Yancy said, catching my eye and mouthing "*help.*" *Translation: Gram tended to make the deceased look like Tim Curry from* The Rocky Horror Picture Show.

"Rebbie can do the makeup. She'll be happy to help," I said, mentally crossing my fingers and hoping Reb wouldn't balk at the idea. I added a quick prayer that she'd have a lighter touch than Gram. Desperate times call for desperate measures.

"Concentrate on getting better," Gram turned and wagged a finger at Yancy. "Everything's under control."

"Right." Yancy threw me a pained look. "This is important, Sadie, you have to tell Rebbie I was planning to go with the number two base. Don't overdo the liver spots on his head and hands. The cotton cheek stuffing is in the drawer directly below. . . ."

"We'll be in the cafeteria," Killian interrupted. "Cassandra, can I buy you something to drink?"

Yancy waited until Killian and Gram left before motioning me closer. "The cell is in my pants pocket, please bring it to me. I was able to access Frobi's GPS on her phone retroactively. I've got addresses of all the places she went to peddle caskets, art, whatever."

I went to the tiny closet. "Great, I think. Could Torture Junkie be hanging out at one of the businesses?"

Yancy thought for a moment while I rummaged through his pants pockets. "I don't think so. Junkie works with computers. He could be sending nefarious messages from some assisted living office but it doesn't feel right. There might be a very sophisticated piggybacking program on the laptop."

"Junkie writes kids games?"

Yancy shook his head. "No. I'll explain it later. I'll make a list of businesses while you go and get the laptop. You'll find it in the casket room, mahogany casket against the wall with the lid closed, third one from the door."

I handed him the cell phone. "Why hide it at the mortuary?"

"Who would think about looking in a casket?"

"Junkie, for one. Yancy, that's the equivalent of painting a bulls-eye on Gram's back! What if the hearse fire was no accident?" I paced to the window and looked out. "Dexter's right. It's time to turn that damn pink nightmare and the cell phone over to the authorities before anyone else gets hurt!"

"You want Brother Dearest to rot behind bars forever?"

"That's low, Yancy."

"Mercedes, one more day. What I'm finding is . . . let's just say my efforts will help exonerate Cary, I swear!" He held up his right hand in the Boy Scout pledge."

"You weren't a scout, Candlemass."

"No, but I can recite their motto. Come on, Mercedes."

I sucked on my lip. "Okay. I'll bring the laptop." I started for the door then stopped. "Just in case your accident was no accident, be on guard for Nurse Ratchet with a deadly hypo."

Yancy paled as I shut the door.

Killian met me as I stepped off the elevator, handing me a plastic cup and a straw. "Just coming to find you. Here, I figured you could use a caffeine boost."

"Thanks." I took a sip of Cherry Pepsi and nearly purred as the cold drink slid down my parched throat. "Is this your form of apology for this morning?"

He cocked an eyebrow and shrugged. "Speaking of earlier, I saw Crocodile Dundee in the parking lot. He a friend of Yancy's?"

It was my turn to shrug. "I'm not privy to Axel's B.F.F. list."

Gram walked out of the ladies restroom and gave her French twist a pat. "Who's in the mood for my special tuna surprise sandwiches?"

THE HARRIGAN FUNERAL HOME CASKET ROOM has the air of a stern librarian demanding hushed tones from all who enter. Opulent burgundy carpet swallows every footstep. Wall sconces and recessed lighting cast a graceful glow over the ivory-striped wallpaper and cherry wood wainscoting. A variety of shiny caskets, ranging from least expensive to opulent, line the perimeter of the room. Of all the caskets placed just so, none resembled the crappy façade boxes in my driveway.

I opened the mahogany lid on the third casket and pulled the laptop from the beneath the white satin pillow. After wrangling it into my shoulder bag, I headed for the kitchen where Gram was making sandwiches. I had just enough time to grab one (and maybe a chunk of peach pie I'd spied as we came in the back door), get the laptop to Yancy, then hunt down Reb. My request for her to do Mr. Brestlin's makeup was best made in person, especially since she wasn't answering her cell.

Gram must have read my mind, for she handed me a paper sack when I came into the kitchen. "Sorry you have to eat on the run. Let me know if Reb is willing to help."

I peeked inside the sack: a sandwich, chips, and big hunk of pie, all carefully wrapped in plastic. Does the woman love me or what? "Thanks, Gram. I'll be in touch." I gave her a quick hug, then hurried out the door.

Yancy handed me two lists when I entered his room. One listed businesses and the other had detailed instructions for Rebbie. Both were barely legible but I didn't have time for explanations, besides, he was busy cussing his bandaged hands and the laptop as I left.

I raced over to Reb's house. She wasn't there, so I left a note to call me, ASAP. Damn, I tried her cell again: no voice mail, nothing. A tingle of alarm wiggled up my spine. Where could she be?

Trying not to let panic rule my mind, I headed home to check on Willie and the dogs. I hadn't heard from Willie, either, and it wasn't like her to stew alone. Maybe she and Reb were together seeking meaningful employment and ignoring their cell phones.

I pulled into my driveway, which was blessedly clear of caskets, and parked behind a maroon LeSabre. No wonder I hadn't heard from Willie. She'd found herself a friend, no doubt a very male friend. I sighed and opened the back gate, anxious to change out of my sticky outfit and slip into something comfortable and cool.

Three ecstatic dogs met me at the gate, leaping around my ankles as though I'd been gone for years instead of hours. I knelt to accept happy-joy-joy kisses from the trio while my eyes zeroed in on Willie and her gentleman caller. They sat opposite each other, holding hands across my aging picnic table on the backyard patio. Seated with his back to me, I noted how the man's white tee-shirt hugged broad shoulders and hid part of an intricate tattoo encircling his tanned right bicep. Black hair curled against his thick neck.

Oh, crap. I knew that neck and tattoo.

FOURTEEN

WILLIE GAVE ME A FINGER WAVE and Todd Sudi turned around and grinned. They both had the satisfied look of my barn cats slurping saucers of thick cream.

I groaned. What type of sexual atrocities had my kitchen table suffered now?

Willie held up a frosted glass. "Just in time, my girl. Todd makes the *best* Long Island Iced Tea. Run and make Mercedes one and another for me, okay, darling?"

Todd patted her hand. "Sure. A proper house guest always does their fair share."

House guest! I did a mental head slap and marched over to the picnic table. "Excuse us for a second, Todd." I grabbed Willie's arm, towed her across the patio, yanked open the screen door and pulled her inside.

Willie wrenched her arm from my grasp, slid her sunglasses onto her head, and stuck her hands on her hips. "Mercedes McCambridge Harrigan, what is your problem?"

"Out!" I hissed and waved a hand at the man lounging on the weathered seat. "I want him out. He is *not* your house guest. And never will be. Need I remind you that while you're drinking and doing God knows what with Sudi, your son, Cary, is stuck in the county jail!"

"According to Dorothy Parker, only martinis lead to sexual misjudgments. Long Island Iced Teas are simply a nice way to quench one's thirst." Willie's perfectly waxed brows puckered and she looked at the ceiling with a pained 'Why me?' expression. She folded her arms over her chest. "I have *not* forgotten Cary. For your information, Todd is giving me free legal advice."

"Todd Sudi gave up a law practice to sell and repair cars?"

"Don't be obtuse. He has family members who've run afoul of the law. He's sharing information from the school of hard knocks. In return, I'm being a good Samaritan, offering aid to the downtrodden. What's the harm if he stays until his apartment is fixed? Just think of Toddy as a stray in need of help, like that gray mop with ears." She pointed at Mr. Wiggins sprawled on the oval rug under the kitchen table, gnawing on something metallic-red.

"What is he destroying now?"

Willie did a palms-up, slid her glasses down over her eyes, gave her pushup-bra a good plumping and strutted outside. The screen door slammed in her wake.

I knelt on the floor and reached for the oblong red plastic thing trapped between furry paws. Mr. Wiggins gave a half-hearted snarl before releasing his treasure. I stood to study the cell phone in my palm. How did Mr. Wiggins wind up with what appeared to be Reb's cell phone? I pushed the mangled power button. The screen remained blank.

"You killed it," I told the furry mutt. He wagged his stumpy tail and barked.

"No, it drowned in the toilet."

I whirled and spotted Reb stretched out on my couch like Snow White awaiting love's true kiss. Judging by the raggedy cut-off sweats and faded Old Navy tee she wore, it could be a long wait.

I hurried into the living room and stood above her. "I've been trying to call you. What are you doing lying on my couch?"

She remained motionless, eyes closed. "Meditating. Contemplating my sad life. Listening to your mom quote dead gossip columnists."

The pity party raged on. "I have a job for you," I announced in my best tell-her-what-she's-won game show voice.

She opened one eye. "Please, nothing that involves sales."

"Gram needs a makeup expert to prepare Mr. Brestlin for the viewing tonight."

"Work with Yancy?" Reb opened the other eye. "Thanks but no."

"Yancy's sort'a out of commission," I said, heading for the stairs to change.

Reb sat bolt upright. "I'd have free rein?"

I nodded. "Just don't make him look like an eighties rock star."

"OMG! Sadie, my karma's turning around." She swung her legs off the couch, stood, and followed me upstairs. "This is it. My new calling," she said as I changed into navy linen pants and a sedate cream blouse. Reb checked her watch. "Viewing's at seven, right?" She grabbed my hand and hauled me down the stairs, scooped up her purse, and was half-way to the back door when she skidded to a halt. "I forgot, Willie and Todd picked me up in his loaner car. I need a ride. What's wrong with Yancy? Nothing contagious, I hope."

I gave her the condensed version of the accident.

"Are you telling me the hearse pulled a spontaneous combustion?"

"Quit with the drama, dear girl. Cars only blow up on the silver screen." Willie came into the kitchen holding Todd's hand.

"Not true, Sweet Cheeks. Anything can combust given the right circumstance." Todd clinked the two glasses he held in his unoccupied hand. "Anyone else care for a drink?"

Sweet Cheeks? I swallowed my gag reflex and asked, "You have personal experience with explosions?"

He shrugged and artfully refilled his and Willie's glasses. "Nah. Strictly thoid party info."

"Let's discuss this later. I have a date with a corpse," Rebbie said, pulling me outside.

Reb opened the passenger door of the Ghia and stopped. "Wait. I thought you'd be my assistant preparing Mr. Breslin.

Pancake makeup doesn't mix well with that boring outfit. Where are you going?"

I pursed my lips and slid into the driver's seat. Reb would want to play Watson to my Sherlock. She could be an asset to have a long while I retraced Frobi's business appointments. She thought fast on her feet and was very glib of tongue. However, there wasn't time for her to get Mr. Breslin ready for tonight and play faithful sidekick.

"I'm checking the businesses Frobi visited. She had to have a contact here connected to the art scam. Could be one of the places she called on is a hotbed for stolen artwork."

"You're going alone? Could be dangerous. Come help me tonight and tomorrow we can present a united front while snooping different places."

Reb's suggestion was tempting. I'd described myself as a grownup Nancy Drew but in reality I didn't have a plan. I gave myself a mental head slap. With the multiple scams Frobi was mixed up in, the murderer had to be linked to one of them. Right? I didn't have time for self-doubt, I had to push forward and ask probing questions, shake things up, whatever it took to help Cary.

"No big deal, really. This will be like the time we turned a Macy's mannequin from basic-boring to whoa-mama on that middle-school field trip, right?"

"What?" Reb's question pulled me from my thoughts.

"Just thinking out loud. I'll be fine if I pretend Mr. Brestlin is a mannequin. I'll make him look fabulous."

I pulled into her driveway and handed her the paper with Yancy's instructions. "Breslin was over eighty. Don't get carried away."

"Do I ever?" Reb winked, slid out of the car and checked her watch. "I just have time to get a new cell to match my new career then I'll pop over to the mortuary. You're coming to the viewing, right?"

"Of course."

I shifted the Ghia into first and headed down Garfield with the intention of driving by my apartments for a quick check. The complex parking lot was blessedly clear of ghost hunters and

Sherrilyn Sanborn stalkers. Even the tenants were behind closed doors, probably hiding from the heat. A gray van advertising Corneilson Construction occupied the slot opposite Sudi's apartment. Two men, one tall and slim, the other medium everything, stood in front of the boarded-up window, hands on hips and ball caps pulled low over their eyes. Sudi's connections?

I swung into the parking spot next to their van.

"Hey, how you doin?" Mr. Medium guy asked as I exited my car. Vibrant blue eyes assessed me from a comfortable face with deep laugh lines.

"Good. I'm Mercedes Harrigan, landlord." I held out my hand.

"Gus Corneilson. This here's my brother, Tom." Gus grabbed my hand and pumped it like we were long-lost friends. Tom nodded, then turned his attention back to the yellow legal pad he held in his hand.

"We're gonna fix up this apartment just like new," Gus said.

"How many just-like-new dollars are we talking?" The calculator in my mind started whirring and I gulped.

"Don't worry your pretty li'l head." Gus waved his hand like he was shooing flies. "This job's payback for services rendered by Mr. Sudi. However, you ever need a job done, we work fast and cheap." He pulled a well-worn wallet from his back pocket, fished out a dog-eared business card, and pressed it into my palm.

I thanked him, stuck the card in my purse, and left. Caring Hearts Assisted Living was my first stop. The beige stucco building shaped like a giant horseshoe had a parking lot nearly filled. Inside, homey Norman Rockwell pictures encased in black plastic frames decorated the creamy walls of the lobby. An expensive painting hanging next to copies would stick out like a tarantula on a wedding cake. I didn't hold out much hope of learning anything helpful but after talking to the marketing director, I surmised Frobi's cheap casket enterprise might be the wave of the future.

Three assisted living facilities later, I'd learned nothing useful. Time to check out the surgery center. I followed my phone's Map

App instructions and pulled into the parking lot, turned the Ghia off and stared at the sight before me. The architect must've been given a mandate to make the massive building as modern as possible and embarrassingly ugly at the same time. It looked like a fifties sci-fi flying saucer painted lime green. Inside, the lobby continued the ultra-modern theme with uncomfortable-looking furnishings on a glazed concrete floor. The large paintings on the walls resembled a series of Rorschach tests. The only thing in common these paintings had with the art I'd found inside the coffins was someone probably used a paintbrush to create it.

Two women, working behind a horseshoe shaped check-in center looked up from their computers. I smiled, nodded, and walked back outside. Without a plan I was feeling so far out of my comfort zone that I needed a passport. I should've brought along a professional type prop; a brief case, or samples bag, or something. Tall, lush ornamental grasses planted along the front waved in the breeze as I stood on the sidewalk hoping for inspiration to strike.

The main door opened and an elderly man joined me on the sidewalk. The top of his bald head gleamed in the sun while the remaining silver-white hair on his head was pulled into a ponytail which hung below the collar of his sport shirt.

Dark eyes regarded me from beneath bushy salt and pepper brows. "Admiring the expensive landscape or trying to figure out who designed this abomination called a medical center?"

I chuckled. "I'm betting someone paid a fortune for this particular design."

"You're talking to one of the someone's. I've been coming to Dr. Bernard Hooks, the neurologist, for about six months. Should've started with Dr. Crystal Hope, she's a damn fine general practitioner. Even their last names are telling, Hope sounds better than Hooks and she doesn't think she knows more than God." He stuck his hand out. "Name's Ben Lautenbach."

His handshake was warm and firm. "Mercedes Harrigan."

"I watched you pop into the lobby then pop back out. Are you looking for a specialist?"

"My neighbor is," I said. It wasn't a total lie, Agatha Heckathorn was always on the prowl for a medical person who would agree with her bizarre self-diagnoses. "You'd recommend Dr. Hope over Dr. Hooks?"

"I'd start with Dr. Hope. If she can't handle whatever problem your neighbor has she's not ashamed to say so and call in a specialist. Dr. Hooks is good enough, I suppose. But the man's obsessed with talking about the latest artwork he's trying to acquire." A white Subaru pulled up next to the curb. "Here's my daughter, right on time for a change. Nice talking to you."

Dr. Hooks collected artwork? Could this be the connection? Was it that simple? In a Nancy Drew novel the answer was yes. Real life was never that simple.

I checked my watch and realized I just had time to race home, feed my menagerie, and get to the viewing. Good thing boring outfits were a staple at funeral homes.

Just as I slid into the Ghia, my cell phone rang.

"Hey, girlfriend," Floydean said. "Tell Rebbie not to get her panties in a twist over the warehouse deal going sour."

"Why?"

"Deal's really gone south. A fire is roaring through Bernhagen's block as we speak."

FIFTEEN

"**S**END IT NOW!" HEADS SWIVELED MY WAY at the tinny bellow broadcasting from my cell phone. I broke the connection on Yancy's tirade and hurried away from the casket, inching my way through a sea of mourners in funereal attire. I'd barely reached the safety of the hall when the offending phone vibrated again. I could ditch it in one of the potted plants, but that would only prolong the inevitable.

"Stop calling!" I hissed. "The casket is surrounded by people. I'm not taking a picture. The whole idea is tacky."

"He must be hideous. I should've never consented." Yancy moaned. "We're ruined! Harrigan Funeral Home will soon be eschewed by anyone with the least smidgen of taste."

I huffed a sigh of frustration and ducked into the ornate coat alcove near the front door. "For the last time, Brestlin isn't up to your standards, but he's passable! Reb did okay. I haven't heard a single complaint, not even from Agatha," I said sotto voice.

"Tell Ms. Hypochondriac she needs a new hobby. Even I find her interest in socializing at viewings bizarre," Yancy said.

"Forget about Agatha. Forget the viewing. Call me when you've found something important to help Cary!" I ended the call on Yancy's snide reply and slipped my phone into my black satin clutch.

From the alcove I could see the foyer, part of the hall, and a sliver of Viewing Room B where Brestlin was laid out. An interesting group was present tonight. Besides family and friends of the deceased, and professional viewers like Agatha, I spied my mother and Todd Sudi feeding each other wafer-thin cookies from the complimentary array on a silver cookie platter. Martin Mangum, trying and failing to look like he belonged, was hanging around a large floral arrangement hoping for a grand tour after the viewing. I hadn't spotted Axel, but Killian was here per Reb's invitation. He'd examined Reb's handiwork, said she'd performed a miracle on the deceased, and now leaned against one of the foyer walls, arms folded, looking cool and dangerous. Several people gave his 'don't-mess-with-me aura' a wide berth on their way to pay their respects. I spotted Bernie Bernhagen angling past a group of elderly women. What a guy. Despite his warehouses going up in smoke, he still found time to pay his respects. Maybe he had the warehouses insured and that might save him from the Pheasant Ridge debacle. Miracles did happen.

An audible gasp filled the room and my eyes locked onto Reb making her way down the hall in killer stilettos, wearing a slinky, form-hugging black dress, while holding aloft a platter of cookies. The platter bobbled some when she passed Bernhagen.

"Nice save," I said, snatching one of Gram's melt-in-your-mouth creations and rescuing the platter from her shaking grasp. *Yancy wanted a picture, why not send one of Reb? It'd be a shame if he missed seeing his replacement. Second thought, bad idea. He might stroke out.*

"His warehouses are turning to ash, what the hell's he doing here?" she snorted, glaring at Bernhagen. She hadn't thought about the insurance angle.

"Must've known the deceased," I said. "Brestlin was a community pillar, big fish among all the movers and shakers before he retired to Phoenix."

"Whatever." Reb inhaled and exhaled. "Now that I've found my true calling, I don't need to play kiss-butt with phony business-types anymore. Corpses are far better to work with. Not much different from making up Barbie and they never cop an attitude." She grabbed the tray from me and stalked to the linen-covered table, replenishing the dwindling refreshments in fearfully precise overlapping rows.

Not wanting to point out that she'd be unemployed once Yancy's bandages came off, I turned and nearly bumped noses with Gram. She grabbed my elbow and yanked me to the nearest corner.

"Ghouls just wanna have fun is *not* proper dress code," she hissed, pointing at Reb. *So the unemployment line was closer than I thought.*

"Mr. Brestlin looks good." I pointed out.

"He's okay. Reb's no Yancy."

Who was?

I watched Gram mingle her way toward the viewing room and noticed Dexter waving at me from just inside the front door.

"Hey, Dex," I said, surprised by his wrinkled shorts, tank top and tennis shoes with no socks, the same outfit I'd seen him in earlier.

"Glad I didn't have to hunt you down, way I'm dressed." He handed me an eight-by-ten manila envelope. "I've made a formal complaint. Now it's your turn."

"What?"

"That nincompoop from the Post Office keeps stuffing my box with the wrong mail. Last week it was the Kendels' and Agatha's. Today it's Sudi's. Since he's stayin' out at your place, Violet insisted I drop it off so you can deliver it."

"He's not staying at my place!" I hissed.

Dexter shrugged, looked around then leaned close and whispered, "Violet's ninety-nine percent sure there's a money order in one of the envelopes. With the weird stuff goin' down around the neighborhood, thought it might be best . . ." His voice trailed off, he glanced around once more, then cleared his throat. "Violet's waitin' in the car; she's dying for a Tastee Treat swirl cone." With a quick two-fingered salute he hustled out the front door.

I hefted the envelope. It felt heavy. If Sudi was still paying his respects to the cookie tray I could deliver the envelope or . . . I decided to retreat to my car and see if a blatant clue was wedged in this bundle. After all, Cary's life was at stake and Sudi was on my suspect list. I know mail tampering is a Federal Offense but simply inspecting various fast-food coupon flyers and bills wasn't considered criminal. Right?

I glanced at Killian; he appeared deep in conversation with some fellow. Perfect.

Outside, the smoky, hot air turned the setting sun into a blood-red orb. Cars crowded cheek-to-jowl under tall shade-splaying oaks in the funeral home's smaller parking area. The larger adjoining lot was a bare macadam rectangle shimmering with heat mirages and promising trouble if one stepped on the soft tar wearing heels. I'd arrived early enough to park the Ghia under an Oak tree, but even with the windows down, the black interior looked like a crematorium ready to consume unprotected flesh. I opted to examine the envelope's contents while leaning against the front fender and, after a quick glance around the shadow-shrouded parking area to make sure I could do this without an audience, I ripped open the manila envelope. Inside was a jumble of the usual credit card offers, a grocery store flyer, a couple of bills and an oblong envelope with Sudi's work address printed neatly in the center. Could contain a cashier's check. Also in the mix I found a letter addressed to R. T. Tripper with Todd's apartment number and address. The letter was from a Stephen Sudi with a New York return address.

Weird.

Todd lived alone, so who was R. T. Tripper? Maybe, like Frobi, the man had an alias? Or did the T. stand for Todd and Sudi was his alias? A shudder ran through me. Who exactly was this guy playing kissy-face with Willie? *Calm down, Harrigan, don't go conclusion-hopping.*

I could march this whole mess to Killian and prove . . . nothing. Okay, desperate times called for a little law-bending. With my heart thudding hard in my chest, I dropped the mystery letter on the blacktop, placed my black suede pump on it and gave a couple of healthy twists.

"Twistin' the night away are we, Luv?"

I squealed, dropped the manila envelope and looked up into Axle's handsome face. I'd have sworn the lot was empty; where had he jack-in-the-boxed from?

"Sorry, didn't mean to give you a fright," he said.

"You didn't. There was a bug. Big, nasty thing."

His eyes slid to the mess of mail littering the ground. "Let me give you a hand." He stooped and picked up the various papers.

"Thanks." I held my hand out.

"Oh-oh, looks like this one didn't fare so well." He held the torn, rumpled envelope between thumb and finger. Blue-lined paper peeked from the ripped corner.

I snatched it from him. "That's okay. I'll take care of it." I shoved everything back into the manila folder and stepped back to take in his outfit. Black tweed sports jacket, crisp white shirt open at the neck, black linen slacks. Talk about trust-inspiring respectability with just a hint of sexuality simmering beneath. "Here to pay your respects?"

He shook his head and grinned, his teeth gleaming white in the deep dusk. "Didn't know the poor gent. Martin called and asked me to join him for the tour. Very nice of your Grandmum to open up her business."

"And you dressed to impress the spooks?"

He chuckled. "Only decent thing to do at a viewing. Didn't want to look like regular riff-raff."

Good thing he hadn't run into Dexter.

"Are you leaving?" he asked.

"No," I said. "Just getting some air. I'll see you inside."

Axel stuck his hands in his pockets and tagged along behind

two elderly couples making their way across the parking lot. A white Cadillac slowly maneuvered from a parking spot as two more cars entered. So much for a nice, secluded spot to look at Sudi's mail. Clutching the envelope stuffed with mail to my chest, I power-walked to the garage, punched in the code on the keypad, waited for the door to creak open, and slid into the nearest hearse. I hit the transmitter button on the opener and waited until I was safely closed away from prying eyes.

Sweat beaded my forehead as I pulled my shirt away from my clammy back. Either the sun-roasted garage had upped my sweat meter or maybe the idea of leaping into felony-land had my anxiety meter overloaded. *Just do it and get it over with.*

I took hold of the ragged envelope and looked at the address again. *Quit stalling.* My shaking hands eased the lined paper from the torn envelope and I quickly unfolded the single sheet. Printed in large block letters smack in the middle of the paper was one line: **TIME TO MOVE.** That was it. No salutation. No signed name.

Yeesh! I'd risked wearing an orange jumpsuit courtesy of the Feds for one lousy cryptic line? Who'd take the time to address an envelope, hunt up a stamp, then send a letter with a few words? Unless. . .*it* was code. But for what? James Bond would know. Too bad I didn't have his smarts, or ultra-cool gadgets, or mega-sexy car.

I squealed and jumped when my cell phone buzzed against my thigh on the leather seat. *Add Bond's nerves of steel to my want list.*

I didn't need the caller I.D. to tell me who it was. "Stop obsessing, Yancy!"

"Using a two-finger hunt-and-peck system on this blasted laptop is bad enough, Mercedes. My concentration is totally shattered. I can't continue until I know Brestlin looks presentable."

I fought the urge to bang my head on the steering wheel. "I'll send the damn picture if you check out Todd Sudi and a fellow named Stephen Sudi. Same spelling. I'll text you Stephen's address."

"Todd's the tenant who ran his truck into his own apartment, right? Didn't you run a credit check when he moved in?"

"Yes, but I want a total looking-up-his-nose-with-a microscope check."

"Send Brestlin and I'll find out what brand of deodorant both Sudi boys buy."

I took a picture of Stephen Sudi's address and sent it to Yancy's phone, stuffed all the mail into the manila envelope, clicked the garage door open and ran to my car to hide the incriminating envelope. Time to get back before Gram noticed my absence. The crowd had thinned enough for me to sidle up to the casket, point my phone and click a quick picture.

"Quirky hobby?" The question, whispered against my earlobe in an Aussie accent, made me drop my phone into the casket. Crap. Silent as smoke, Axel had caught me off guard. Again! I snaked my hand into the casket, and fumbled around between Brestlin and the silk lining to yank my phone free.

I explained how Yancy was Gram's right-hand embalmer and with him out of commission in the hospital he wanted a picture of Mr. Brestlin to make sure Rebbie had followed his instructions when she applied the makeup.

Axel nodded. "He sounds extremely efficient."

"Extremely is a perfect adverb to describe Yancy."

"Martin says your grandmum is nearly ready to give us a look 'round. Thought you might like to come along," Axel's hand skimmed my cheek as he tucked a stray curl behind my ear. Tingles erupted in my stomach then spread south, making my knees rubbery. He made touring the all-too-familiar funeral home sound like a romantic weekend getaway.

"Mercedes, you have to talk to your grandmother!" Reb made her way across the room, hands on her hips, eyes narrowed and blazing. "She called my ensemble outrageous." She cocked her head at Axel and gave him a sultry grin. "Do you find my outfit outrageous?"

If Axel spent one moment impressed with Reb's sexy outfit, he was careful to remain neutral. I had to give him points, lesser men have fallen to their knees on her account.

"Not my place to say. Please excuse me, looks like Martin needs a word."

Reb frowned and watched him walk away. "Gorgeous and gay." She *tsked* and shook her head. "What a waste."

I swallowed a smile and checked my watch. "Almost nine. Let's get a Tastee Treat swirl cone and discuss some other possible fashion options?"

Reb walked over to the casket and ran her hand along the quilted silk drape. "He looks good, don't you think?"

I came and put my arm around her shoulder. "Yes."

"As good as Yancy could do?"

The wistful sound in her voice made my heart clutch. I crossed my fingers behind my back. "Yes. Just as good."

MY HOUSE WAS DARK WHEN I PULLED INTO the driveway, no sign of Sudi's car. Damn. Where was Willie? I dialed her cell and got her voice mail. Double damn. I left a message to call me and plodded to the back gate. Exhaustion had me feeling lightheaded and ready to collapse on the kitchen floor. Three fury bodies leapt around my legs as I opened the gate. I knelt down and petted each wiggling torso, wishing I could absorb some of their energy through osmosis.

"Hey, guys, were you good? Want a treat?"

At the mention of the "T" word, Bogart and Bacall took off for the doggie door. Mr. Wiggins gave my hand a final lick and we entered the house together through the unlocked back door.

Damnit, Willie! Would she leave *her own* house unlocked?

I switched on the kitchen light and hit the play button on my answering machine. Nothing from Willie, but I listened to a robotic voice explain my car's warranty was about to lapse and I should call ASAP to avoid this fate. Considering my Karmen Ghia left the showroom floor sometime in nineteen sixty, a mere phone call wouldn't restore anything on my classic baby.

I snagged a handful of dog treats from the clown cookie jar and fed a couple to each happy face, all the while listening for sounds from upstairs. I wanted to make sure Willie wasn't home and engaged with a gentleman before I traipsed up to my bedroom. Quiet. No creatures stirring. I unlatched the baby gate from the kitchen doorway and let the trio gallop into the living room.

Locking the back door and turning off the kitchen light, I moved into the moonlit living room unbuttoning my wilted crepe blouse as I walked. I stopped mid-button in the middle of the room. Something was different. There was a scent in the room, an essence both exotic and manly. Not a scent I was familiar with, but one I could get very used to if the right guy wore it. I stood still and listened. Nails scrabbling on the floor above. One of the trio was scratching covers to make a nest. No heavy breathing. No footsteps. The dogs had thundered through this room, not stopping to bark at any boogey-type men or a late-night Lothario. Still . . .

I turned on the table lamp beside the couch and looked around. Everything seemed in order. Torn cushions back on the couch, round braided rug covered the hardwood plank floor, no shoe tips sticking out from behind the closed drapes. I looked closer, letting my eyes roam every surface, every nook, every . . . I walked over to the built-in bookshelf. There, on the third shelf, my Dachshund figurine sat in front of *The Best Of James Herriot*. Only it was supposed to stand guard in front of my Nancy Drew collection.

So, I moved it the last time I dusted. Only I was sort of anal about the Dachshund and Nancy. I checked the front door. Dead bolt secure, doorknob locked. Frowning, I walked upstairs, grabbed my gun from between my mattress and box springs, and began checking closets, under beds, behind the shower curtain: nothing. Had Sudi moved the Dachshund? Was it his scent? Maybe. Maybe not.

I padded downstairs and made the rounds shutting and locking all windows and double-checking door locks. It was a hot night and by morning my closed-up house would be hot as hell. Better to swelter than wake up dead.

Upstairs I wrangled and shoved my dresser beneath the half-open bedroom window, plunked the box fan on top, then switched the knob to high. If a crazed killer wanted to spidey-walk up the side of my house, deal with hefting the stubborn window higher, and answer to a pack of ankle biters, he was welcome to try it. I'd already decided to sleep with my gun and heavy-duty flashlight on my night stand. I added the shrill police whistle for good measure. Stripping to my panties and pulling on a light tee-shirt, I crawled into bed and sank into a deep sleep.

The metallic voice hissing through the phone mimicked Darth Vader's tone and kept demanding I divulge my favorite color. The black, old-fashioned receiver clutched in my hand felt hot, heavy. When I pulled it from my ear it began to twist and writhe all the while ringing, ringing, ringing!

I bolted upright, clutching the pillowcase to my ear, gulping air like a dying swimmer. Still, the ringing continued. I untangled the sweat-clammy sheet, grasped my cell and steeled myself. Heart galloping, I waited in silence for the eerie metallic voice from my dream.

"Mercedes? Are you there, girl?"

Floydean? I blew out a whoosh of relief. Floydean Mollicker.

"I'm here. Just making sure you're not Darth Vader."

"What?"

"Never mind. Bad dream." I rubbed a hand across my eyes and looked at the whirling fan. Behind the blades, the night's black curtain pressed against my window. My gaze shot to the digital clock next to my weapon arsenal. 1:30 a.m. Great! "What's wrong?"

"I'm privy to classified info about the artwork in the caskets."

"They're the real deal and now Cary is facing more than suspicion of murder charges?"

"What? No. I mean, I don't know if the paintings are real or not. Rumor has it that Frobi Fisher scammed someone known as the Curator. That's like cheating the Godfather! The Curator put a price on her head."

"Come on, Floydean. A hit man? Go prank someone else." I grabbed the bottle of water on my nightstand and took a gulp. Ugh, warm.

"Not a prank, I swear on new Fendi knock-off sandals."

"I'm listening."

"This has to remain between us but I thought you'd want to know. The Curator hired an assassin to take care of Frobi and return the paintings."

"Great. This proves Cary didn't kill Frobi." My fingers tightened around the water bottle, and it protested with a loud crunch.

"Maybe."

"Maybe? Cary is not a hit man. He hates stepping on ants!"

"That's your perception. This new wrinkle has people scrambling, checking contacts, sending out all kinds of feelers."

"Who knows about this?" *Holding Cary because of circumstantial evidence was no longer possible. Right?* "I need to call Mr. Barkley. He can use this to get Cary released."

"Girlfriend, this isn't about getting Cary out of jail. I called to warn you. The hit man had two jobs; murder Frobi and return the paintings. The FBI took possession of the artwork and you are responsible."

I gulped. "The caskets were shoddy, ready to fall apart. Anyone could've stumbled onto them."

"I don't think an assassin cares about such details."

SIXTEEN

I RUBBED MY EYES, DRAGGED MY FINGERS through my hair, and blinked at the yellow legal pad before me on the kitchen table. Under the glare of the overhead light, some of the doodles were pretty good. However, my pitiful notes put me . . . is there a square before one? My .38 pistol lay on the table. Silly. But, I wasn't taking chances.

A hit man in Portneuf Gap? Either that was beyond a ridiculous supposition or this had all the markings of a cheap detective thriller circa nineteen fifty. Funny, though, earlier Dexter had mentioned something about a hit man.

Forget the assassin theory. I needed to concentrate on Frobi and her chosen lifestyle. She was very stranger-danger aware, and she wouldn't have admitted anyone she didn't know into the apartment. Who besides Cary was Frobi acquainted with? One of my tenants? I'd laughed at Willie's list but maybe she'd stumbled onto something. Frobi had made a living bilking victims out of money. If someone took Gram's life savings and she died penniless I would want revenge. Could I take the life of the person responsible? And why did the killer add the dramatic flair of a vintage James Bond movie? Suffocation by gold paint did make a symbolic statement. But, again, why?

The day Cary and Frobi arrived, Agatha met them with the exciting news that cooking diva Sherrilyn Sanborn was hiding out in the complex. Hush, hush info according to Albert Lechman, aka Creepiest Fan. Had he been at the complex the night Frobi died? If he murdered Frobi for revenge, or justice, or whatever why was he still hanging around? *I refused to entertain the idea of Lechman as a hit man.*

Like Agatha, Todd Sudi had joined our little group on the pretense of paying his rent, but he'd left in a hurry without paying because . . . he recognized Frobi? No. Maybe. He also owned a body shop where cars were sprayed to look like new. The same equipment could also spray a person. No problem.

Mark Sandborn had made a fool of himself in front of the entire complex the night Frobi died. In a drunken stupor he'd mistaken Frobi for his ex-wife Sherri. Hmm. Hard to imagine him spray painting someone when he could barely walk a straight line.

Was Martin Mangum really a would-be ghost hunter? What about Axel Danforth? My heart gave a lurch, thinking he might be involved, but hard facts needed thorough examination. Axel had followed Gram and me to the hospital. Out of simple consideration? Or murderous curiosity about Yancy's condition?

My mind kept going in circles like the doodles I'd sketched around each suspect's name. Someone was desperate to get Frobi's laptap, desperate enough to send Yancy to the hospital. . .or to the morgue? Someone had also left morbid warnings at Grams' and cut Sudi's brake line.

I had no proof. Not a shred of evidence. But my gut instinct told me Todd Sudi was somehow involved right up to his thick neck. Had he cut his own brake line? Possible. And from his accent I could see him involved in something illegal. I know, I was stereotyping again, desperation brought out my worst traits. But could he be the mastermind behind Frobi's murder? I had serious doubts. He'd been renting from me for about ten months and the timeline didn't add up. Right now nothing added up.

I stood, stretched, and poured another cup of coffee. Outside my kitchen window the horizon loomed pitch-black against a pewter sky. Soon dawn's colors would wash away this dismal night. Returning to the table, I sat tapping the pencil against the pad, determined to come up with a plan to flush out the killer and free Cary. I sighed and wrote assassin near the bottom of the page and doodled a rectangle around the word. Improbable or possible?

The hinges on my back screen door screeched in protest and I was on my feet, gun in hand. All three dogs raced into the kitchen, hackles up, barking in unison.

The murderer? He'd deduced I was onto him and had come to clean-up a loose end. Me!

I watched in horror as the doorknob twisted right then left. *Don't panic. The dead-bolt is secure.* I backed into the corner beside the fridge, heart thumping, arms shaking as I raised the .38 and cocked the trigger.

The knob twisted harder.

"Blast it all to hell!"

I nearly fell down with relief. Willie. The dogs settled, hackles flattened and tails wagged. I gently eased the hammer down, opened the fridge, hid the gun in the vegetable drawer, and hurried to unlock the back door.

"Why is the door locked?" she demanded, brushing past me, purple Fendi heels dangling from two fingers. "You live in the boonies. What are you afraid of, marauding cows?"

I folded my arms. "And you're traipsing home with the dawn because . . .?"

"Because Toddy didn't want to quit playing with his damn pool cue."

Please don't let that be a euphemism. "Excuse me?"

"It's all rather droll, dear. I thought the man was a stud. Turns out he's a dud."

Sounded like Sudi'd lost his sleep-over status. "Willie, I tried calling you. I've been worried," I said through gritted teeth.

She fumbled in her deep leather bag, laying the contents on the table. "After the viewing, Toddy and I joined a couple of his co-workers at some pseudo-cowboy bar. Horrid place, I probably wouldn't have heard my phone. Then the party moved to some Joe-Schmoe's house for a spur-of-the-moment pool tournament." She frowned, laid the empty purse on the floor and poured herself a cup of coffee. "Now where did I leave my cell? Maybe in Todd's car?" She huffed a sigh. "That means I'll have to deal with him again." She took a sip, put the cup down and folded her arms. "I must rent some transportation today or I'll go mad. I'm going to visit Cary come hell or whatever." She started toward the living room, stopped and turned. "But first I need to catch a couple of winks. Be a darling and wake me around noon. If Todd calls about my phone take a message, and please keep the mutts quiet."

Taking my squinty-eyed, silent stance as a yes, Willie flounced toward the stairs singing the chorus of *Friends in Low Places*.

Wake her at noon? Oh-kay! I went into the narrow laundry room off the kitchen and hunted around in the cupboard above the washer. Ah-ha. Aunt Vie's old wind-up alarm clock. Guaranteed to jar anyone awake within a three-block radius. I wound the clock, set it to the current time, and turned the alarm knob for straight-up twelve. I'd slip this little beauty on the floor under Willie's bed.

Settling back at the table, I reviewed my list. Still not enough evidence to convince myself, let alone Killian, but I planned to lay out my suspicions anyway. I'd hunt Sudi down, deliver his mail, and see if the odd letter caused a reaction. And I'd get Yancy to run a check on every suspect. Even Axel and Martin.

I hurried upstairs for a quick shower. Time to commence Operation Flush. Someone was going down.

Revived from the shower, I pulled on shorts, and a red tank top and walked into Willie's room toweling my hair. I poked her shoulder. She mumbled something and pulled the sheet over her head. I yanked the sheet back, leaned over and shook my semi-wet hair like a dog.

"Mercedes McCambridge Harrigan!" She jammed the pillow over her head.

"Where's Sudi staying?"

"Not here," she mumbled against the pillowcase.

I grabbed the pillow. "Tell me and I'll leave you alone."

She rolled onto her back and opened one eye. "I think he mentioned one of your renters offering him a couch, spare room, dog-house, something like that." She snatched the pillow and gave it a good plumping. "Close the door on your way out."

I slid the alarm clock under the nightstand, just out of reach, and did as she requested.

Downstairs, the rising sun slanted through the kitchen window illuminating dust motes in the cheery light. I fed the dogs, poured myself a bowl of Frosted Flakes (nothing like caffeine and sugar to make me feel invincible) and made a list of people to see, places to go. I heard Eclipse whinny from the corral and a second later, Killian's truck rumbled down my driveway.

Show-time.

I poured a cup of coffee, added just a hint of sugar, pasted on a smile, and managed the back door without slopping a drop.

"Aren't you the early bird," Killian said, taking the cup I offered him. His wind-tossed hair shone like fine silk in the morning light.

"Gotta catch those worms," I said. "Jack, I need to run something by you."

His face morphed from friendly to wary. "Shoot."

Concentrating on laying out the facts without wandering off on tangents, *think bullet points, Harrigan,* I told Killian about all of the strange warnings left at the funeral home and my thoughts about Yancy's "accident." I left out the hit man theory . . . for now. I needed Killian onboard not laughing his butt off.

His beautiful lips disappeared in a straight line and his thick brows inched together. "Shit, Sadie. Why didn't you . . ."

"Wait! Just hear me out."

He took a deep breath, let it out, and gulped some coffee. "Okay, Sherlock, I'm listening."

"Whoever's behind the threats is most likely behind Frobi's murder. If we set a trap . . ."

"We? Trap?" Killian shook his head. "No trap setting. Leave the investigation to the proper authorities. Understood?"

I narrowed my eyes and clenched my teeth to corral any snide remarks. I wasn't falling for the make-me-storm-off-mad ploy. I continued as though I hadn't heard him. "I plan on using Frobi's laptop as bait. I need backup. Are you in or not?"

"The laptop you asked me about, you've had it the whole time? You never stopped to consider it might be evidence? Mercedes . . ." He studied the sky as though praying for strength or possibly guidance not to strangle me.

"Yancy is working his tech magic investigating the digital footprints left by Torture Junkie."

Killian pressed his lips together and stared at his boots for what seemed forever. "Would it make any difference if I say no to this harebrained scheme?"

I shrugged.

He gulped more coffee, slowly nodding. "Okay. But you're going to owe me. Big time."

It was my turn to gulp.

NEXT ON MY HIT-LIST: REBBIE. Because of the early hour, and to sweeten my proposition, I stopped at Albertsons and grabbed an assortment of doughnuts. I parked in her driveway, walked to the front door, and leaned on the bell.

"Someone better be near death!" Reb grumbled behind the door before opening it a crack. She glared from me to the box full of doughnuts. She blinked, yawned and opened the door. "Is that an apple fritter? Come in."

I followed her into the kitchen, grabbed a plate from the cupboard, and arranged the yummy, deep-fried calories in a mini-pyramid.

Reb yawned and opened her fridge. "What's your pleasure, Pepsi or orange juice? I'm out of coffee."

"I'll make a Mocha Java run."

Reb slumped into the nearest kitchen chair and lifted a can of Pepsi. "This'll do. Why are you here before the crack of dawn?"

My watch read 7:45 a.m., but pointing out dawn had come and gone wouldn't help my cause. Besides, bed-head didn't begin to describe Reb's hair which stood out like it was trying to abandon her scalp. Smudged mascara pointed to a half-hearted makeup removal. Hard night for sure.

I hid a smirk behind my first doughnut. "I would like your help. We're gonna get the sicko who turned Frobi into a life-sized Oscar."

Reb reached for an apple fritter, took a nibble, and chased it with a slurp of soda. "Wonderful. You have a plan?"

I nodded and between bites of glazed glory gave her the basic idea.

"You sure the hospital will release Yancy this morning?"

I gave her a look.

Reb thunked her head with her hand. "Right. One night of that cry-baby and some orderly is bodily removing Mr. Whiny as we speak." She took another nibble and slurp. "Your plan needs a little tweaking. You wearing a wire is not the best idea. Killian and I have a history in undercover work. I should wear the wire."

I hadn't considered the intricacies of wearing a wire or who would be taping what to where. Whoa, mama! A flash of heat shot straight to my stomach. *Steady, girl.* I swallowed the last of my doughnut along with the sexual fantasy. "Nope. This is my responsibility."

"Huh?"

"My brother brought this mess to town so I'm the wire-wearing bait. Besides, you don't look so hot. Did preparing Brestlin knock you off your feet?"

"No! That gynormous, chocolate-dipped cone gave me a super sugar high. I ended up watching *Top Gun* until the wee hours."

She took another nibble of fritter, chewed, and grinned. "Course, watching Tom Cruise in his flight suit made it almost worth it."

I nodded. Back in our pre-teen years we'd nearly worn out my mother's VHS tape of *Top Gun.* Our naive minds considered him the sexiest man ever created and we both secretly knew he'd propose marriage if we could only meet him. "How long until you're ready to roll?"

Reb rubbed her eyes, stood, and stared at her reflection in the toaster. "Yikes. Better give me a couple of hours."

"One hour max." I said, licking my fingers before digging into my purse for keys. "Gotta deliver Sudi's mail and gauge his reaction."

PULLING INTO THE PARKING LOT, I spotted Dexter tossing peanuts to a squirrel. "Morning, Dexter. New pet?" I asked, exiting my car.

"Cute lil' devil loves to beg. Looks like you're on a mission," he said, pointing to the manila envelope containing Sudi's strange letter. "Did you happen to notice the sleaze ball across the street?" He pointed to the silver Taurus with Lechman dozing behind the wheel.

I shrugged. "Yeah, the ever-present boil on humanity's butt. Do you know where I can find Sudi?"

"Rumor has it he's bunking with Agatha."

I raised my eyebrows. "OMG!"

Dexter grinned and winked. "Sorry, just pulling your leg. He's in twelve with James."

I gave him my best eye roll, crossed the lot, and banged on James Katseanas' front door. No answer so I banged again. A blood-shot eye filled the oval peephole near the top of the door.

"James ain't home." Sudi's voice sounded like gravel bouncing down a tin roof. *Must've been some pool tournament.*

I shook my head and held up the manila envelope.

The dead-bolt clacked like a gun shot in the early morning stillness. The sun, a relentless orb climbing a cloudless sky, baked the deathly calm air. Sudi opened the door. From his wrinkled tee-shirt and khaki shorts, I suspected he'd fallen asleep fully clothed. He rubbed his eyes and stroked a hand along his ten-o-clock-shadow. "The putz mailman gave it to you?"

"Delivered to Dexter."

Sudi's scowl tripled and he held out his hand. "You see what we gotta put up with round here?"

"Unprofessional." I tipped the large envelope toward Sudi and watched in mock horror as his mail dumped onto the porch. "Oops." I stooped and picked up the scattered mail making sure the odd, mangled letter was on top.

"Just look at this letter." I held it up for Sudi's inspection. "Some postal sorting machine had its way with this one."

Sudi blanched. He reached for the tattered paper, but I whisked it out of reach. He looked at me with a puzzled expression that morphed swiftly to panic. He slammed the door and the dead bolt tumbled closed.

"Idiot." I unzipped the little pocket inside my purse and plucked out my master key. I opened both door locks and shoved my way into the little foyer. No sign of Sudi.

"Don't make me chase you, Todd. I just want to ask you a couple of questions." I gathered my purse close, a handy bludgeon if need be, and went into the living room. The couch, two chairs and end table looked early thrift shop and contrasted with the state-of-the-art flat-screen TV. James Katseanes had defined his priorities. A flash of color in my peripheral vision, a sense of tumbling over a chair, and an instant later I lay on my back staring up at the living room ceiling. The front door banged shut. I sighed, then collected myself and the scattered contents of my purse. "Of course, you know, this means war!"

SEVENTEEN

I TORE OUT OF THE FRONT DOOR and ran smack into Axel. His nimble reaction and strong grip prevented me from ricocheting onto my butt.

"Whoa, luv. What's the rush?"

"Did a grungy-looking guy run past here?"

Martin stepped from behind Axle's jeep and pushed his glasses back in place. "Yeah, the jerk peppered me with dust when he peeled out in some old junker." He brushed his pant leg and scowled. He tilted his head up like a dog sniffing the wind. "Man, he left a ton of bad karma hanging low. Air's totally tainted."

"What kind of car?"

"Old LeSabre. Real oil burner. Headed east from here," Martin said, pointing toward Benton Street.

"There a problem, luv?"

I shoved my exasperation aside, pasted on a smile and stared into Axel Danforth's beautiful eyes. "No, no problem." *Except you're high on my suspect list, you always pop up at odd moments, and you have my libido working overtime.* "I needed to return something to my renter, Todd Sudi. Guess I'll have to catch him later."

Axel cocked his head and frowned. "The bloke in a hurry was Sudi? Never would'a guessed, way he looked and all, like he was running from something. Weird."

There's weird and then there's WEIRD. "How do you know Todd Sudi?"

"We've met a couple of times. He's trying to get me to trade the Jeep in for something a bit newer."

Typical Sudi.

"Hang on a sec." Axel grabbed my hand. I couldn't help noticing the way his muscles moved under his black tank top and the way his army drab shorts accentuated his trim waist and long legs. My heart fluttered as he drew me closer. "I came to say g'bye."

A lump formed in my throat, plummeted to my stomach, tied a couple of knots and bounced back to clog my throat. "You're leaving? Right now? When . . ." *I'm on the verge of flushing out Frobi's murderer?* "Uh, when you and Martin are on the verge of his first big psychic discovery?"

"My crew's been called to California."

Ghost-busters had crews? "Let me guess, someone made a positive Elvis sighting and you're going to do lunch with the King."

Axel tipped his head back and laughed. Martin snorted and clapped me on the back. "Axel's a smoke-jumper. Psychic research is his hobby."

"You chase spirits as a hobby?"

"Yeah, after a brush with lightning a couple of years back it seems I have a real knack for cluing into paranormal activity."

"Cool, huh?" Martin said.

Mind racing, I nodded. "Yeah, cool." *And leaving now put a checkmark next to slightly suspicious.* Hard to track a suspect in the middle of a raging inferno.

Axel misread my silence. "Not to worry, luv." He brushed his thumb across my knuckles. "I've battled thousands of blazes. Just another day in Mother Nature's office. I'm not leavin' until tomorrow. Maybe we could grab a bite to eat tonight."

Tonight! I had less than twenty-four hours to set my plan in motion.

"Sounds great." I smiled to add weight to my words in case galloping panic trembled in my voice. "Let me check with Gram, see if she needs any help. I'll get back to you."

Axel plucked a pen from Martin's shirt pocket, turned my palm up, and wrote a string of numbers. "That's the best number to reach me at." He leaned close and I inhaled his masculine scent. His lips brushed my cheek and I had my own brush with a lightning bolt. "Give me a holler when you're ready."

"Will do," I rasped, and pulled my hand from his warm grasp. With equally unsteady mind and legs, I made it to my car, opened the door and gave Axel and Martin a quick wave. Axel flashed a killer smile and my muddled mind began chanting please don't let it be him, please don't let it be him! After two fumbled attempts, I managed to insert the key in the ignition. *Get a grip, Harrigan.* If Axel was the killer, so be it. But, as Rebbie had wisely noted, what a waste.

Five minutes later, I spotted Reb standing on the curb, cell phone pressed to her ear, right foot tapping out a frantic internal rhythm. Dressed in yellow spandex shorts, top, and lemon wedge sandals, she resembled a banana popsicle with curves. She climbed in the car, ended the call, and plopped her cell into her oversize yellow bag. "Yancy's back home and totally on board with Operation Flush. He's already sent a *let's negotiate* message to Torture Junkie."

While I'd driven to her house in a daze, Reb had contacted Yancy with instructions. Yeesh! I needed to get in the game. Get my head on straight. Execute my A game. Get some new clichés.

"How'd it go with Sudi?" Reb asked.

"He freaked and bolted."

"Aha. He *is* the killer!" Reb clapped her hands. "Thanks to us, Cary will soon breathe free."

"Not yet, Watson. Too many questions, too few answers. Plus we're running out of time. Axel leaves for California in the morning."

"He called to say cheerio?"

"No. He came by the complex to tell me in person."

Reb frowned. "Convenient. He splits just when we decide to set a trap?"

"Exactly."

"Wait a minute!" Reb swiveled in her seat to face me. "Suppose Axel *is* a real psychic, with the ability to read minds. They do exist, you know. Now he's cutting out!" She drummed her nails on the dashboard. "Quick, turn around. We'll follow him and nail him when Yancy leads him to the laptop. No wire-wearing, bait-and-hook nonsense. Just straight-out brilliant detective work." Reb pumped the air with her fist.

I raised an eyebrow. "And if he's not the murderer?"

She sighed, scowled, and went back to drumming her fingernails. "Shut-up and drive."

I parked next to the extra-wide double garage door which housed the funeral home's hearse and limo, and we hurried up the side stairs to Yancy's apartment above. I gave his door a quick rap and we walked into his art-deco abode. Dressed in royal blue pajamas, Yancy sat at the kitchen table, hunched over Frobi's laptop. His long index fingers hunted and pecked the keyboard with amazing speed, considering the bulky gauze bandages on his hand and the bottle of pain pills at his elbow.

"I'm in. Come take a look at what I found." he said, voice tight, eyes staring at the screen.

Reb and I looked at what his bandaged finger was pointing to. At first glance it looked like a typical site for ordering works of art. Or good imitations.

"Is this Frobi's website?" Reb asked.

"Yes and no. When I tried to hack into this site, to learn everything about it from the inside, I couldn't."

Reb patted him on the shoulder. "Too many pain pills, Candlemass."

Yancy shot her a sour look. "Because it doesn't exist."

I opened my mouth and he held up a hand. "Don't argue. Remain silent. It's like a front for the real website. Whatever data comes in, it goes to the real site, but the info is routed so it cannot be followed."

"Like a riddle within a riddle?" I asked.

"No. When you get on this particular Web site the connection doesn't take a direct route. Someone has found a way to direct the routing and send it through such a complicated pattern that it's almost impossible to follow and penetrate."

"You've lost me," I said.

"I don't have time to explain. Bring me the laptop on the counter by the sink." Reb placed the smaller computer next to Frobi's. Yancy pointed to the screen. "I downloaded a couple of Web sites from the pink laptop to my little workhorse." He opened the laptop and tapped some keys. "Look at the activity icon. This icon means the computer is being used; there's a program running."

"So?" Reb and I said in unison.

"I'm not using it. Someone else is. Because I downloaded a program from Frobi's computer, someone now has complete access to anything on *my* laptop. Most people wouldn't detect this. A devious program used the fake program to piggyback onto my computer. Once downloaded all the info put onto the computer is available. There are no secrets." He took a sitting bow. "Please, hold the applause."

"I still don't understand." I said.

"People who use body parts to write notes wouldn't."

I glanced at the numbers scrawled on my palm. "Yeah, new developments. We've got to snare Junkie tonight."

Yancy raised the few remaining scorched hairs on his right eyebrow. "Why the sudden rush?"

"Axel's unit has been called to California, seems his other job is fighting fires," I said.

"Be still my heart." Yancy patted his chest and looked at the ceiling. "Wish that hunka-hunka-burning-Aussie would switch teams."

Reb snorted. "That explosion must've messed-up your radar. The man's as gay as they come."

I held up my hand to stop Yancy's reply. "You two can debate Axel's sexual orientation later. Let's focus, people. We have less than twenty-four hours to solve this."

The front door swung open, and Gram entered carrying a tray covered with a blue gingham cloth. "Solve what?"

Yancy closed the laptop and pushed it to the opposite side of the table. "World hunger, starting with me." He snatched the cloth away and moaned with pleasure. "Cassandra, you are heaven-sent."

Wearing a floral chiffon dress, Gram looked as cool as an English rose garden, despite the fact she'd been cooking a small breakfast buffet for her patient. She placed the tray before Yancy, then sat in the chair next to Reb and repeated, "Solve what?"

I snatched a slice of bacon and made a show of chewing thoughtfully. Reb studied her nails while Yancy stuffed his face with Eggs Benedict.

Gram folded her arms. "I'm waiting."

"You might as well clue her in," Yancy said, patting his lips with the blue gingham napkin.

I gave Gram the *Reader's Digest* condensed version of our plan, emphasizing the fact that our strategy still needed some fine-tuning."

"Well fine-tune yourself right out of this nonsense. This is a matter for the police. Not the Three Stooges."

"The police *are* involved," I said, choosing to ignore her remark. "Killian will be monitoring my every move."

"You are *not* wearing any damn wire," Gram stood and eyed each one of us. "None of you are!"

"Who would you have wear it?" I asked. "And don't you dare say Willie."

Yancy swallowed a bite of biscuit. "Mercedes, *intelligent* people find it unwise to cross Cassandra."

Gram's nostrils flared. Her eyes opened wide and anger flashed from their chocolate depths. "Mercedes McCambridge . . ."

"Sorry. Okay? But I can't sit on my hands and do nothing."

Gram picked up the pink laptop and shoved it at me. "Turn this over to the police. Let them track down Junkie. They're paid to take risks."

"And while they're jumping through all types of bureaucratic hoops, Junkie does something bolder . . . like blowing up the hearse and sending Yancy to the hospital? It could've been the mortuary."

Yancy paled to a mottled pink. Gram gasped and Reb swore. I placed the laptop back onto the table and straddled a chair.

Silence settled on the room as we each contemplated how far Junkie was willing to go. Yancy was the first to speak. "Your idea is a bit nebulous, Mercedes. We may be in over our collective heads."

The laptop beeped. In unison we all jumped and stared at the putrid pink rectangle. "Someone has mail," Gram said.

Yancy opened the lid, poked a few keys, and grimaced. "Junkie wants the exchange to take place at midnight. I'm supposed to come alone with the laptop to the Simplot fountain in Old Town."

"Exchange?" I said.

"I couldn't offer up the laptop for nothing. Junkie would've smelled a trap. My asking price is twenty thousand. And FYI, if Junkie even smells a cop in the area the deal is dead . . . and possibly me along with it."

"Wonderful. You've done the groundwork, now the police can take it from here," Gram said. "Agree to whatever Junkie wants. Mercedes, you call Killian and arrange to turn the laptop over to the proper authority."

"Cassandra, did you not hear what I just said about cops?" Yancy said.

Gram flicked her hand at Yancy. "That's so cliché, it's almost laughable. The police will handle this with the utmost stealth. The police force must have an undercover cop so close to your double that your own mother couldn't tell the difference."

Reb and I exchanged glances. *Only in Gram's most naive dream.* My cell phone played Willie's ring tone, ending the bizarre comedy routine. I glanced at my watch, 10:30. Hmm. Guess she craved transportation more than beauty sleep.

"Yes, Willie," I said.

"Listen up, 'cause I'm only gonna say this once. I have youse mama. To get her back all safe and sound, bring ten-thousand in the usual unmarked bills and Frobi Fisher's laptop to the alley behind my body shop in an hour. No cops. No heroics. Or bye-bye mama. Got that? One hour."

"Let me talk to her."

"You can have a nice conversation in an hour."

The line went dead.

"Mercedes, what's wrong?" Gram asked, taking my hand and leading me to the nearest chair. "Sit down before you fall down, honey. Take some deep breaths."

I sat and stared at my cell phone. "Todd Sudi is holding Willie hostage."

EIGHTEEN

"**R**EALLY?" REB COCKED HER HEAD LIKE a puzzled parakeet, and frowned at the bacon she'd pilfered from Yancy's tray, as though she had no idea why she was holding it. "Willie and Sudi, I wonder who is holding whom hostage?"

"This is serious!" I brushed at a stray hair wishing I could brush away the horrid pictures my 3-D imagination had conjured up.

"Why on earth would Sudi kidnap Willie?" Gram's eyebrows drew together.

"He wants ten-thousand dollars and that atrocious pink nightmare, that oblong putrescence!" I pointed to the laptop next to Yancy's elbow. "That spawn of Satan that started this whole mess."

"OMG, Torture Junkie is Todd Sudi?" Reb grimaced and placed the uneaten bacon back on Yancy's plate.

"No. No, this is all wrong," Yancy said, tapping the bottle of pain meds with his fork. "Junkie's supposed to pay me twenty-thou. Now he wants us to pay him ten?"

"Sudi doesn't know we're with you. He might figure it's time to get whatever he can and bolt," Reb said.

"Did you hear Willie in the background?" Gram asked.

I shook my head.

"Then you can't be certain Sudi has her, right?"

"The call came from her cell phone." I stood and started for the door, rummaging through my purse for keys. "Connect the dots, the man's from Jersey. I'm not taking any chances."

Reb lifted an eyebrow. "So in stereotypical frenzy world, you're headed where?"

Her question stopped me mid-stride. Rushing home to search for Willie equaled stupid with a capital S. Yet, that had been my first impulse.

"One hour to form a battle plan." Yancy tapped his fork against his juice glass. "Come on people, use that gray matter between your ears!"

"Call the police," Gram said.

Of course. I dialed Killian's cell, praying he was still with Eclipse and within cell range.

"Hey, Sadie." His deep voice had never sounded so sweet.

"Where are you?"

"In the barn, cooling down Eclipse and listening to your mutts whine behind the fence. Why?"

I told him about the kidnapping, Sudi's demands, and explained the problem. "I'm not sure if this threat is serious."

"I'll check the house; don't do anything until you hear from me."

"Killian's checking the house for Willie." I looked at the ceiling and sighed. "Sudi must think I can conjure up money like a freakin' witch."

"There is *one* person who could gather that amount," Yancy said. He glanced sideways at Gram. "And she'd hardly break a sweat in the process."

Gram rolled her eyes. "I suppose. If it becomes absolutely . . ."

If this was a Willie drama, was she counting on Gram coming through? I hated myself for thinking such thoughts, but loose cannon ran in my family.

Killian's ring-tone cut short her answer and my thoughts. "Willie's not in the house. There's a note on the table saying she went to get her cell, but from the looks of the blue bedroom, there might've been a struggle."

My heart stuttered and I choked back a sob. "Struggle, as in stuff broken, or . . .," I gulped past the knot clogging my throat. "B-blood?"

"No, no blood. Clothes and shoes scattered everywhere, blankets and sheets heaped on the floor. That new pooch is shaking under the bed."

I let out a sigh, as reality shoved aside the ghastly images in my mind. "Sounds more like Willie rushing to go somewhere. Just guessing, but the quivering dog must've eaten another one of her shoes. Thanks for checking, I'll let you know when I find her."

"Mercedes, a threat's been made and we have to treat it as though it's legitimate. This possible kidnapping is now a police matter." Killian's tone brooked no argument.

Logic argued that I should turn the whole mess over to him. Give Portneuf Gap's seldom-used SWAT Team a real mission. But, on the one hand, assembling that much manpower with the clock ticking could take too long, forcing Sudi to do something rash. On the other hand, what if this did turn out to be another Willie drama multiplied to the tenth power? If the SWAT Team found Willie and Sudi sharing yucks over my naïveté, Killian would be standing in front of the fan when the crap went airborne.

My head was spinning with so many different scenarios, I was out of hands to count on.

"Jack, this stinks like a Willie prank cooked up to teach me a lesson for leaving her stranded without decent transportation. If the SWAT team finds this is a huge prank what will your superiors think? Sudi might be a simple pawn in her little scheme."

Dead silence.

Finally Jack cleared his throat, his voice low enough I had to strain to hear. "If you're wrong? If Sudi has kidnapped your mother?"

His words brought me up short. At the auto repair shop, Sudi had access to all sorts of painting apparatus. A mental image of

Frobi naked, dead, and sprayed gold sent icy dread slithering up my spine.

Yancy cleared his throat and tapped his watch.

"Jack, I *have* to be the one to deliver the money to Sudi. If you can work with that and keep all the players completely out of sight, fine." *Would he ever forgive me if this turned out to be a Willie antic?*

A disgruntled snort exploded in my ear. I pictured Killian looking upward as he shoved a hand through his hair.

Damn it, Mercedes."

"My mother," I said between clenched teeth. "Either my way or . . ."

"The highway," Killian finished for me. "Got it. Okay listen up, here's what I want you to do."

THE ATTACHÉ CASE, LOADED WITH ONE LAYER of crisp bills on top covering stacks of ordinary paper beneath, dragged heavily on my right arm, its handle sticky-slick from my death grip. I stared over the top of my Karmann Ghia down the long ribbon of hot asphalt winding through a series of never-ending alleys. I could hear Reb chomping gum to my right. The police hostage negotiator, Gary White, stood to my left.

"Let's run through the plan once more," Gary said, leaning against the hood of his truck, peering through a set of high-tech binoculars at the back door of the auto shop, two blocks away. Dressed in worn cowboy boots, black tee, and form-fitting Wrangler jeans, Gary looked more like a ranch hand than the police department's whip-sharp negotiator. At fifty, he must've dealt with more human sewage than the average officer, yet he seemed upbeat.

"You're sure the undercover guys are well hidden?" I said, bumping the case against my right knee and fighting the urge to pick at the tape holding the communication wire against my stomach. Yes, I was wired. No, Killian hadn't been the one to attach it. A female officer had made sure the wire worked properly and that it remained invisible under my shirt.

"Take a gander." Gary handed me the binoculars.

I scanned the area with the powerful lens and noticed a woman lounging on a bus stop bench at the corner where the alley ended. Three stuffed shopping bags took up the rest of the bench.

"The woman waiting for a bus is part of the operation?" I asked, handing Gary back his binoculars.

He nodded. "See anyone else?"

I shook my head. A smile creased his sun-worn face. "Counting officer Killian, there are three officers in place, ready for the take-down."

Impressive!

My cell beeped with a new text alert. I looked at the one-word message sent from the designated lookout's phone: *Showtime.* I took a deep breath, walked to my car, and opened the door. Reb gave me a hug and whispered, "Show no fear!"

Officer White leaned in the passenger-side window as I climbed behind the wheel and started the Ghia. "Nothing to worry about. Just get that Sudi fellow into the alley, give him both cases and leave the rest to us. If things go south, I'll step in." He gave me a thumbs-up signal.

I rumbled down the alley, zipping across a side street before I pulled to a stop beside a sagging chain-link fence that separated the adjacent run-down neighborhood from the alley and auto body shop. I cut the engine and listened in the still, mid-morning heat to the sound of metal banging on metal reverberating through the shop's open back door.

I scanned the backyard of the weather-beaten frame house on my right. The gate bisecting the middle of the fence was propped open with a half-crumbled cinderblock. A menagerie of rusted junk covered most of the mean, hardpan dirt yard below two large Chinese Elm trees and a tumble-down back porch. A once-white Buick with four flat tires dominated my view, and the morning light gleamed metallic on the car's lone hubcap. Was Killian in position behind the car? Or was he crouched farther back behind the tilted camper shell with busted windows resting on a heap of old tires and scrap lawn mowers?

A bead of sweat slid from my hairline. *Best not to think about officers hiding, ready to pounce.* I swiped it away and turned back to the shop. The open doorway provided an occasional glimpse of two men dressed in gray coveralls, working on a truck. I checked my watch. 11:45. Fifteen minutes later than Sudi's deadline.

Was the Showtime message a mistake? Was Sudi pissed I hadn't shown up on time? Had we blown it getting everything setup? I blotted the perspiration on my forehead with the back of my hand. A guy from the shop stepped out into the blistering heat, pulled a bandana from his head. Dreadlocks tumbled to his shoulders, and he used the bandana to wipe his face. He leaned against the grimy brick, pulled a pack of cigarettes from his front pocket and shook one out. He lit up, inhaled deeply, tilted his head back and blew a plume of smoke skyward.

Waiting in the car made my stomach crawl. I opened my door and got out with the idea of talking to Smoker Dude; find out if he knew Sudi. A vintage LeSabre turned left into the alley and stopped alongside my Ghia.

The driver's black-tinted window slid down about an inch and Sudi peered out, eyes roaming the area before switching to me. "You come alone?"

I nodded.

"You got the laptop and money?"

"Yes."

He inched the window down, exposing his whole face. "Let me see."

I took a breath. "I want to talk to Willie."

"Not 'til I see what you got."

I shrugged, hoping my face didn't betray my galloping heartbeat. "Seems we're at an impasse."

Sudi rolled his eyes. "What I got' ta put up with." He hit a button on the driver's side door and the backseat window slid down.

Willie popped into view sitting serenely against the backseat. She didn't appear restrained, nothing on her face to prevent her from speaking or screaming.

I blinked and bent down to get a better look. "Willie, you okay?" I asked.

Willie said. "All a big misunderstanding. I'll explain later, just please do as Mr. Sudi says."

What the hell was going on? Willie held hostage was the drama coup of a lifetime. Where were the anguished sobs? The histrionics?

"Enough with the yakking." The backseat window powered back up and Willie disappeared behind the tinted glass. "Show me the money."

I retrieved the attaché case from the passenger seat of the Ghia, opened it, and angled it so Sudi could see the top layer of twenties.

"Okay. Where's the laptop?"

I snapped the attaché closed, set it down next to my feet, turned, and grabbed the laptop from the passenger floor mat.

"Good. Now . . ." A flash of gray and Bus Stop Lady slid across the LeSabre's trunk, landed and yanked open Sudi's door before I could blink. She jerked Sudi from his seat and shoved him to the blacktop. I half expected the theme song from the TV show *Cops* to start as a burly guy exploded from the office attached to the body shop. Killian sprang from behind the rusted camper and rushed into the alley, weapon drawn, hollering at Sudi to stay down.

Killian opened Willie's door and helped her out. He tried to usher her toward the open shop door, but she pulled loose and ran toward the two officers scuffling on the ground with a writhing Sudi.

"Wait a minute," she screamed, waving her arms. "Leave that man alone."

"Stay back, ma'am!" Bus Stop Lady shouted.

"You don't understand," Willie said, twisting away as Killian made a grab for her. She changed direction, ran to the passenger side of the LaSabre, and snatched her purse. As she rounded the front of the car, the bus stop officer yelled for her to stay put or risk getting Tasered. A crowd had gathered on both sides of the alley. *Terrific. An audience for Willie to play to.*

Willie stopped and put her hands on her hips. "If you'll just listen, I can explain everything." She marched forward, purse open, rummaging around for who knows what.

"Willie!" I cried, and lunged for her as the officer took aim and pulled the Taser trigger. Willie dropped her purse, fell to the ground, shrieking and writhing.

Killian put his hand on my shoulder, clamping down in case I decided to join the fracas. "She'll be fine. Won't leave much of a mark."

I nodded and closed my eyes, not wanting to watch my mother flop around like a landed trout.

"Does she have a license to carry?" Killian asked.

I opened my eyes. "What?"

Killian pointed to the contents of her purse scattered on the hot asphalt. Among several tubes of lipstick, tissues, wallet, and various sales receipts lay a small handgun with what looked like a pearl handle.

"Oh crap," I said.

"My thought exactly," Killian replied.

Two patrol cars turned into the alley and parked behind the LeSabre. A subdued, handcuffed Sudi slid into the back of the first patrol car. Willie embraced the role of ultimate martyr, and shuffled head down, shoulders slumped, as an officer escorted her to the next squad car. With a tear-streaked face and anguished cry, she allowed the cop to help her into the back seat.

I turned to Killian. "I'm sure there's a logical explanation."

"Usually is." He picked up the gun, examined it and grinned. "Wow, it's a vintage lighter."

"Probably a prop used in a fifties or sixties movie."

He picked up the attaché case and frowned. "Where's the laptop?"

"What?" I turned in a complete circle, then stooped low and peered under my car. Nothing between the wheels but cracked asphalt and tenacious weeds. I stood and dusted my hands off. "It was right here." I pointed to a spot next to my feet. "Before all hell broke loose." I searched my car and Sudi's while Killian combed the surrounding area. The putrid pink thing had to be magic. It had vanished.

NINETEEN

"**W**HAT DO YOU MEAN VANISHED? How can a hot-pink laptop vanish in the middle of a police sting?" Yancy screeched. I held the cell phone away from my ear as I paced the sidewalk in front of the police station. The late-afternoon sun felt like a hot iron attempting to press the world into submission.

"I think I can use my laptop to continue communicating with Junkie." After his initial outburst, Yancy's voice was calm, almost quiet, like he was talking to himself. "But my laptop is not performing right. Remember, I explained there's a type of piggy back program running in the background."

I blew out a frustrated breath. A wide slick of perspiration plastered my shirt to my back as though the two were fused for eternity. "Yancy, do the math. Sudi is very likely Mr. Junkie. He's in custody and being grilled as we speak. You won't be communicating with Junkie." My stomach growled, reminding me it was way past noon and the doughnut I'd eaten at Reb's was just a fond memory.

"Mercedes, your math equation is totally erroneous. Sudi and Junkie *cannot* be the same person! Frobi was not just scamming people with caskets and art. She was on the verge of introducing what appears to be a harmless software program but hidden very deep on the benign program is what's called a piggyback program that tracks everything one does. The ramifications of this are astounding! Has anyone stopped to consider that maybe, just maybe, Sudi and Junkie crafted this Machiavellian scheme to throw everyone off?"

"And Sudi takes the fall for Junkie because they're such great pals? Even if Sudi and Junkie are separate people, Todd Sudi doesn't strike me as the self-sacrificing type. Willie swears he's not a kidnapper. He was only using her as insurance against trigger-happy cops. Sudi's a bone-head who wanted to make some quick money and leave town."

"That's what he wants everyone to think! He's totally oleaginous in all aspects of his perverted life. And think on this, why the sudden need to depart Portneuf Gap? Hmm?"

Hmm was right. Suddenly people had the urge to depart Portneuf Gap and I suspected it wasn't the heat. "Candlemass, pop a couple more pain pills and go take a long nap in a casket." I ended the call and returned to the air-conditioned police station lobby where Reb and Gram waited.

"Gram, I owe you big time for leaving Yancy home," I said, taking a swig from the can of Pepsi Reb offered. The cold swallow glided down my parched throat. "He's throwing a huge hissy fit about the missing laptop. He claims it holds a devious program that could start an apocalypse."

Gram sighed while her hand sought the pearls around her neck, polishing one between her fingers. "Yancy's a little freaked out right now. He doesn't believe this whole nightmare is really over."

I would never admit it to Yancy, but I felt the same way. Something was off. But what? The police felt certain Sudi would eventually confess to Frobi's murder. But I wasn't convinced and the feeling I'd missed something was like an itch deep inside I couldn't reach.

The door to the police inner sanctum opened and Willie emerged clutching Barkley Worthington's arm. "I am eternally grateful to you, Mr. Worthington. And I want to apologize for my role in helping Todd with his scheme. It all started out as a gag when Todd stopped by the house to return my cell phone."

"What?" Reb and I said in unison. Gram huffed something under her breath.

Willie shook her head and sighed. "Toddy seemed like such a gentle soul. You think you know someone."

"Why was he in such a rush to get out of town?" I asked.

Willie frowned, as well as her Botox treatment would allow. "Someone was threatening him."

"What type of threats?" Was Yancy right? Could the threats be related to Torture Junkie? Seemed like a stretch but stranger things had happened. The letter with the New York postmark had to enter into the equation, but how?

"He didn't say. At first I thought he was playing a practical joke, but after he called you he became all business. Didn't want to stop by his apartment to pack or gather anything, just wanted to put Portneuf Gap in his rearview mirror."

I turned to Barkley. "This has to help convince the police that Cary's innocent, right?"

"Too soon to tell," he said. "It depends on what Todd Sudi admits to during the interrogation. If he does confess, not a likely scenario but let's say he does, then Cary would be released. This isn't a one-hour police drama though. Criminals rarely confess."

"All of the painting equipment in the body shop will be tested for gold paint, right? It's the perfect setup to cover a person. There have to be fingerprints, hairs, fibers, something that can prove Cary's innocence." Reb said.

"There's definitely probable cause for a judge to issue a search warrant for the shop." Barkley said. "All of that testing takes time. Most likely the evidence will be sent to Boise for testing. Again, we're not in a one-hour TV drama."

Willie clapped her hands and cleared her throat. "I appreciate your insight, Mr. Worthington. You are certainly right about justice moving slowly, but, from here on out we must all have positive thoughts about Cary. If a negative thought enters your mind, you must banish it. I have great techniques I will share to help remove negativity. We will build a positive circle around my son. I suggest we gather later and have dinner somewhere nice? My treat for the stress I've caused everyone. We can brainstorm ways to help Cary breathe free once more."

Barkley coughed into his hand. "I appreciate the invitation, but Cassandra and I have business to discuss this evening over dinner." Gram's face softened and her relief was palpable. "If I hear any news about Cary I will call you immediately."

"Sorry, Willie. I'll take a rain check," Reb said, rummaging in her shoulder bag. "I have plans with Jack." She found her cell phone and began frantically punching numbers as she inched her way toward the door.

Willie wrapped her arm around my shoulders, "Guess it's just you and me, kiddo. Where should we eat?"

Eat? The word sounded foreign. Minutes before, I'd been hungry. Now, filling my knotted stomach was the last thing on my mind. I wanted a notebook and a quiet place to corral and write down my spinning thoughts. I was hoping to capture the elusive idea that I knew was locked somewhere in the nether regions of my mind. It might be the final piece to this insidious puzzle.

"We can put our minds together and brainstorm. It will be great."

"Right," I agreed. Brainstorming with someone other than Willie might just help. I considered and discarded Killian, he and Reb had plans. The best dispatcher ever, Floydean Mollicker, would be an asset if she wasn't working. Yancy? If he could shelve his paranoia and stay alert through his pain med haze he had more to gain by finding Torture Junkie if Junkie was the killer, and not sitting in jail.

"First, things first, dear." Willie rubbed a splotch of dirt off of her red Capri pants. "I know I look a fright, after the police brutality I've had to endure, but you simply must take me to Rent. A. Decent.

Car!" She strode toward the door, muttering her favorite line from
A *Streetcar Named Desire* about never relying on the kindness of
strangers ever again.

I hugged Gram, thanked Barkley for helping Willie avoid jail,
and asked him to let me know if he heard anything about Cary,
then hustled outside after Willie.

"I'm thinking something sporty in either red or yellow. And
with an air conditioner that could freeze the balls off a brass
monkey," Willie said as I unlocked the Ghia's passenger door. She
climbed in and quickly rolled down the window. "Kick this baby in
gear before I melt."

I turned right onto Yellowstone Avenue and headed north.
The Avis car rental agency was about five blocks from the police
station, housed in a converted gas station. I knew the chances of
finding exactly what Willie had in mind were slim to none. We
would persevere.

An hour later, the shiny red convertible VW bug parked in the
driveway made my poor Ghia look a little like the rattle trap Willie
had dubbed it. I took comfort in the fact that what the Ghia didn't
have in looks or creature comforts it made up for in speed and pure
classic style.

With the three dogs happily crunching dinner in the kitchen
and Willie singing in the shower upstairs, I decided to do
something productive and check my phone messages. I'd missed a
couple of calls while we were at the car rental agency. The first one
was Killian's deep voice asking me to please feed and water Eclipse.
Hmm. Guess Reb hadn't lied about their date. The next voicemail
was from Axel. A problem had come up so he'd have to take a rain
check on dinner. Damn. In all the excitement I'd forgotten about
our date. Forgetting a date with a sexy hunk proved stress could
dissolve brain cells. If this continued, I was doomed to inhabit an
assisted-living facility before my mother.

Axel's message left me both disappointed yet agitated. I trudged
out to the barn to take care of Eclipse. The big, black horse trotted

to the fence and hung his head over the rail as soon as I turned on the hose and stuck it in the trough.

"Hey, big guy. Want to hear about my day?"

He whinnied and tossed his head to scatter away pesky flies. I dug into my pocket and produced a couple of sugar cubes. His velvet muzzle brushed my palm and I stroked his sleek neck, explaining my problem as he savored the sugar.

"You agree, this whole idea of Sudi as a savage, calculating killer feels off?"

Always a great listener, Eclipse tossed his head in the affirmative. I patted his rump and headed to the barn to check his feed.

I poured oats into his bucket. "An unforeseen emergency makes Axel cancel our dinner plans is no big deal, right?" Eclipse had no answer, he was busy munching. "If it's no big deal, why is my gut instinct quivering a solid six on the Richter scale?"

My cell phone rang its generic ring making Eclipse shy away from his oats.

I dug it out of my back pocket, hoping, for once, that it might be a renter with a clogged toilet.

"I'm nearly ready. Are you done fiddling about in the barn? We have to get this show on the road." Willie said, each word rising in tone until she was nearly singing soprano.

Her announcement might make the average person assume she'd been making margaritas again. Nope. This was classic Willie, back in charge, with a new set of wheels.

"Great. I'll shower and change."

"Don't be silly, dear. You look great. Besides I'm starving, I could eat that big beast you're feeding."

"Okay. Just give me a couple of minutes, I'm almost done mucking out Eclipse's stall."

"On second thought, probably best you do shower. I'm going to pop down to the Gas n Go at the end of the road and pick up some staples. There's nothing fun to munch on and I'm in the mood for something spicy and salty. I'll be back in a New York minute."

She clicked off and Eclipse snorted.

"Right, I lied; your stall's fine." I tucked the phone back in my pocket. "Sometimes small white lies are essential when dealing with Willie." I explained, scratching between his ears as he bent his head to eat.

I left the barn and gave a quick sniff-check under my arm. Eeew. Guess it wasn't a lie after all. Trudging upstairs, my cell phone beeped a text-message alert from Reb's cell: *Meet me in the embalming room. Discovered something EXCITING!* Hmm. Had her date with Killian ended early? I sent back one word: *Now?* The reply: *Yes. Now. Now. Now!* Too bad I couldn't text an eye roll. However, this could be the excuse I needed to get out of Willie's brainstorming session.

I grabbed my keys from the hook by the back door along with a black marker from my purse. I printed on the back of a junk-mail envelope, Meeting at Mortuary. Back Soon. I was fairly certain Willie wouldn't follow me. She wouldn't want to run into Gram and face the inevitable elephant in the room that Yancy had alluded to? Gram had resources and Willie knew it. She wouldn't plan a harebrained kidnapping to bilk Gram out of money . . . would she? This subject was best left alone, at least for now.

On my way into town, I phoned Reb. Two rings and her voicemail came on. I clicked off and pressed harder on the gas pedal, praying I wasn't breaking the speed limit for some new makeup technique Reb had discovered that would give the deceased a totally natural appearance.

A strong north wind picked up, sending obsidian clouds scudding across the sky, blotting out the vanishing sunset. I rolled down my window, letting the heavy scent of impending rain wash over me.

The funeral home looked dark and deserted as I drove down the long driveway. I guessed Gram and Mr. Barkley were out, hopefully enjoying a cozy dinner for two. No lights shone from the apartment above the garage, either. Yancy must've taken my advice, popped a couple of pain pills and was blissfully floating in la-la land. I parked next to the back porch as lightning split the dark sky. Fat raindrops pinged off the Ghia's roof and I made a dash for the back door. Fumbling for the right key, I leaned against the kitchen door and nearly fell face first across the threshold as the door swung open. Weird. Gram always locked the doors when she went out.

"Gram?" I shouted into the dark interior. My only answer was a rumble of thunder. "Reb?"

Silence. A shudder had the hairs on my neck tingling. *Come on, Harrigan. Pull up those big-girl boots. Dead bodies are harmless.* I flipped on the kitchen light and strode to the door that connected Gram's living quarters with the mortuary. Opening the heavy door, I switched on the wall sconces softly lighting the hallway that ran the length of the building. The deep burgundy carpet muffled my footsteps as I made my way to the elevator that would take me down to the embalming and preparation rooms. This hallway had terrified Cary as a child. He'd been convinced lost and angry souls wandered it's length seeking revenge; Reb and I had played along feeding his fear every chance we got. Now, as another volley of thunder boomed and the lights flickered, a shudder raced up my spine and I had to gulp down an anxiety knot. *Payback really can be a bitch.*

The lights dimmed again as I pushed the button and waited for the elevator to rumble up from the basement. The doors slid open. I peered into the ancient box and changed my mind. If the power failed I'd be trapped.

Not trusting Reb to start the backup generator, I opted for the staircase around the corner. I gripped the handrail and hurried down while trying to ignore my queasy stomach.

Don't be such a baby, Harrigan. You've been in the basement thousands of times.

"Reb, what's the big surprise?" I called as I reached the bottom. Again, silence.

The hallway stretched dark and daunting before me, the only illumination coming from beneath the closed storage room door at the end of the hall. I flipped the light switch at the bottom of the stairs. Nothing.

Uh-uh. This is the part where the hapless movie heroine goes bumbling into the monster's trap. "Not this time," I mumbled, sneaking down the cement corridor. I crept up to the storage room, listening, hoping Reb would make some tell-tale sound. I heard a rustle and burst through the door, ready with a loud "Gotcha" that died before it reached my lips.

In the center of the room was a polished oak bier. Atop the bier sat a pine casket, the top half open revealing Yancy, clad in silk pajamas, eyes closed, hands carefully folded across his chest in the classic eternal pose. Stricken mute, I watched his chest rise and fall before letting out a painful pent-up breath. Marching to the open casket, I put my face close to Yancy's and through gritted teeth whispered, "I'm *not* amused."

He didn't stir. Just as I thought; zonked on pain pills. *But what was he doing in the basement in a casket? Pre-arranged plan with Reb or his own sick joke?* I straightened and surveyed the room. The only illumination was a recessed light directly over the casket, the rest of the room was cloaked in shadows with numerous places from which Reb could pounce. *Two can play this game.* I punched her number and waited for the ring, ready to do a little pouncing of my own.

Her phone rang behind me. The door slammed shut. I turned ready to give Reb hell.

A tall figure stepped from the shadows, wearing a black ski mask and holding Reb's cell phone in a gloved hand. Definitely not Reb. And definitely not good.

TWENTY

T HE EYES STARING OUT FROM THE SKI MASK were intense blue and glittered with demented excitement.

"Put your phone on the floor and kick it to me," Ski Mask said, voice deep and muffled.

"You have my friend's phone. You don't need mine," I said, very cool and calm . . . except my voice came out a cracked mixture of Minnie Mouse and Goofy.

Where the hell was Reb?

Tied up and stuffed in a closet? Or worse?

Ski Mask stepped farther into the light and raised his right arm; his gloved fingers curled tightly around a huge black handgun with nary a weapon in sight for yours truly, unless I counted Yancy's block head.

"I will only tell you once more, kick your phone to me!"

Give up my phone? I might as well crawl into the casket with Yancy. Wait!

I could dive into the casket, knock it over, and use it as a shield. Then what? I glanced at Yancy, still sleeping away, and noted a trickle of blood snaking from behind his left ear down into his collar. *Freakin' great. The poor guy wasn't loopy on pills, he was knocked out!*

Unless I wanted a giant knot on my own head (or worse), I had to keep my phone. I bent slowly, placed my phone on the floor, stuck my finger down my throat and made retching sounds.

"Son-of-a-bitch. Are you going to puke?" Ski Mask asked. "No puking. I hate puke!"

From the corner of my eye I watched him lower his gun. I got out one more retch, scooped up my phone and ran, head down, straight into his stomach. He let out a muffled "Oof." I sprinted for the door and yanked it open. A shot whined past my head, my ears echoing from the blast. *Feet, don't fail me now.*

The hallway stretched before me like a millennium of darkness. My back tingled at the thought of a bullet exploding through me before I could reach the staircase. A second shot zinged the wall next to me. Dodging into the closest embalming room, I slammed and latched the flimsy lock, and flipped on the light. Now what?

"Open the door, Mercedes, or I'll blast my way in."

I wanted to tell Ski Mask his impersonation of a Big Bad Wolf stunk, except the way he said my name sparked a memory. I knew that voice. But where and when had I heard it? Carefully modulated syllables with a petulant, yet arrogant quality. I closed my eyes, letting my mind pull together the voice, body posture, intense blue eyes, and . . . no way! Albert Lechman, supposedly the biggest fan of Sherrilyn Sanborn the one of the cooking channel's southern diva's was ready to huff and puff and blow me away?

I glanced around the room for something to shove in front of the door. A slug slammed through the middle of the flimsy wood, the blast reverberating like thunder. I hit the ground and scrambled under the embalming table. Two fumbled misdials and my shaking fingers finally punched 911 on my phone. To my horror nothing. No signal. I forgot the embalming room was a dead zone in more ways than one. A sob erupted from the pit of my stomach.

Lechman pounded a quick shave and a haircut against the damaged wood. "Open the door and I'll make this quick and painless. Otherwise . . ."

"Cops are on the way!" I screamed, shoving my useless phone into my back pocket.

A hailstorm of slugs tattooed a crazy pattern across the hollow-core door. A couple of wood-rattling thuds and the door slammed open. Lechman stepped into the room, ski mask in one hand, gun in the other. A leer plastered on his sweaty face. Jack Nicholson's eerie crooning, "Here's Johnny" sprang to mind.

Scrambling out from under the table, holding back a shriek, I ran to the nearest counter and grabbed a Trocar stick. The thought of ramming the sharp point of this fluid sucking instrument into Lechman gave me some small satisfaction. Especially when the man looked crazed enough to eat his young and put a bullet neatly between my eyes.

"Lie down. On your back." He motioned with the gun to the embalming table and produced a small roll of duct tape from the back pocket of his black jeans.

Serpentine!

Thoughts of moving targets being harder to hit and sprinting in a zigzag pattern jammed my brain. I heaved the Trocar like a javelin at Lechman and took off for the opposite corner. Great plan. Too bad I tripped. I sprawled on the cold tile floor, the impact knocking the air from my lungs with a solid whump.

Pain seared the back of my head as Lechman lifted me off the floor by my hair and pressed me tight against him. His breath smelled like peppermint-tinged blue cheese as he whispered, "Time's up."

"Cops . . . on . . . way" I said, hitching air into my lungs.

His expression switched from eager, wide-eyed, almost salivating, to can-we-spell-robotic control.

Whoa, scary!

"Fine. Plan B it is," he said. With the gun barrel kissing my temple and his hand twisted in my hair, we marched in tandem out of the embalming room and back to the storeroom. I shot a look at Yancy still lying in the casket, willing him to sit up or groan, anything to create a diversion. Bad news; Yancy didn't move. Good news: his chest rose and fell in a slow rhythmic motion. At least he was still among the living.

Lechman shoved me toward a folding chair behind the casket. "Take a seat."

I grabbed the chair and whirled, holding it in front of me like a lion tamer, ready to rush Lechman. He put the gun against Yancy's right eye.

"Ready when you are," he said.

I swore under my breath and put the chair down.

"Now sit."

Seething inside, I did as I was told. He tossed the duct tape to me. "Tape your ankles together."

"Not on your life," I said.

"Running out of patience here," he growled and tapped the gun against Yancy's eyelid.

Panic bubbled in my chest. I bent and taped my ankles, while my mind raced through different escape methods.

"Good girl. Now toss the tape to me and put your hands on your head."

"No," I said, folding my arms and praying he wouldn't put a bullet in Yancy.

His head jerked up, eyes narrowed.

"Not until you tell me what's up with that freakin' pink laptop! And where is Rebbie?"

He shrugged. "That laptop holds a computer program worth more wealth than you could possibly imagine."

"A computer program?" Damn, Yancy had either solved the mystery or was close. Now if he'd only wakeup and create a diversion.

A smile quirked his lips. "I know you're not computer savvy like your friend, Candlemass. He's close to brilliant, but I'm better. I had lots of time to hone my computer skills in prison after Frobi Fisher, aka Samantha Schultz, framed me for the money laundering scheme we were running. Our third partner, Tripper, disappeared into the wind leaving me the convenient scapegoat."

Tripper? That name sparked a memory . . . from where? Not a recent rental application but something to do with my rentals. I gasped. Tripper was the name on the envelope in Sudi's mail. Todd Sudi was a wanted man?

"Your poker face sucks but I'll give you points for figuring out that Sudi isn't who he claims to be."

"You used Sudi's repair shop to spray Frobi?"

"I thought using gold paint was brilliant. Totally symbolic of Fisher's money-grubbing persona. Too bad symbolism is wasted on the Portneuf Gap Keystone Cops. Your mother getting the Taser treatment was the perfect distraction. No one paid attention in all the commotion to a guy shoving a laptop into his coveralls and strolling away."

"You were dreadlock dude?"

He gave a little bow. "That be me. As for your ditzy friend, she isn't here. I trailed her from the police station to her house. While she sang in the shower, I helped myself to a container of pasta salad, a couple of bucks, and her cell phone."

I gulped past the repulsive thought of Lechman rummaging through Reb's house while she lathered away in the shower. "A container of salad?"

"Guy's got'ta eat. I also searched your house, FYI your dogs are pathetic deterrents. Searched your house top to bottom for the laptop while they followed me wagging their tails.

Eww! Leachman had violated my home? It was his scent I'd detected.

Double eww!

"Oh-kay, questions answered, let's move on to the part where you put your hands on your head before I make mincemeat of your friend's face."

His smooth manner and dulcet tones sent cold fear crawling through my stomach, making me quake inside much more than if he'd gone on a hate-filled rant. His words spilled from his pouty lips, covering his calm demeanor like coal dust on snow.

I slowly did as instructed, eyes darting, mind rushing through evasive maneuvers.

Lechman hurried behind me and I felt hard steel pressed against the back of my head. "Nice and easy, put your right hand down to your side."

The duct tape stuttered as Lechman fumbled to unroll it one handed. In my mind I saw Frobi, naked, glittering with gold spray paint, eyelids taped shut. Raw panic clawed my throat. I gritted my teeth, raised my heels, leaned forward a little and shoved backward with all my strength. The chair toppled knocking Lechman and me to the floor.

I scrabbled and shoved, belly-crawling across the floor, frantic to be rid of Lechman and the stupid chair.

"Yancy!" I screamed. A knee jammed between my shoulder blades cut my scream short. Lechman rolled me onto my back, jerked my arms together at my waist and taped my wrists in one smooth move.

"Try to be a nice guy and this is the thanks I get." He hefted me over his shoulder and stomped back to the embalming room, straight back to the refrigeration unit with closed heavy metal doors that concealed two coffin-like body compartments.

Lechman dumped me on the floor and opened both doors. He tugged on the top body drawer. It slid out with a slight screech. I thrashed and screamed, but Lechman wrestled me into the holding tray.

"Wait," I wheezed through claustrophobic lungs. "You have the laptop! I'll cover whatever money you lost on the paintings."

Patting the bottom of the tray beside my feet, he grimaced. "What the hell, this feels about room temp." He ducked behind the metal door. "Why isn't this unit running?"

"You want the rest of your payment, right? I can get you lots more money!" I cried out.

He poked his head around the door. "Really? Where is it?"

"My grandmother has a safe deposit box."

He pursed his lips then checked his watch. "Too risky." He started to roll the drawer in and stopped. "Is embalming fluid as flammable as gas? Maybe I'll try mixing the two."

I pulled my knees to my chest stopping the compartment's progress. He pulled the drawer back out then gave it a quick shove. The metal casing rammed my knees straight. The drawer slammed shut.

Claustrophobia. Fear of fire. Add spiders and the man would've hit my top three phobias.

The pungent odor of gas and formaldehyde reached deep inside my steel tomb. *Oh crap. He was serious.*

I screamed until my throat hurt. Tears wet my cheeks. I stopped. Screaming wasn't working. The funeral home would burn with me and Yancy. Gram would lose all her life's work and more.

Hot anger knocked panic out of the way, clearing my mind. I slowly worked my arms up until my bound wrists were close to my teeth. I ripped at tape and flesh, working my hands and mouth from side to side, tasting salty blood, until finally my wrists separated.

Smoke. I smelled smoke. I worked first one arm and then the other over my head, found the end of the locker and pushed. Nothing. Lechman placing me backwards in the drawer meant I couldn't use my legs to leverage my way to freedom. I pushed again. My metal coffin slid forward ever so slightly. I shoved harder, again and again making the drawer move inch by inch. With each shove, smoke filtered through the gap, stinging my eyes, filling my lungs. Coughing made it harder to push.

"I'm trying, Gram," I whispered and continued pushing.

Wham. The door slid all the way out. I scrambled upright, tumbling onto the floor, blinking through the haze. A hand reached down. I latched on and heaved myself upright, punching at the hazy figure before me. My fist connected, sending a zinging pain clear to my elbow. Steel-like arms wrapped around me pinning my flailing arms to my side.

"Luv, I'm here to help, not harm," a soothing Aussie accent breathed next to my ear.

Axel? My knees threatened to fold.

"Can't go soft yet, luv. Buck up a bit longer, I need your help."

Axel released me, his eyes roamed my face. He frowned and wiped his thumb gently across my lips, then bent and ripped the tape away from my ankles.

"Easy does it," he said, guiding me through the smoke to a figure slumped on the floor.

"Plan is, I'll break the window and boost you to safety. Then you need to lean back in and grab ol' Yancy here under the arms while I hoist him out. Reckon you're up for that?"

I nodded, hoping I could be all that Axel needed.

He pulled a bunch of paper towels from a wall dispenser, and climbed onto a chair. "Fetch something to smash this glass with."

I grabbed a broom from the corner. "Wait. How will you get out?"

"No worries." He bent, gave me a swift kiss, then smashed the pane with the broom handle until the opening was clear of glass. Wrapping his hand in paper towels, he swept away stray fragments, hopped off the chair, and made a cup with his hands. "Up you go."

As soon as my foot touched his palms, Axel nearly launched me through the ceiling. I grabbed the window ledge and pulled myself out into the night air. Blessed, cool night air.

I took a deep breath, turned and angled my body back into the smoke-belching hell. My fingers grasped the top of Yancy's over-gelled hair, then his shoulders and I finally slid my hands under his armpits. "Go!" I screamed. With some effort we managed to get Mr. Deadweight out. I dragged Yancy a safe distance, then raced back to help Axel. We collided next to the yew bush and I found myself tangled in a heap of arms and legs for the second time that night.

Axel gently took my face in his strong hands and kissed me, long and slow. His soft lips pressed against mine, sending serious clanging through my numb brain, or maybe the clamor was coming from all the emergency vehicles and squad cars converging on the funeral home. At the moment, it was hard to tell.

Axel reluctantly broke away, lifted his head, and blew out a breath. His beautiful eyes clouded for a moment. "Had me worried, luv. Thought you and Yance there were goners."

"How . . . ?" I began.

He placed gentle fingers against my lips. "Call it gut instinct . . . wanted to see you before I left. Tried your cell. No luck. Came here to see if your lovely Grandmum might know your whereabouts." He climbed to his feet and helped me up, wrapping me in strong arms for a gentle squeeze before we crossed to "ol' Yance". Axel placed a hand on his chest.

Yancy's eyes fluttered, opened, and then widened as he took in his surroundings. He coughed and pulled a face. "What the hell?" His right fingers tapped his forehead. "I must be febrile, seeing lights, ugh, tasting smoke." He groaned and shifted his gaze to me. "Be a dear one and fetch me another pain pill. I want to return to la-la land and my comfy bed."

"Febrile?" Axel repeated, checking Yancy's pulse.

"Thinks he's either delirious or hallucinating," I laughed, patting Yancy on the shoulder. "You'll be fine, Candlemass."

From the corner of my eye I caught sight of Killian racing across the grass. Axel's head snapped in Killian's direction. He stopped assessing Yancy's condition. A huge grin split his soot-smeared face. He pulled me into an embrace and kissed me again before adjusting his wrinkled shirt. "I fear someone will notice how you've seduced me."

I giggled "Lucky you. Now you have bragging rights, pal."

Let the games begin.

TWENTY-ONE

I WATCHED JACK AND AXEL EGO-WRESTLE like Bandy roosters while a very capable paramedic poked, prodded and asked me questions. Gram, Rebbie, and Willie made a half-circle behind the paramedic, on guard like frantic mama bears each one ready to leap into the fray and play Florence Nightingale. Tired to the bone, I wished I could raid Yancy's pain pills and join him in la-la land.

The fire was out and I shared Gram's obvious relief that the damage had been contained mainly to a couple of rooms in the basement. Another plus: not a single deceased loved one had ended up cremated instead of properly prepped for burial in the family plot.

"Enough!" I cried. "Gram and Willie, stop fawning." I turned to the paramedic who wore the name tag "Gretchen" over her right breast pocket. "I don't need stitches, nothing's broken, no severe smoke inhalation, right?"

Gretchen mulled over her answer before nodding her head. "It'd be good to take a ride to the E.R.," she said. "Maybe let one of the doctor's there take a look."

I scooted off the gurney I'd been trapped on for what seemed a century, started to shake my head and thought better of making any sudden movement. "I need to go home, take a shower . . ." thoughts of Lechman prowling Reb's house made me amend that to sponge bath." . . . feed my poor dogs, and sleep for a week or two."

Willie piped up. "I'll drive you home and get you settled all comfy in your bed, dearest."

Dearest?

"Nursing a loved one comes easily to me since I played a background nurse on a short-lived daytime medical drama." Willie favored the closest male paramedic with a comely smile.

"She's coming home with me," Reb said, hands on her hips; eyes blazing a scorched-earth glare. "I can check on her between showing houses and looking for new employment."

Gram cleared her throat. "That's very nice of both of you, but I insist Mercedes stay with me. What she really needs is good home cooking for a day or two."

Visions of fresh-from-the-oven cinnamon rolls danced in my head and tempted my taste buds. I banished such thoughts and said, "I can't leave my dogs." *At least not in Willie's care.* "Plus, I'm babysitting that Tasmanian devil disguised as a Schnauzer."

"Not to worry," Gram said. "The dogs can stay in the kitchen and keep me company while I cook."

Does the woman love me or what?

THE NEXT AFTERNOON, STUFFED WITH EVERY comfort food I ever craved, I pulled into my driveway, cut the engine on the Ghia and sighed. "No place like home," I mumbled into Bacall's furry ear as she bounded into my lap and stood on her hind legs, tail slapping the steering wheel. The three dogs bolted for the front porch as I climbed from the car and eyed the peeling paint on the window trim, yellowed patches of lawn begging for water, and weeds choking out the poor petunias lining the front walk. My place had never looked better.

The front door opened. Cary stepped out onto the porch as the three pooches raced inside. He bounded down the stairs and had me in a bear-hug before I could blink.

"Damn, but you still look like something the cat wouldn't drag in," he laughed.

"Yeah? Brave words from the guy who started all this."

"I know." Cary set me back on my feet. He shoved his hands in the pockets of his khaki shorts and studied his bare feet. "Man, if I could turn back time, believe me I'd find a way."

I tousled his hair. "Sounds like the makings of a Cher ballad. Sure to be a hit."

Cary gave a half-hearted shrug and tried for a smile.

"Make yourself useful. Lift that barge, tote that bale of luggage inside and all is forgiven," I said motioning to the two big suitcases Willie had crammed with almost everything I owned and sent over to Gram's.

Inside I found Willie in a packing frenzy. Suitcases, clothes, and shoes had taken over my upstairs. She gave me a quick peck on the cheek when I reached the top landing, then resumed hollering into her cell. I walked back downstairs and discovered Cary in the kitchen feeding leftovers to the dogs.

"Cary!"

"Just look at those faces. They need a treat after all they've been through."

"Treat yes. Half a pan of lasagna, no." I snatched the pan from him and shoved it back in the fridge. "What are your plans now?"

He opened the fridge, retrieved the lasagna and started shoving cold forkfuls into his mouth. "I'm headed back to sun and surf territory. Buddy of mine just opened a school, claims he needs a partner to help satisfy all those high-paying tourists dying to hang ten." He grinned and the last of my anxiety melted. My surfer bum brother was back.

"Who's Willie yakking at?" I asked, grabbing a Pepsi from the fridge.

"Her latest agent. Tryouts for a new commercial start in two days." Cary answered around a mouthful of lasagna. He swallowed and continued. "She's exactly the type," he sketched quotation marks in the air with his fingers, "the commercial dudes are lookin' for. Once she nails the audition, her flagging career will soar into the stratosphere. Or so she says. We board a little prop plane this afternoon, fly to Boise and eventually catch a red-eye flight to John Wayne Airport. Tomorrow at this time I'll be staring at that beautiful ocean."

"She rushed to your aide in a tiny plane and now she's returning home in one? Willie hates flying in anything smaller than a 747." I said, sipping my drink. The first swallow down my raw throat burned, but the next numbed and tasted wonderful.

"One must suffer for true art!" Willie waltzed into the kitchen, eyes glowing, grinning like she'd won a million-dollar lottery. "Franz says the part was written for *moi*." She grabbed the can from my hand and finished it.

"Wonderful." I didn't ask what the commercial was about fearing a long explanation about the artistic value of selling Preparation H or some such middle-age staple.

"I hate to leave you in your hour of need, so I've arranged for Rebbie to come stay with you." Willie took me by the shoulders and stared hard at me. "She's confused and needs your wisdom right now as much as you need her help."

I nodded, not sure how to reply to that statement. No surprise, Willie had turned the past week into some little melodrama with me and Reb in the starring roles. I intended to play along until she was safely aboard the twin-engine plane.

Willie stroked my cheek. "That's my brave little soldier." Luckily she flounced from the room before Cary and I started laughing.

I sobered as a thought hit me. "You are so lucky Lechman confessed everything to me or you'd still be behind bars. And you're double lucky I survived his plan to roast me alive!" I shuddered.

Cary pulled me into a gentle hug. "I owe Danforth, big time, for saving my big sis. I would've been there for you if I wasn't locked up." His eyes filled and a lone tear slid down his cheek.

"You've always wanted to play fireman." I brushed the tear from his face. "All charges have been dropped, right? Local authorities and the FBI are okay with you returning to California?"

"Yeah. Sure. All charges are null and void. They have my number if they need any more info." Cary released me, turned and picked up Bogart, holding him close, talking into his fur.

Uh-huh. "What about those shoddy caskets and the artwork? Are the paintings real or fake?"

"I honestly do not know. Frobi played me for a total patsy."

"You never met the Curator?" He shook his head. "Guy's powerful. He hired a hit man to retrieve the paintings and shut Frobi up permanently."

"Lechman?"

"That's the popular opinion. You know, when I thought I was about to be barbequed a crazy thought hit me. Maybe Lechman is the pyromaniac who's been terrorizing the town. He seemed almost sexually aroused when he was splashing accelerant around. Pretty sure I heard him giggle." I shuddered and hoped nightmares about fires were not in my future. "Guess we'll see if the fires stop."

"Again, sis. So sorry I brought this to your doorstep." He raised his eyes for a moment and took a deep breath.

I waited.

He blew out his breath, petted Bogart's ears and stared at a spot above my head. When his blue eyes finally met mine, I could see that he knew I knew. He wasn't blameless. But he'd learned a hard lesson. We'd let it go at that.

I threw my arms around him and hugged him tight. Bogart grumbled and Cary planted a kiss on the top of my head.

"Love you, sis."

"Right back at ya, bro," I whispered past the lump in my throat.

My cell phone broke the moment. Nuzzling Bogart, Cary left the kitchen while I answered the call. A woman with a slight accent wanted to see the apartment listed on Redfin. *Apartment? Earth to Harrigan, life goes on. Get your butt in gear.*

We arranged to meet in twenty minutes, I hollered up the stairs that I'd be back and headed out the back door. I met Killian at by the gate.

"Hey," I said.

"Hey yourself. How're you feeling?" He took hold of my hand.

"Good. Great. You?"

"Good. Thought you'd like to know we found Lechman's rental parked near the airport. He didn't show up on any of the passenger lists, didn't rent a plane, and no one recognized his picture, but man like him must have fake ID's out the wazoo, he's quite the chameleon."

Cold goose bumps dotted my skin. I shuddered and Killian pulled me into his arms. "We *will* find him, Sadie. I promise that son-of-a-bitch'll never bother you again."

"Right." I let out a shaky breath.

"Hey, the FBI is all over this. APB's on the guy have gone to several agencies. We'll catch him."

I nodded against his chest. "Speaking of APB's, Cary's cool to leave for California, right?" *Not that I didn't trust my brother, but . . .*"

Killian stiffened for a fraction of a second. "Yeah, he's been cleared. Does your brother always land on his feet?"

"You mean after doing something supremely stupid? Pretty much, yeah."

Eclipse whinnied from the corral. "Better go see the big guy," Killian said. Still, he kept me in his gentle embrace. "Where are you headed?" he asked.

"To show an apartment." I sighed and moved away.

"You have your cell? It's charged?"

I patted my purse. "Yes, locked and loaded."

He stroked my cheek. "Take care."

I drove into town on auto pilot, my mind occupied with thoughts of Axel and Killian. Axel had breached Gram's stronghold last night to kiss me goodbye and tell me he'd be back ASAP. After he and his crew got the California fire under control.

Considering California fires, that could be awhile.

Now Killian was showing more than friendly affection. Was it because of Axel's interest? Or the fact I'd nearly become a crispy critter? I sighed. My muddled brain wasn't ready to tackle such issues. I chose to fall back on the Scarlet O'Hara plan: I'd think about such things tomorrow.

I pulled into the parking spot in front of the vacant apartment Cary and Frobi had shared. It would be good to rent it, get back to reality instead of living in the nightmare of a week dominated by greed and deception.

Dexter stepped out of his apartment. "You look good, Mercedes. How're you feeling?"

"I'll be fine once Lechman is caught."

He nodded. "Amen to that. The other day, you asked me if I remembered anything about the night that poor gal was murdered."

"Did you?" I climbed out of my car, and used my hand to visor my eyes against the blazing sun.

"Watching the news last night about the fire and looking at Lechman's photo jogged my memory. Night of the murder, I saw Lechman and that ghost buster guy standing together across the street. They looked right chummy, talking, gesturing while the coroner removed the body. But next time they were together they acted like they'd never laid eyes on each other. Agatha ended up doing the introductions between them."

"Lechman and Martin?"

"No. Lechman and that fellow from Australia. Danforth. Not sure if it means anything but I thought you'd want to know. Showing the apartment?"

"Yes."

Violet hollered from inside the apartment. "Dexter, I need your help."

"Duty calls." He disappeared inside.

I opened the vacant apartment and flipped on the living room light. Dexter had to be confused about Lechman and Axel. Axel hadn't arrived in Portneuf Gap until after Frobi was murdered. I walked into the kitchen and hit the light switch. The front door slammed shut. I whirled and squealed like a little girl. Axel, sexy and rugged, leaned against the door jam.

"Hey," he said.

My hand flew to my chest, my heart beating wildly against the palm of my hand. I blew out a breath and forced myself to relax. "Hey, yourself. I thought you were fighting fires in California."

He grinned. "Few things I need to tie up before I join my crew."

"Ghost busting with Martin?"

He barked a short laugh. "No. I've had more than enough of that delusional fellow."

A flash of pink caught my eye. To my right, tucked into a corner of the kitchen counter, Frobi's laptop lay open. The Web site on the screen looked like the site Yancy had discovered. *Oh, crap. I knew where Lechman was.* I inched closer to Axel and whispered, "Lechman's here. We need to leave."

"No worries, Luv. I'm on top of this."

"You don't understand!" I hissed. "He's a hit man!"

Axel tipped his head back and laughed.

I wanted to shush him but his laugh clicked the last puzzle pieces neatly into place.

"Lechman isn't the hit man, is he?"

His grin widened. He looked more feral than handsome.

I turned to run. His fingers twined around my hair and he slammed my head against the living room wall. Pain pulled me up short as tears filled my eyes. Strong arms wrapped around me and he half-dragged, half-carried me down the hall and into the back bedroom where he shoved me down in the middle of the floor.

I landed on my hands and knees, panting, head throbbing, eyes level with the open closet. I gasped.

Lechman *was* here.

His body was sprawled against the corner of the closet, a neat bullet hole in the middle of his forehead. Bile rose in my throat.

"Lechman a hired assassin? That's rich." Axel shut the bedroom door. "He had a gift for duping the gullible, IRS scams, bogus emails from AT&T . . . but he lacked foresight. He did have a thing about fire, it was his idea to trap you and ol' Yance then burn down the funeral parlor. I nixed that plan, but he was as stubborn as he was stupid. Lucky for you I knew he wouldn't listen. Rule number one: a true professional doesn't cause collateral damage unless there are no other options. I only teamed with Al Lechner, that's his real name, to get hold of that sweet computer scheme."

"Lechner?"

"Lechman, Lechner, close enough he wouldn't screw up his new identity. Google Lechner and you'll find he was once charged with murdering his father and trying to cover it up with fire. Also has a long history of fraud investigations, recently big in Bitcoin, crypto BS. Just like dear Frobi. Difference was she mastered becoming a ghost, never got caught. Never enough evidence to charge her. She never did time, always made sure other people took the fall."

A gun with a silencer appeared in his right hand. "Sorry, Luv. Time to wrap up all loose ends."

I closed my eyes, bent over and stuck my fingers down my throat, hoping it would work the same as it did with Lechman, aka Lechner.

"No. No! Stop!" Axel cried.

I shook my head and continued making retching sounds.

"That's so vile. Stop!" Axel lowered the gun and grimaced.

Gathering my courage, I ran head down, ramming Axel in the stomach. He let out a "woof" and I bolted for the kitchen. Grabbing the kitchen door jam, I skidded into the kitchen, snatched the pink laptop from the counter and raced out the back door.

Axel burst from the apartment bellowing like a wounded bull. I scaled the chain-link fence that separates my complex from the river, and let the laptop dangle in the air above the water.

"No!" Alex lunged a second too late. The laptop made a perfect arch, landing with a beautiful splash in the river below.

Hands locked around my neck, Axel dragged me from the fence. I kicked and flailed with all my strength, but his brutal grip only tightened. Ears ringing, vision blurring, I thrashed, failing to break his hold.

Then I was on the ground, gasping air, looking through a blurry fog at two figures rolling and cursing on the grass. One of the figures went limp, the other one stood and pushed his glasses back onto his nose. Martin Mangum smoothed his stripped polo shirt, picked up some sort of large square gadget he'd used to bean Axel and gently placed it in his backpack.

"He is not a paranormal investigator. Guy's a total phony! He laughed at me!" Martin jostled Axel's shoulder with the toe of his shoe. "Who's laughing now? Huh? Who's laughing now?"

TWENTY-TWO

"**B**ASICALLY NO ONE WAS WHO THEY claimed to be, yet they were all chasing after the pink laptop." Willie said, "This truly is life imitating art, the whole thing is very similar to that marvelous vintage movie, *It's A Mad, Mad, Mad, Mad World*," she sighed. "You know, I should've tumbled to Sudi's deception."

"Really?" Yancy said. He gave my front porch swing a nudge with his toe and he and Willie continued a slow sway.

"Yes. Right from the get-go he just didn't seem like a Todd." Willie tsked-tsked and shook her head. "He is a perfect character study though; criminal charges from New York to Atlanta." She clapped her hands and smiled. "Up close and personal experience like that cannot be taught in drama class."

Turned out Sudi/Tripper was wanted by authorities in connection with a cold case murder of a bookie in New York, plus a charge of embezzlement from a former employer in Atlanta. His auto repair shop was a perfect well-oiled money laundering venture. Stephen Sudi, Tripper's silent partner in New York, had learned Tripper's past was closing in; but I figured, even if the letter had been delivered on time, Tripper would've ignored the 'Move Now' message. The man was obsessed with getting the laptop once he figured out Frobi had stumbled onto the scam of the century. Greed and Willie were his eventual downfall.

Cary loaded the last of Willie's suitcases into the trunk of the little VW rental. "Shame the laptop is somewhere in the Portneuf River. A program worth killing for now sleeps with the fishes." He looked at Yancy reclining next to Willie. "Scout's honor you didn't make a copy?"

"No. I. Did. Not." Yancy scratched at a scab on his eyebrow. "And FYI, FBI divers found the laptop. Government top secret computer geeks are doing their best to retrieve the data. Too bad they haven't asked for my help."

Cary chuckled, closed the trunk, then wrapped an arm around me. "Thanks for everything. After devouring all those Nancy Drew books," he gave me a squeeze. "Criminals don't stand a chance." He ruffled my hair. "Are you really okay? We can postpone our flight for a day or two."

"We most certainly *cannot*," Willie cried. "Our departure is already twenty-four hours late." Cary and I bit back a laugh at the stricken look on her face. Willie smoothed her perfect hair-do and stood up from the swing. "I mean, Rebbie is here to help your sister. And goodness, your grandmother is in the kitchen making all kinds of food. That wonderful officer Killian will no doubt . . ."

I held my hand up. "I'm fine."

It wasn't a lie. Alex Danforth's days of fighting fires and murdering people for money had come to a halt. Languishing behind bars can crimp even the best hit man's plans.

Reb came out of the house carrying a small paper sack. She handed the sack to Willie. "This is that special potpourri I mentioned, it's a Middle Eastern recipe that a client shared. It's supposed to bring the recipient powerful luck in business ventures."

Willie clutched it to her bosom with one hand and hugged Reb with the other. "Thank you, my dear girl. I'll tuck some in my bra before the audition. I'll call and let you know how it goes."

I caught Cary's raised eyebrow and gave a shrug. If Willie and Reb had bonded, so be it. Willie calling Reb with her latest drama instead of me was not a bad thing.

Gram joined the group on the porch as goodbyes, smooches, promises to keep in touch, and more smooches were exchanged. Gram even held Willie's hand when they said farewell. We all waved in the afternoon heat as we watched the VW drive away.

"Axel, that gorgeous hunk, actually was a fire fighter?" Yancy asked.

"Yes," I said. "Killian said he confessed dropping into the middle of a raging inferno gave him the same thrill and adrenalin rush as committing murder for money. He's also claiming Lechman was solely responsible for the recent rash of fires."

"You mean Lechner," Yancy said.

"Potato pahtahto. Still equals evil."

"Weird a fire fighter hooking up with a pyromaniac, both looking for untold wealth." Gram said. "Axel was a wily one, using ghost busting as an excuse to come to Portneuf Gap; very smart and resourceful. I'm glad Martin was partly responsible for Danforth's capture, good for that sweet boy's self-esteem. Plus, the reality show, *Ghost Hunting,* has contacted him. They might want to use his fifteen minutes of fame in a future episode. He asked me if they could film inside the mortuary."

Yancy gasped. "Cassandra . . ."

"I haven't said yes. Let me grab my purse and we'll talk about it on the way home." She disappeared into the house and Yancy shuffled off the porch.

"Mercedes, please, talk to her. I've had about as much drama as I can stand." Yancy grimaced. "My eyebrows may never grow back."

Gram came out, they both got into her car and drove away with Yancy looking pitiful and Gram smiling.

I stretched until my back vertebrae popped and opened the screen door. "Want a Pepsi?"

Reb followed me into the kitchen. "Yes. With tons of ice." She took a seat at the table. "Were the paintings fake or real?"

"I don't know. Floydean's got feelers out among her friends who work at the FBI but no word yet."

"You'd love to have the one with the Dachshund catching bubbles, right?"

I handed her a Pepsi in a tall glass nearly over-flowing with ice and sat across from her. "It would look good on my wall. But even a fake is out of my price range."

"I've been thinking and I've got a sure-fire plan that could net you the painting and air-conditioning for your vintage house."

Oh-oh. "Nothing illegal, right?"

She took a gulp of her drink, sat it on the table, and steepled her hands under her chin. "Okay. Now don't talk. Just listen."

The familiar phrase from our childhood had my radar humming. Whenever Reb uttered those words, it usually ended badly for both of us. I made the motion of zipping my lips and waited.

"This is the second murder we've solved. Right?"

I nodded.

"Unlike the authorities, we take thinking outside the box to a new level. We do what it takes to really get to the nitty-gritty center of problems. Right?"

I opened my mouth, but she held up her hand. "Not that Jack didn't work his tail off, but he happens to be hampered by all that rigid, cop thinking. On the other hand, we are free thinkers, willing to look at a situation from every angle." She paused to gulp down another swallow. "You might even say we're naturals at solving sticky problems.

"I'm so done showing real estate. Too many times I've worked my butt off putting together a great sale, only to have some snake-bellied realtor slide in and snatch it out from under me. Or some phony like Bernhagen proposes a mega-deal. I waste all kinds of time and effort then watch the deal crumble like your Gram's piecrust." She plopped a cube of ice into her mouth and crunched.

"You've nearly been killed twice dealing with weirdo people! We've both been busting our butts while a veritable gold mine was sitting right in front of us. It's the whole forest for the trees thing."

"Reb, you're talking in circles. Get to the point."

She waited a beat and finished crunching the ice. "We should start our own detective agency."

I snorted a laugh. "Are you nuts?"

"Most P.I's spend time snooping out insurance fraud and catching cheating spouses. It's exciting yet tame. We could make big money and there's really no danger, unless someone comes to us seeking help above and beyond what the authorities can give."

I shook my head. "Reb . . ."

"Just think about it. I've already checked. In Idaho, there's no test to worry about. All we have to do is pay our money and hang out our shingle. We should think of something catchy . . ." She stopped and gasped as Mr. Wiggins ran through the doggy door carrying her new cell phone.

"There's your first case," I said, as she took off after the little thief. "How does he keep stealing your phone?"

J. W. HODGE LOVES COMMITTING MURDER on paper. She finds it very therapeutic. She grew up playing in her grandmother's mortuary so she might be more comfortable with death than most. She and her husband are kept busy cleaning and repairing their many apartments. When she's not cleaning or writing her next book she's busy rescuing dogs, feral cats, and battling with a flock of wild turkeys who are determined to rule her hillside. She's a member of Mystery Writer's of America and Sisters in Crime and belongs to two critique groups.